MW00327103

E.R. PUNSHON
INFORMATION RECEIVED

Ernest Robertson Punshon was born in London in 1872.

At the age of fourteen he started life in an office. His employers soon informed him that he would never make a really satisfactory clerk, and he, agreeing, spent the next few years wandering about Canada and the United States, endeavouring without great success to earn a living in any occupation that offered. Returning home by way of working a passage on a cattle boat, he began to write. He contributed to many magazines and periodicals, wrote plays, and published nearly fifty novels, among which his detective stories proved the most popular and enduring.

He died in 1956.

Also by E.R. Punshon

E.R. PUNSHON

INFORMATION RECEIVED

With an introduction
by Curtis Evans

DEAN STREET PRESS

INTRODUCTION

When E. R. Punshon (1874-1956) launched his Bobby Owen mystery series in 1933 with the publication of *Information Received*, his new detective novel got from Dorothy L. Sayers, already one of England's most renowned mystery writers, the kind of book review most novelists have only ever dreamed of getting. Excerpts from the Sayers review would emblazon the dust jackets of Punshon mysteries for the next twenty-three years, until Punshon's death in 1956, one year before Sayers's own passing.

"What is distinction," Sayers asked rhetorically in her *Sunday Times* crime fiction column review of *Information Received*, before concluding that distinction's name was Punshon. Sayers made clear that what she referred to here was not *plotting* distinction but *literary* distinction. It was literary distinction, she declared, that was "missed by scores of competent mystery writers who can construct impeccable plots. The few who achieve it step—plot or no plot—unquestioned into the first rank." Sayers asserted that Punshon's tales possessed qualities more important than those which arose from "the mere mechanics of puzzle-making," namely "that elusive something which makes them count as literature" and "that enhanced and glorified reality which is the highest art." The current Punshon mystery, *Information Received*, was, in Sayers's view, "a real book, not assembled by a journeyman, but written, as a book ought to be, by a man who is a writer first and foremost."

Dorothy L. Sayers's review of E. R. Punshon's *Information Received* was a career-making moment for the lesser-known mystery writer, an epochal event in the life of a man who in 1933 was nearly sixty years old and had been publishing novels since the year of Queen Victoria's death. Punshon's novel *Earth's Great Lord*, a romance of the Australian outback, had appeared in 1901, to be followed in 1905 by *Constance West*, a romance of the Canadian wilderness. After publishing a third mainstream novel, *Rhoda in Between* (1907), Punshon gave an early hint of his penchant for mystery-mongering, producing a couple of crime tales, *The Mystery of Lady Isobel* (1907) and *The Spin of the Coin* (1908), both more notable for sensational melodrama than sober detection. "Thrill succeeds thrill," observed *The Bookman* of *The Mystery of Lady Isobel*, while the *Morning Leader* confidently declared: "Lovers of sensation will rejoice over *The Spin of the Coin*."

Of Punshon's next dozen novels, at least four—*Hidden Lives* (1913), *The Solitary House* (1918), *The Woman's Footprint* (1919) and *The Bittermeads Mystery* (1922)—can be characterized as crime novels, though to each still clings the heady aroma of Edwardian melodrama. Only in 1929 did Punshon make his bid as an author of more firmly puzzle-focused, fair play detective fiction in the modern, Jazz Age manner, with his Inspector Carter and Sergeant Bell mystery series, which ran through five novels into 1932. Although Dorothy L. Sayers had praised the Carter-Bell series as well, the plaudits she lavished on *Information Received*, Punshon's first Bobby Owen detective novel, must have been, for both Punshon himself and his publisher, Ernest Benn, an unexpected blessing.

Why was Sayers so powerfully struck by *Information Received?* Certainly at the time Sayers reviewed the novel she had become, through her reviews in the *Sunday Times* and other critical writings, perhaps the most vocal British exponent of transforming the traditional puzzle-oriented detective story into more of a novel of manners with crime, a process which she believed would lead the genre out of what she deemed its body-in-the-library creative dead-end. She saw in Punshon's books, particularly *Information Received*, a mystery writer who could really *write*, someone interested in creating compelling stories of crime as it impacts psychologically credible people rather than merely fabricating intricate puzzles involving clichéd, cardboard characters.

Information Received introduces a new series character, a handsome, modest young policeman named Bobby Owen, who features in all thirty-five mystery novels Punshon published under his own name between 1933 and his death in 1956. (He also published two mystery novels under a pseudonym, Robertson Halket, that do not feature Owen.) Eventually attaining the rank of Commander, Bobby, as Punshon calls him, starts as a lowly constable in *Information Received*. An Oxford graduate (pass degree only), Bobby turned to the Metropolitan Police Service after finding before him "a world with but scanty openings to offer to young University graduates with only pass degrees." At the start of *Information Received*, Bobby has served on the force for three years, during which "his most exciting experiences had been escorting old ladies across the road and satisfying the insatiable thirst of children for the right time." Yet things are about to change, most drastically.

Bobby is on the scene shortly after financier Sir Christopher Clarke is found in his billiard room, fatally felled by a couple of gunshot wounds to the chest. ("Close by lay a revolver, and an acrid smell of powder still lingered in the room. From two round, burnt holes in the dead man's chest bubbles of blood were oozing with a slow and dreadful regularity.") Soon on the scene as well is Superintendent Mitchell of the Criminal Investigation Department, a big, bluff, garrulous man who serves as Bobby's mentor and the lead investigator in the early novels in the series. Given to quirky pronouncements ("A good detective never forgets his sandwiches.... That's the first law of all sound detective work—don't forget the sandwiches. We may have to wait here all day."), Mitchell nevertheless has a wise head on his shoulders.

Mitchell's wise head is needed in the Sir Christopher Clarke murder case, where a goodly number of people seem to have had reasons for wanting the dead man permanently out of the picture. Although, to be sure, *Information Received* has a proto-Cluedo-style opening, with a rich man found murdered with a revolver in the billiard room, the ending is anything but a standard Golden Age device, drawing as it does on an older, richer literary source and Punshon's "own keen insight into the characters of those under pressure," as mystery scholar Nick Fuller has put it. As Dorothy L. Sayers wrote over eighty years ago, with *Information Received* E. R. Punshon crafted a detective novel of distinction—and even better ones were yet to come from the new mystery master's hands.

Curtis Evans

CHAPTER 1

Two Theatre Tickets

SINCE that formidable personage, Sir Christopher Clarke, square built, square jawed, iron of fist and will, with fierce little eyes that gleamed from under bushy brows as though they sought whom they might devour next, was by far the most important and influential client of Messrs Marsden, Carsley, and Marsden, Lincoln's Inn, the well-known and long-established firm of solicitors, it is perhaps no matter for surprise that a certain nervousness, or even more than that, was apparent in the manner of the senior partner of the firm as he rose to greet him.

But Sir Christopher was well used to seeing people nervous and uncomfortable in his presence. Was he not the strong, successful man, the man who knew what he wanted and saw that he got it; were not respect, deference, consideration, even fear, his rightful due? and if it was now even more than fear that peeped from the dark, sharp eyes of Basil Marsden, Sir Christopher took that more as a compliment than anything else. After all, is it not natural to fear the strong, and was he not strong with the strength of a quarter of a million in cash and a credit as high as that of any man in the City of London? Why, but for the recent slump he would have been a millionaire by now, and even the slump had affected him as little as any man.

So if he noticed the terror that seemed to show in the dark, sharp eyes, if he noticed a certain trembling in the white, well-cared-for hands that moved about the papers on the lawyer's desk, he took no notice. He said:

'About the Belfort Trust?'

'I have the papers here,' answered Mr Marsden. 'The accounts show a total of a little over £20,000. A large sum,' he smiled, 'and as in these days of smash and grab raids,

7

one never knows, I asked Carsley to go himself to the Safe Deposit to fetch it, and take two of the clerks with him, just so as to be on the safe side. It's nearly all in bearer bonds, you remember. Better safe than sorry is a good motto. I think Carsley was almost disappointed nothing happened.'

'Carsley is a partner now, isn't he?' Sir Christopher asked.

A little surprised at the question, Mr Marsden nodded.

'Now he's passed his examinations,' he said, a trifle maliciously. 'He didn't find it too easy, I'm afraid.'

Sir Christopher made no comment but the tone in which this was said had not escaped his notice. It was perhaps not unnatural that Basil Marsden, who had had sole control of the firm for a good many years, was not altogether pleased at having to admit as a partner on equal terms young Peter Carsley, the son of the original Carsley. But as partner he had had to be admitted, or else bought out at a price it would not have been convenient to pay. So installed in a partner's room young Peter Carsley sat, though as yet very insecurely in the saddle and with hardly more knowledge of the business than any junior clerk – and indeed as a very junior clerk Marsden seemed more than half inclined to treat him.

Now Marsden got up and opening the door called into an adjoining room:

'Peter, bring me the Belfort Trust papers, will you? securities and all. They're in the safe, you know. Dickson has my key.'

Closing the door, he came back to his seat.

'Carsley won't be a minute,' he said. 'May I ask, is it the intention to close the Trust?'

'You don't want that, eh?' chuckled Sir Christopher. 'Pretty profitable bit of business, eh?'

Marsden laughed, too.

'Well, we've had it a long time,' he said. 'I suppose old Mr Belfort ...?'

'Fussing a bit,' admitted Sir Christopher. 'He wants to see all papers, bonds, securities, everything himself. Natural, in a way, as he is taking over now his brother's died. I shall tell him if he can find another trustee to act in my place, I shall be grateful. I have quite enough on my hands, as it is, and the hundred a year I get as trustee doesn't pay me for my time.'

Mr Marsden gave an acquiescent murmur though, as, to his certain knowledge, Sir Christopher had never given to the Trust more time than was required for the signing of an occasional paper now and again, he was inclined to think Sir Christopher earned his hundred easily enough. Still, it was true this old Mr Belfort, suddenly imported into the affair through the death of another trustee, seemed inclined to be officious. But then again Sir Christopher wouldn't mind that, provided Mr Belfort confined his officiousness to worrying not his fellow trustee but the Trust's solicitor. Probably Sir Christopher would not care if this fussy old man wanted to do everything himself, instead of leaving everything to the others, as his recently deceased brother had been content to do.

There was a pause while they still waited for Peter Carsley. Sir Christopher, little used to waiting, looked frowningly at the door, and Mr Marsden suddenly remembered.

'Oh, Sir Christopher,' he said, 'a boy left your theatre tickets this morning – here they are.'

'Theatre tickets?' repeated Sir Christopher. 'What theatre tickets?'

'From the Regency,' explained Mr Marsden, producing an envelope with the imprint of that well-known theatre and marked 'Two stalls'. He added: 'I went with a friend the other night. I had no idea Shakespeare was so interesting. I didn't find it at all boring, not at all.'

He paused, for Sir Christopher was looking in a puzzled way at the envelope the lawyer had handed him.

'Some mistake,' he said. 'I've not booked any seats any-where. Who left it here?'

'A boy from the theatre,' Marsden explained, looking puzzled in his turn. 'It's addressed to you, in our care, so we thought it was all right.'

'I see it's my name,' grunted Sir Christopher, opening the envelope. 'Two stalls for to-night, apparently, but there's no – '

He paused abruptly, and Marsden saw that he had become pale, that in his small, fierce eyes had crept what almost seemed a sudden terror. His hand shook that held the tickets, and all at once he looked a smaller, frailer man, as if in that one moment something had gone out of him, something that left him naked and afraid.

For the moment Marsden almost supposed that he was dreaming, for what could there be in two theatre tickets to throw into this sudden panic the strong, the successful, the prosperous wealthy man of business?

Sir Christopher got up suddenly and went to the window. He threw it open and leaned out, far out, as if he had great need of air, and for a moment Marsden played with the idea of creeping up behind and taking him by the legs and throwing him out.

A foolish, impracticable idea, of course. Besides, the Marsden, Carsley, and Marsden offices were on the first floor of the building and a fall would hardly have been fatal, not immediately fatal at any rate. Anyhow, the opportunity passed, for Sir Christopher turned back into the room and very slowly, very deliberately, tore envelope and tickets in half and threw them down on the floor.

'Trying to frighten me,' he said between his teeth, more to himself than to Marsden, and Marsden wondered be-wilderedly why a gift of two stalls for a successful Shakespeare revival should be supposed to be an attempt to frighten a man like Sir Christopher. It was said that the finest per-formance of *Hamlet* for two generations was to be seen just now at the Regency, and what was there about that to alarm any man? But Sir Christopher was looking straight in front of him as grimly as though he saw there some strange enemy, and though his great clenched fist on the table before him was steady enough, there was still that dark look of terror in his eyes – of terror mastered and held down no doubt, but of terror all the same. He said heavily: 'It doesn't matter ... it makes no difference ... Marsden, I'll make a fresh will.'

'Now, to-day?' stammered Marsden, more and more astonished.

'Now, to-day,' repeated Sir Christopher, glaring at him as if daring him to say a word, and the door opened and young Peter Carsley came in rather quickly, carrying a sealed packet in his hands.

'I'm so sorry I've been so long,' he said. 'We couldn't get the safe open at first.'

Peter was a tall, fair, good-looking youngster, with grey eyes, prominent, well-shaped nose, a strong, even obstinate-looking mouth and chin, and a direct, rather blunt manner. That he had had some difficulty in passing his final examinations is a fact that must not be concealed, but at any rate he had got through in the end, even though the intensive effort required had quite likely cost him his chance of representing England against Wales at Twickenham – and whether the gain was worth the sacrifice he was in his secret heart not quite sure.

He greeted Sir Christopher now with a certain restraint and Sir Christopher's manner to him was far from cordial, indeed almost rude. Peter flushed a little, he had a trick of flushing, it was the secret shame of his inner life, and put down on the table the sealed packet he had brought with him.

'This is the list of securities,' he said, producing a type-written document. 'It's not been checked yet.'

'We'll do that now,' growled Sir Christopher. 'Make

sure they're all there for Belfort to see. He's coming to dinner to-night, and he can go through them afterwards to his heart's content.'

'Shall you be keeping them all night?' Marsden asked, a little startled. 'Isn't that a trifle – dangerous? £20,000, almost all in negotiable stuff.'

'I've a good safe,' Sir Christopher retorted, 'and I'm sorry for the burglar I lay hands on.' He held out his hand as he spoke and certainly it looked one of which the grip would be formidable enough. 'Besides, I keep a loaded six-shooter in my bedroom,' he added.

'But –' began Marsden hesitatingly.

'But what?' grunted Sir Christopher. 'I've had diamonds worth as much as that in the safe for three months now or longer – they've been all right.'

He had rather a grim look as he spoke, and indeed his square-set figure, his fierce, glittering eyes and great hooked nose all gave him the look of some huge bird of prey it would be best not to meddle with. One felt it would be a rash thief indeed who ventured within his reach.

Peter turned towards the door, and, as he did so, noticed the torn theatre tickets lying where Sir Christopher had thrown them down. He paused, surprised, and Sir Christopher said with an evident sneer:

'Two stalls for a theatre. You can have them, if you like. I'm engaged.'

Looking still more surprised, Peter picked them up.

'Oh, thank you,' he said, with the gratitude a gift of theatre tickets always evokes, and then with a certain disappointment: 'Oh, Shakespeare.'

'Prefer a musical show?' asked Sir Christopher.

'Well, yes, I do,' confessed Peter. 'They ram Shakespeare down your throat so at school, you do get fed up with him.'

'Better go,' grunted Sir Christopher. 'It'll improve your mind. They're for to-night.'

'Oh, for to-night, sorry, I'm engaged to-night,' Peter

answered, and put down the tickets on the corner of the table from which, with an angry gesture, Sir Christopher swept them to the floor as the door closed behind Peter.

'Young puppy, infernal young puppy,' Sir Christopher snarled. 'Did you hear that? – like his insolence. He meant he was engaged because he knows Jennie's going to the Amherst ball and he's going, too. Does the young fool think I'll ever let her marry him?'

CHAPTER 2

The New Will

MARSDEN judged it prudent to make no answer to this question, especially as it was evident that Sir Christopher did not expect one. That Peter had met Miss Jennie two or three times and had been duly smitten by her fresh young beauty, Marsden already knew. He had even heard that Miss Jennie seemed inclined to show his good-looking young partner rather more favour than as a rule she bestowed on the eager youths who dangled in her train. But obviously the idea of a marriage between the young solicitor, only just admitted to practise, and the daughter of a man of Sir Christopher's wealth and standing – and ambition – was not one to be taken seriously. Very certainly Sir Christopher entertained quite other views for the disposal of his daughter's hand. Indeed, Sir Christopher's frowning brows and angry eyes told plainly how he regarded this project that he evidently knew the young lawyer had been rash enough and foolish enough to entertain.

But without saying anything more he drew the Belfort Trust documents towards him. Marsden had everything in order, everything clear and simple, and Sir Christopher was soon satisfied. The list of securities was checked and given back to Marsden, and the securities themselves, and the other documents, Sir Christopher thrust into his dispatch case, all ready for the inspection of old Mr Belfort that evening.

'Nothing Belfort can find to grumble at there,' he said. 'If he wants to realize I shan't object and it could be done at once – everything realizable at short notice. Now get my will. I'll destroy it at once and I'll give you instructions for a new one.'

'I'll go and get it myself,' Marsden said.

It was kept in the strong room in the basement and Marsden was absent a few minutes. When he returned, he was surprised to find Sir Christopher had picked up the torn pieces of the theatre tickets and had put them together on the table before him. With so strange an intensity was he staring at them, as though they concealed some secret his angry and determined eyes were resolute to discover, that at first he did not hear Marsden re-enter the room. But when Marsden spoke, once again with that same angry gesture he had used before, he swept the tickets to the floor, almost as though defying them to do their worst.

'Got it?' he asked, holding out his hand for the will. 'Humph, good many years since this was drawn up. Half to Jennie, half to Brenda.' He looked up in his fierce, abrupt way, as if expecting a challenge and eager to reply to it. 'Brenda's nothing to complain of,' he declared, almost with defiance. 'Not everyone would leave his money equally between his own daughter and a stepdaughter, eh?'

'I must say I thought it very generous to Miss Laing,' agreed Marsden, who was far indeed from any intention of challenging anything whatever the firm's most important client chose to say.

'Bound to provide for her, of course,' Sir Christopher went on. 'But equal shares – that shows I meant to do the right thing. Different now she's getting married, though.'

'Shall I take your instructions, Sir Christopher?' Marsden asked.

'You know Brenda's engaged to Mark Lester?' continued Sir Christopher. 'Clever young fellow, Mark, and has a very good post with Baily's; his mother's some relation of Mrs Baily. Excellent prospects. He writes poetry and plays and stuff, too, I'm told, and of course there's not much harm in that so long as he keeps it just as a hobby – might make some money too, perhaps, you never know. Very much in love with Brenda, apparently.'

'I heard something about it,' Marsden answered

cautiously, not quite sure yet how Sir Christopher viewed the engagement, but very certain that anyhow Miss Jennie would never have been permitted to engage herself to this young City clerk with literary tastes, however promising his prospects might be.

Rumour, indeed, said that Sir Christopher had done all in his power to bring their engagement about, so much so that it had been hinted he was anxious to be rid of his step-daughter and for that reason was marrying her off to the first man he could find. But even if that were so, and he had rather imposed a husband upon Brenda than allowed her to choose for herself, at any rate she had seemed willing enough and no reasonable objection could be taken to Lester, who was a presentable young fellow with a career before him and good prospects. And then perhaps it was not altogether un-natural that Sir Christopher should wish to see his own daughter, now that she was of age, taking over the manage-ment of his house. Up to now, by virtue of her seven years' seniority, and also possibly by reason of her more forceful character, the household reins had been quite naturally in Brenda's hands, though that had never caused any disagree-ment or jealousy between the two girls. Jennie had never found anything to question in an arrangement that had always seemed to her the obvious one, and indeed, ever since her early childhood, when their mother had died, had been accustomed to look up to her big sister for help and sym-pathy, almost as to a second mother.

'Everything to Jennie, this time,' Sir Christopher said in is gruff, abrupt way. 'The same executors, the same legacies, otherwise everything to Jennie for her sole use and benefit.'

'But – Miss Laing?' Marsden said, hesitatingly, not quite sure whether Sir Christopher had not forgotten her.

'Just say,' directed Sir Christopher, 'that I have already provided for her in another way. I told her this morning what I meant to do for her – some people would have thought it generous. Anyhow, she knows. We'll attend to that afterwards. At present, everything to Jennie – provided, provided,' repeated Sir Christopher slowly, 'that at my death she is unmarried. Make that clear. Everything to her if she is unmarried. If she is married, then – then everything to the King Edward Hospital Fund. Have I got to say it again?' he barked suddenly, as Marsden sat and stared, very much astonished at so unexpected a conclusion.

'No, no, I quite understand,' he said hurriedly now. 'Everything to Miss Jennie, provided she is unmarried. If she is married, everything to the King Edward Hospital Fund. A clause to say Miss Laing is otherwise provided for. All smaller legacies and everything else to stand.'

'That's right,' said Sir Christopher. 'Now draw up a deed of gift or settlement or whatever you call it transferring to Brenda the whole of my holding in the three and a half per cent War Loan – '

'The whole of it?' asked Marsden, more and more surprised at arrangements that seemed to him more and more eccentric.

'Forty thousand, isn't it?' asked Sir Christopher.

'A very large sum,' commented Marsden.

'No one shall say I didn't do my duty by her,' declared Sir Christopher, getting to his feet.

'The money is to be settled on her absolutely?' Marsden asked.

'Absolutely, for her sole use and benefit,' Sir Christopher replied. 'For her to play drakes and ducks with, if she wants to. I shall consider my responsibility to her fully discharged.'

'Very generously discharged indeed,' murmured Marsden; and indeed was inclined to think it a generosity almost excessive.

'No one shall be able to say she's anything to complain of,' Sir Christopher repeated.

He went across to the empty grate, and there, striking a match, put light to the old will and watched carefully to see that it was entirely destroyed. When the last little flame had flickered out, and the thing was utterly consumed, he collected hat, umbrella, gloves, nodded a good-bye to Marsden, and then, just as he was in the act of going out, he said:

'Oh, by the way, let young Carsley help you draw up the new will. He may as well know about it.'

With that he went off and Marsden whistled softly to himself.

'That's that,' he mused, 'and that explains the will – puts a spoke in Mr Peter's wheel very effectively indeed. Anyone who marries Miss Jennie now marries a pauper, unless and until the old man makes another will, which of course is what he'll do as soon as he gets her safely off to someone he approves of. Meanwhile, checkmate to Mr Peter. But I wonder what's making him so generous to the other girl? Jolly queer, not like him a bit; not many people, anyhow, would make marriage settlements on such a scale for a stepdaughter. Forty thousand in the three and a half per cents is a jolly nice wedding present.'

He went to the door and called to his young partner.

'Old Clarke's been giving me instructions for a fresh will,' he said. 'Everything to the Jennie girl, unless she is married at his death. If she is married, everything to charity. He specially mentioned that I was to tell you.'

There was a faint, malicious smile on Marsden's lips as he said this, and for a moment or two Peter made no reply. Then he said slowly and deliberately:

'We rather expected something of the sort.'

'Who is "we"?' demanded Marsden.

'Jennie and I,' Peter answered. 'You see, we were married three weeks ago.'

'What?' shouted Marsden. 'What?'

But Peter did not think it necessary to repeat what he had said.

'Good Lord!' said Marsden, slowly taking it in. 'Does he know?'

'I don't suppose he knows,' Peter answered. 'I expect he has some idea.'

'Well, I'm blessed,' said Marsden, coming into the room and sitting down. 'You young fool, you've done it now – the girl won't get a penny.'

Peter said nothing, and Marsden sat staring and thinking till another and startling idea came to him.

'Good Lord!' he cried, 'ten to one he'll take it out of the firm – he'll ruin the firm for this. You fool, you've done me in, too.'

'I thought of that,' answered Peter calmly, 'so I'll get out. You can tell him you've given me the sack, if you like. That'll calm him down as far as you're concerned. My wife' – he flushed crimson, the words were still new to him, still wonderful and lovely – 'my wife and I talked it all over. We expected something like this. That is one reason why we thought it better to get married privately – that can't be undone, and Sir Christopher can do what he likes, but he can't undo our marriage, so it will be no good his trying to bully Jennie. There's no telling what he mightn't have been up to before, but now he can't do anything. But very likely he would try to get at me and perhaps at you as well, if I was still here. So I'll get out. I shan't be sorry to chuck the job, anyhow. I'm no good at it, and never shall be. I should never make a lawyer and don't want to, either. I've talked it over with Willy Simmonds. He's willing to buy me out and come in with you. It'll be a good thing for you, he's a jolly smart chap and he has lots of experience and a fair practice already.'

Marsden had become very pale. He said nothing, but his expression had become so strange that Peter was quite alarmed.

'What's up?' he said. 'I thought you would jump at the idea. You will get a clever brainy fellow as partner instead of a duffer at the job like me – you were cursing heaven only yesterday for having landed you with me for a partner.

Simmonds is coming along to see you any time you like –
what's the matter? You don't object to Simmonds, do you?
You told me yourself last week you wished to the Lord you
had someone like him to work with.'

'You fool – you fool – you infernal fool,' Marsden stammered, 'you've ruined me and yourself, too.'

'What on earth – ?' began Peter, but Marsden jumped to
his feet in a fury.

'You fool,' he almost screamed, 'you may as well know
now, you would have sooner or later. There's a deficiency
of Lord knows how much – I don't. I had to take money
where I could get it to make up the Belfort Trust. I was
afraid old Clarke would spot something was wrong, but I
suppose as long as the totals were right, he didn't care. I've
had to take money from half a dozen other accounts and do
you suppose Simmonds will buy without finding that out,
and when he does – '

He left the sentence unfinished, and Peter tried hard to
understand, but found it difficult.

'Do you mean,' he said in a whisper, in a low, awe-
stricken whisper. 'Embezzlement?' he asked.

'That's what the courts would call it, I suppose,' Marsden answered, laughing harshly. 'I could have put the
money back in time, I always have till now. It's that Belfort
Trust upset me – once I could get that back I should be all
right. I could use it and carry on till I had got things square
again, but now, you fool, you utter fool, you've ruined
everything. If you stay with the firm Sir Christopher will
smash it; and you can't sell out and clear out – you've nothing to sell except your share in a bankrupt swindle.'

CHAPTER 3

Murder

EARLY that same evening, about the time when the great, daily tide of humanity ebbs from work to home, Police-Constable Robert Owen, B.A. (Oxon) – a pass degree only – took shelter from a light passing shower under one of the tall cedars that grew on either side of the gate admitting to the imposing Hampstead residence of Sir Christopher Clarke. The wide stretching arms of the trees, reaching out over the roadway, protected him well enough from the rain as he waited for his sergeant, who, in the ordinary routine, was due soon to meet him thereabouts.

As yet there was no sign of him, and, stifling a yawn, Bobby Owen reflected that a policeman's lot, whether happy or not, was at any rate sufficiently dull. During the three years he had spent in the force his most exciting experiences had been escorting old ladies across the road and satisfying the insatiable thirst of children for the right time. Of course his luck had been atrociously bad. Any little turn up with Communists blazing to overthrow civilization, or with Irish more modestly content with the destruction of the British Empire, always took place when he was off duty. Smash and grab raids never happened on his beat, no burglar ever troubled his tranquillity, even motorists themselves seemed to suffer from an epidemic of good behaviour when he was near. Indeed Bobby was almost reduced to wishing that when, on coming down from Oxford, he had found a world with but scanty openings to offer to young University graduates with only pass degrees, he had decided to join the army instead of choosing the police – even though an army in peace time had always seemed to him the last word in futility.

Of course, his athletic record was good enough to have

secured him a post on the staff of almost any school in the land, except the few where the standard is so high that besides the necessary athletics, some scholarship also is demanded. But towards the teaching profession he felt no attraction whatever – quite the reverse, indeed – and an offer of a post in the haberdashery department, known as 'habys', in one of the great London stores he had also declined in spite of the alluring prospect it held out of becoming in due course a super-Selfridge, of out-harroding Harrods, of aiding the flag of Kensington High Street to blaze yet more terrific through the advertisement columns of all the papers in the country.

So here he was in the police, very bored, and uncomfortably aware that he was not in too good odour with his superiors. For as soon as they realized that he was an old St George's College man, he had been selected for night club work, and to that job he had shown his dislike so plainly that he had been at once shot out to Hampstead, there to be engaged on ordinary patrol duty. Not that his superiors really minded much, for there is no lack of good-looking young constables who can wear evening dress as though midnight had never seen them in any other attire, and who are perfectly prepared to spend a fiver of their country's money on bad champagne and worse whisky. But all the same neither in 'The Force' nor anywhere else is it wise for the ambitious to get a reputation for being 'difficult'.

So Bobby was not only a little bored, but also a little depressed, as he sheltered outside 'The Cedars', and waited for the sergeant who did not come. Indeed, no living creature was in sight till down the drive from the house pattered an elderly man whose air of bland dignity, of grave responsibility, stamped him instantly as either a bishop or a butler, the lack of gaiters on his nether limbs however tipping the scales of probability in favour of the second alternative.

He had on a mackintosh, carried an umbrella, and was evidently on his way to the post, for he carried two or three letters in his hand. Seeing Bobby, he stopped and commented gravely on the deplorable weather. Constables on duty are warned against entering into conversation with strangers, but also it is prudent for them to be acquainted as far as possible with the domestic staffs of the neighbourhood. For it is surprising how many interesting and occasionally curious events the apparently humdrum lives of butler and maid are brought into contact with.

So Bobby responded genially, learnt that the stranger was butler at 'The Cedars' and was named Lewis, and that he was on the way to post these letters himself, because one of them was of some importance, being no other than Mr Lewis's instructions to his turf agent with regard to backing a certain double at the race meeting beginning the next day. Being informed what this double was, Bobby gave it as his considered opinion that the choice was a good one and might well come off.

For Bobby was an expert on the form of race-horses, that is to say, he read every day the pronouncements, equally authoritative and contradictory, of Captain Go, Major Know, and 'The Spotter', and, having done so, selected when possible a horse none of the three had mentioned. In this way he had brought off some remarkable coups, and had the reputation of knowing a lot, so much so, indeed, that even an inspector had been known to ask him for a tip. Not that Bobby took any real interest in racing, but in police work it is sometimes necessary to open conversations with strangers or to win the confidence of reluctant witnesses, and for both purposes a brief discussion on the prospects of to-morrow's three-thirty is the best possible introduction. Indeed it is quite certain that any observation on this subject is more likely to draw a prompt and instructed reply from any Englishman anywhere than is any other imaginable remark.

That his approval of the proposed double was based upon solid knowledge Bobby was thus able to demonstrate, and, much cheered, Mr Lewis trotted off to drop his letters into the pillar-box across the way. Coming back, he stopped again to speak to Bobby.

'You haven't noticed a little old chap, thin face, long nose, grey whiskers, rather shabby, boots down at heels, hanging about here, have you?' he asked. 'If you do, you might keep an eye on him.'

'Right,' said Bobby. 'What's the trouble?'

'Been talking a bit wild,' explained Lewis, 'not using threats exactly but talking as if he meant to. Sir Christopher told me if he come again to make sure I saw him off the premises, but what's the good of that? Nothing to stop him coming back.'

'Sir Christopher your guv'nor?' asked Bobby.

'Yes,' answered Lewis, 'big City man – it's him as nearly owns United Firms and he's chairman of the City and Suburbs bank, too.'

'I've heard of him,' said Bobby. 'Made a speech about getting back to gold the other day, didn't he? Said gold was gold and when you had gold, why, then you had it. Made a big impression in the City, the papers said. What's the trouble with the grey-whiskered bird?'

'Expect,' said Lewis with appreciation, 'it's someone the guv'nor's done in the eye. Guv'nor told me, if he gave any trouble to clear him out quick and see he didn't hang about the house or garden. But how can I stop that? Nothing to prevent him slipping back again any time he wants. We don't keep the gate locked, and, if we did, he could go in next door now it's empty and get over the wall, couldn't he?'

Bobby agreed that that was possible, promised to keep on the watch for any elderly and grey-whiskered gentlemen who looked as if they might 'give trouble', and Lewis, apparently easier in his mind, returned to the house.

Even yet the sergeant had not put in an appearance and Bobby began to wonder if something had occurred to prevent him from coming. Bobby decided to stroll to the corner and see if any sign of his approach were visible. Coming back, for no sergeant was in sight, he saw across the road an elderly man who certainly appeared to be paying a somewhat unusual attention to 'The Cedars', as though for some reason he took a special interest in the house. True, he did not fully answer the description Lewis had given, for he was not a little man but of middle height and size, and he looked more prosperous than shabby. A glance Bobby gave at his boots showed that, far from being down at heel, they were quite new, and he noticed, too, that they were unusually long and narrow, though that was not a point which interested him at the moment or to which he thought of attaching any importance. Nor had he grey whiskers but, instead, a sandy beard. Still, even Bobby's short experience in the police had taught him that personal descriptions offered by apparently trustworthy witnesses were often wildly inaccurate, and it was at least certain that this stranger was elderly and that he was showing an unusual degree of interest in 'The Cedars'.

'Elmhurst', the next house to 'The Cedars', was empty, except for a caretaker, and stood also in a fairly large garden of about half an acre or more. Deciding that it might be as well to watch this elderly stranger for a time, Bobby pushed open the 'Elmhurst' gate and took up his position behind one of the trees lining the short drive that led to the house. And scarcely had he done so when he heard, coming from the direction of the empty house, the sound of angry shouts, of a dog barking, of running footsteps.

All this seemed to require investigation more pressingly than did the movements of the elderly stranger, and Bobby ran up the drive towards the house, where he met the caretaker, a man named Walters. Walters, it seemed, had seen from the kitchen window a strange man in the garden, in which there was a fair amount of fruit growing, unripe still, but all the same subject to many raids. At once, fearing for the fruit, Walters had dashed out in pursuit, armed with an over-ripe tomato his wife had just been indignantly displaying to him as having been foisted off upon her by a too enterprising greengrocer.

'Chap was after the apples,' complained Walters indignantly, for the produce of the garden he regarded as part of the emoluments of his office. 'I saw him from the kitchen but he must have spotted me, too, for he ran like a good 'un – off he was and over the wall in quick time, but I let him have the tomato and it took him clean in the middle of the back – spoilt his Sunday suit for him, I hope,' said Walters, chuckling, 'but the cheek of it and in broad daylight, too.'

He and Bobby walked down the garden together, but could not discover that any fruit had been taken or any damage done.

'I spotted him too quick,' said Walters with satisfaction. 'Got to be on the look out all the time, so you have.'

He enlarged on his troubles with naughty little boys, as well as with more serious, older raiders, and declared that sometimes the very apples and pears and plums stolen from the garden were offered by the thieves to his 'missis' for purchase. Bobby listened and sympathized, and looking at the wall, he said:

'Good height, topped with glass, too. The chap must have had a bit of a job to get over.'

'Had to, else I'd have copped him,' said Walters proudly.

They went along to the wall, and soon found the place where it had been scaled, for the flower bed beneath was badly trampled, and several flowers broken. Complaining loudly of the damage done, Walters fetched a rake to smooth the soft mould, while Bobby found a ladder, and, mounting it, examined the top of the wall. He said:

'He cut his hand getting over, at least, it looks like blood on some of the broken glass.'

Walters, finishing his task of smoothing the mould of the flower bed, expressed a wish that the broken bits of glass had cut the intruder to mincemeat, and then Bobby returned to his post in the road. There was no sign now of the old man he had noticed before, no sign either of his sergeant, and more for the sake of having something to put in his notebook than because he thought the incident of any real importance, Bobby began to write a brief report of it. He noted the time, now a quarter to seven, and, deciding to give up waiting any longer for the sergeant, who must, he supposed, have been somehow detained, he was on the point of moving away to resume his patrol, when he heard someone crying out for help. Looking round he saw a man standing at the open French window of a room built out from 'The Cedars' on the ground level, and beckoning to him with a certain wildness and urgency of gesture. Bobby began to run; quickly and lightly he ran up the gravel drive towards that gesticulating figure, which now, seeing him coming, ceased to gesture but waited with hardly less of urge and concentration in its intense, still attitude.

'Murder,' this man said as Bobby, leaving the drive, came running across the lawn to him, 'it's murder – it's Sir Christopher Clarke and he's been murdered.'

CHAPTER 4

The Billiard-room

WHEN he had called out this, and seen that Bobby had heard and was coming as quickly as possible, the stranger went back into the room. Bobby followed him through the open French window. It was a billiard-room he found himself in, containing a full-sized table, and at one end three or four comfortable-looking chairs grouped before the fireplace. A game had apparently been in progress, for the balls, and one cue, were on the table, and another cue was lying on the ground. The scoring board showed thirty-four for one player, forty for the other. Between the head of the billiard-table and the chairs before the fireplace lay the body of Sir Christopher, supine and still. Only a glance was needed to tell that here was death, for there was that about the prostrate form which told that all rendering it significant had fled, leaving it void, a deserted habitation. Yet there was something, too, in the contorted features, and the eyes still glaring upward under those bushy brows, that seemed to say the soul had parted from the flesh in anger and tumult and most fierce hatred.

Close by lay a revolver, and an acrid smell of powder still lingered in the room. From two round, burnt holes in the dead man's chest bubbles of blood were oozing with a slow and dreadful regularity. From some other room in the house came the sound of music, one of Wagner's stormy pieces somebody was playing on the piano, and playing very well too, as even Bobby's limited knowledge of music told him. The crashing, reverberating chords seemed somehow a fitting accompaniment to the tragic scene on which he was gazing.

He said to the man who had called him:

'What do you know of this?'

'Only that I found him lying here, and I remembered I had seen a policeman at the gate, so I thought I had better call you at once. My name's Gregory,' he went on, 'Dr Gregory. I'm Sir Christopher's medical attendant. I came across to-night to see him – my God, who can have done it?' he broke off, as if with a fresh realization of the horror of the thing.

'You didn't see or hear anything else?' Bobby asked, and when the doctor shook his head, he added: 'No one else knows, you've told no one else?'

'No,' answered the doctor. 'I came in by the window there. I saw it was open and I thought Sir Christopher might be here. As soon as I got into the room I saw him, like that, dead. Someone's shot him.'

'It couldn't be suicide?' Bobby asked, and then: 'That doesn't matter now. The first thing is to get help. I suppose they have a phone here I can use. Will you wait till I get back and make sure no one comes in? Please don't touch anything, don't even close the window. Just stand by and see no one comes in. I'll lock the door behind me to stop anyone coming in that way. No one seems to have heard the shots. Has that music been going on all the time?'

'I think so,' Gregory answered. 'It's Miss Laing, I expect. I don't think it's ever stopped.'

Bobby didn't wait to ask who Miss Laing might be. He went out into the corridor, locking the door behind him and putting the key in his pocket. The music sounded more loudly here. Evidently it came from a room just across the passage in which he found himself. The door a few steps farther along was half open and looking in Bobby saw that it was a large, well-furnished apartment, the drawing-room apparently. At one end was a grand piano at which, with her back towards him, a woman was sitting. The crashing chords of the Wagnerian music she was playing seemed to fill all the air, and Bobby thought it was no wonder that the pistol shots had not been heard, or, if heard, had merely been taken for a specially vigorous outburst. The music swelled now into the notes of a triumphal march, played with something of the vigour and the passion that characterized the music itself, and Bobby wondered what the player would think if she knew of the dreadful event that had just taken place while she poured out these strains of victory. Without entering the room, he walked on and came to the large inner hall, where he found himself face to face with his recent acquaintance, Lewis, who looked very bewildered and surprised at his unexpected appearance.

'He doesn't know anything either of what has happened,' Bobby thought, 'that's plain enough.' Aloud he said. 'There has been an accident. Have you a phone here? I want to use it at once, please.'

'An accident?' Lewis repeated. 'Them motors, them motors,' he said, shaking his head, 'never know where you are with 'em. Is it bad?'

'Yes,' said Bobby impatiently. 'I must get help at once. You've got a phone?'

'We've two,' answered Lewis proudly. 'One in the outer hall with an extension to my pantry, and Sir Christopher had one put in for himself. In his study, that is.'

'I'll use that one,' said Bobby, thinking it would be more private. 'Where's the study?'

'But Sir Christopher mightn't like – ' protested Lewis. 'Very particular gent, Sir Christopher.'

'Not now,' answered Bobby. 'There'll be no objection from him now. Show me the room, quick, don't waste any more time.'

Impressed by Bobby's manner, trained, too, by lifelong habit to obey the orders given him, Lewis led the way, though still a little uneasily, to a large comfortably furnished room, the principal features being an enormous writing-table in the middle of the apartment and a correspondingly enormous safe against one wall. The door of the safe hung open and the contents seemed somewhat disordered. The window, of the sash type, was open and the curtains pulled aside. As the house stood on a pronounced slope, the flooring on this, the east side, was not on a level with the ground as was the case on the west where the billiard-room was situated, but was raised several feet above the ground. On the big mahogany writing-table stood a phone. Bobby picked it up and called the police station.

'Well, now,' said Lewis, staring hard at the open safe, ' I never knew the guv'nor leave that open before, I never did.'

Bobby was through now and briefly reported. He was told help would be sent at once and that meantime he must see nothing was interfered with. Lewis, hearing what was being said, stood as if utterly paralysed, till at last he burst out in a sort of shout:

'Murdered? Sir Christopher? The guv'nor shot? Good God Almighty, who done that? Who...?'

He looked as if he were going to run out of the room in his excitement, but Bobby caught hold of his arm and pulled him back.

'Now, don't lose your head,' he said sharply. 'Pull yourself together.'

'But it can't be,' Lewis protested. 'It isn't possible, not him...it can't...'

He was silent, abruptly realizing that all the same – it was. To him, his master had seemed the very embodiment of authority and power, and to imagine him now, the victim of such a deed, was almost beyond his power.

'Murdered? Him? Are you sure?' he asked weakly.

Bobby was still at the phone.

'I think the murderer was seen escaping,' he said. 'The caretaker at the next house – it's empty – saw a man in the garden there and thought he was stealing fruit and went after him. He got away over the wall, and the caretaker only had a passing glimpse of him, so I'm afraid that won't be much help.'

'I know who done it,' cried Lewis. 'It's that old chap in

the grey whiskers what the guv'nor told me to look out for. That's him. The guv'nor did him down in the City and now he's got his own back.'

'You'll have to tell the C.I.D. people that when they get here,' Bobby said, a little worried, though, for while that seemed a plausible idea on the face of it, nevertheless it was certain that whoever had escaped with such agility and speed through the next door garden and over an eight-foot wall studded with glass, could hardly have been an old man. 'You had better come back to the billiard-room and identify the body,' Bobby added. 'Dr Gregory is there. You know him?'

'Dr Gregory? Yes, but how did he get there? I didn't know he was in the house; no one's let him in that I know of.'

Bobby offered no explanation. He asked:

'Who else is there in the family? Anyone else staying here?'

'There's the two young ladies,' Lewis answered. 'Miss Brenda and Miss Jennie. That's Miss Brenda what's playing. Miss Jennie's upstairs resting before dinner. There's no one else staying here; there's a Mr Belfort coming to dinner.'

'What servants are there?'

It seemed the staff consisted of Lewis himself, the chauffeur who lived in a cottage a short distance away, and was presumably there now as he had been told he would not be required again that day, and four maids, cook, parlourmaid, housemaid, and 'tweenie' in order of dignity and rank. They were probably all now in the kitchen, busy with preparations for dinner. The fairly extensive gardens were kept up by contract, and there was a woman who came in daily to do the rougher work and always left again at five.

It was not information that seemed to promise much towards the elucidation of the mystery, and Bobby and Lewis went back together to the billiard-room. As they came into the inner hall, the music, which had been going on all this time, came to an end. A moment later a tall, handsome girl, with strongly-marked features, dark hair, dark, heavy-lidded eyes, altogether a striking and commanding personality, came out of the drawing-room. Seeing them she stopped and looked at Bobby, as if asking for an explanation of his presence there. She did not speak, but all the same had the air of waiting for and expecting an answer as she stood and watched them. Offering the explanation he felt she was demanding, Bobby said:

'I am sorry to have to tell you, madam, there has been an accident.'

'An accident?' she repeated, turning her dark, strong gaze on him. 'What accident? Who to?'

'To Sir Christopher,' he ventured. 'You are Miss Brenda Laing?'

With a slight gesture of one hand she seemed to acknowledge her identity and put it aside as unimportant.

'But Sir Christopher is in the house,' she said, 'he came back from the City an hour ago. I did not know he had gone out again. Is it serious?'

'He is dead,' Bobby answered, for somehow he felt he was facing a personality strong enough for the truth and desirous of it above all else. 'He has been found shot. There is nothing as yet to show whether it is accident, suicide, or – murder.'

She might not have heard, so still did she stand, so unmoved were her features, so level and so steady was her gaze. But very slowly she lifted both her hands, and put them to her throat, and one felt that she was struggling desperately to maintain her self-control. In a low voice she said:

'Accident, suicide, or – murder.' And then again: 'Accident, suicide, or – murder.' Then more loudly, she said: 'Someone must tell Jennie, someone must tell Jennie at once.'

'Let that wait for a time, madam, if you please,' Bobby said. 'You heard no report of any pistol shot?'

'I have been playing the piano for nearly an hour,' she answered. 'I heard nothing. When did it happen? Where is he? You are sure there is no mistake?'

'There is no mistake,' Bobby answered. 'I expect officers here immediately. Until they come do you mind waiting in the drawing-room?'

'Someone must tell Jennie,' she repeated. 'That will be dreadful, telling Jennie.' To Lewis she added abruptly: 'Have you seen Mr Lester? I thought I saw him go by the drawing-room window just now.'

'I didn't know he was here, miss,' Lewis answered. 'I haven't seen him.'

'If you do, ask him to come to the drawing-room,' she said, and then to Bobby: 'Accident, suicide, or – murder? Accident? Accidents never happened to him; he never let them. Suicide? Oh, that's impossible; he never would, it was life he wanted, not death. Murder? No, it was not murder.'

'I am afraid it was, madam,' Bobby said, 'but that will be decided soon.'

She lifted one hand high in the air.

'If it is murder,' she said, 'it will be punished. Murder is always punished, for that is God's will.'

For a moment she stood there, her hand uplifted, almost like some inspired prophetess of old. Then she turned and went away quickly, and in silence and motionless Bobby and Lewis watched her go.

CHAPTER 5

The Open Safe

WHEN they reached the door of the billiard-room, Bobby for a moment could not find the key. Manfully though he strove to control his excitement and to remain cool and collected, he was too conscious of the responsibility that rested on him, too well aware of the importance of the chance fate had offered him, to be quite normal. Any slip he made, any blunder, any trifling negligence or oversight might mean that this atrocious crime would go unpunished. And if he handled these preliminaries well, a transfer to the C.I.D., with a good mark against his name, might easily be his reward.

But in which pocket he had put that wretched key he could not imagine, and he grew hot all over as he reflected that even so trifling an incident as this might ruin all. What would Mitchell, the famous head of the C.I.D., think of a man who at a critical moment lost the key – ah, there was the wretched thing, in the very first pocket he had felt in, too. To hide the delay from the waiting Lewis, who was besides much too excited and over-wrought to have noticed that there was any delay at all, he said:

'Was that Miss Laing we were talking to?'

'Guv'nor's stepdaughter; Lady Clarke had her by her first marriage. Miss Jennie's his own daughter.'

'Where's Lady Clarke? Is she in the house?'

'Oh, she's been dead years – when Miss Jennie was only a kiddie, she died. Before my time that was.'

'Miss Laing's a striking-looking young woman,' Bobby observed, for he had been a good deal impressed both by her manner and appearance.

'Oh, I've nothing against her,' answered Lewis. 'Quite a nice lady to have in the house if you do your work proper, but it don't do to get in her bad books. She's one of them as don't forget.'

'Who is the Mr Lester she mentioned?'

'That's the young gent she's engaged to,' Lewis explained. 'Don't see what he can have been doing outside the drawing-room window, though.'

'And Miss Jennie you speak of?' Bobbie asked. 'Is she engaged, too?'

'Like to be, only her pa won't let her,' Lewis grinned, and then with a sudden realization: 'And now he's dead, just think of that.'

'Was there any special reason for his objecting, do you know?' Bobby asked.

'Only as he wanted better for her,' answered Lewis. 'You can't wonder, either. Mr Carsley's only a lawyer, does work for the guv'nor, that's how he's been here sometimes. But of course when the guv'nor found out what was going on he put his foot down hard – like the way he could. And now he's dead,' Lewis added, evidently hardly able to believe it.

Bobby had the key in the door by now. He turned it and they went in. A little to his relief Dr Gregory was still there, patiently keeping watch by the window. An absurd fear had been in Bobby's mind that possibly the doctor might be the murderer himself and have used this interval to make an escape for which he, Bobby, might he held responsible. However, nothing of the sort had happened, and Bobby said to him:

'I got through; they are sending help as soon as they can.'

'That's him all right, that's Sir Christopher, that is,' said Lewis, staring with a kind of fascinated horror at the still and prostrate form upon the ground. 'That's him . . . dead,' he said, his voice suddenly high and shrill, and he sat down heavily on the nearest chair as though collapsing beneath the weight of that knowledge. 'He's dead all right, he is,' he muttered, 'and who's done it?'

A new idea came into Bobby's mind, one he realized he ought to have given more weight to before.

'Do you know if there were any valuables in the safe in the study?' he asked Lewis. 'It was open and the window was open, too.'

Lewis shook his head slowly, his eyes still upon that prostrate form from which it seemed he could not remove them.

'I don't know what he kept in it,' he answered. 'I've never seen it open before, never. Whoever would have thought of a thing like that happening in a house like this?'

There appeared suddenly at the window the burly form of that Sergeant Doran for whom Bobby had been waiting. He gave a quick look at the body but did not seem much surprised.

'Bad business, Doctor,' he said to Gregory, whom apparently he recognized. 'Gent done himself in, eh? Done anything, Owen?'

'I've reported by phone,' Bobby answered. 'They said they would be along at once.'

'That's right,' said Doran approvingly. 'I suppose it is suicide?'

'I don't think so,' Gregory answered. 'He has been shot twice, both times near the heart. A man can hardly shoot himself twice through the heart.'

Doran looked startled and stepped into the room.

'Murder, eh?' he said. 'That's murder, if it's like that, only what did the old cove mean, telling me the gent at "The Cedars" had shot himself? So I came along quick as I could. Old lady knocked down by a motor in the High Street stopped me being here before,' he added to Owen.

'Do you mean someone told you Sir Christopher had shot himself?' Gregory asked, looking puzzled. 'How could he know anything about it?'

'Things like that get about quick enough,' Doran answered. 'All over the place they are, before you can turn round.'

'I don't see how anyone could know,' Gregory repeated, 'except your man here and myself – and the murderer.'

Doran's jaw dropped and he looked very much taken aback.

'You don't mean you think the old chap who spoke to me was the murderer himself,' he protested. 'Murderers don't give information themselves about what's happened.'

'I don't see how he can have known,' Gregory repeated once more.

'Was he a man about middle height and size, well dressed, sandy beard, grey felt hat?' Bobby asked, describing as well as he could the elderly man he had noticed and who had seemed to be showing so much interest in the house.

'You know who he is?' Doran asked sharply.

Bobby explained; and added that the caretaker of the empty house next door had seen someone rush through the garden there and climb the wall into the street.

'He cut his hand doing it, I think,' Bobby added, 'for there was what looked to me like blood on the broken glass on the top of the wall.'

'May turn out a useful clue, that,' commented Doran. 'Good thing you noticed it.'

'There's another thing, Sergeant,' Bobby went on. 'The study window is wide open and there's a safe there with its door open, too. It looks to me as if someone had been at it. I don't know if that can have anything to do with what's happened here.'

'It may have,' agreed Doran. 'Sounds a bit queerish. You had better go back there and see nothing's interfered with or touched. Can't be too careful in these cases.'

Bobby went off accordingly, though he would much rather have stayed in the billiard-room, on which he supposed the investigation would centre. But orders must be obeyed, and as he passed the drawing-room door, which was wide open, he saw Brenda standing within, between the grand piano and and a large and expensive-looking combined gramophone and wireless cabinet. Close to her, looking up at her from an armchair in which she was crouching down, as though she had just collapsed into it, was another girl, of a very pretty and graceful appearance. She had nothing of Brenda's rather imposing and striking manner and presence, but her features were good, and her small, well-shaped head was crowned by a mass of fair curls that owed all to nature and nothing at all to the hairdresser. Her wide-opened eyes were of a singularly clear, bright blue, and though now her whole attitude was one of startled terror, there was about her still something of lightness and of gaiety, so that the thought came into Bobby's mind that she was like a butterfly caught in a sudden storm. Seeing Bobby pass, and noticing his uniform, she gave a quick cry, and Brenda put out a hand towards her as if to soothe and reassure her.

'Hush, darling,' she said, and then, to Bobby: 'Has anyone come yet? Is there anything we can do?'

'I must go to him,' the younger girl cried, and Brenda said again:

'Hush, Jennie, darling, hush.' She added to Bobby: 'I had to tell Miss Clarke.'

'I must go to him. Why can't I go to him?' Jennie repeated.

'Not yet,' Bobby said to her. 'It is better not, not yet. We are doing everything possible. We will do our best to find out what's happened.'

He went on, feeling very sorry for the two girls, more especially for the younger one who looked so pretty and so fragile. It seemed to him sad that her young life should be darkened by such a tragedy. The elder girl, he thought, seemed like a tower of dark strength, able to stand up against worse things still.

'Must be a dreadful shock for them both,' he thought. 'Unbelievable thing to happen, they must think it.'

By now the maids, too, had become aware that something was amiss. He found them all four clustering uneasily by the

39

service door at one end of the hall. He told them that their master had met with an accident, but that Dr Gregory was in charge, help had been sent for, and that there was nothing for them to do but to go on with their ordinary duties.

Then he proceeded to the study where he looked very thoughtfully at the open window and the open safe against the wall, for it seemed to him strange that when Sir Christopher went to the billiard-room at the other end of the house, he should have left his study with the door of the safe wide open like this.

Only had he?

Certainly there was no sign that the safe itself had been tampered with in any way, but then as he had noticed before the contents seemed disarranged and in disorder. One large envelope, apparently containing papers, had fallen on the floor, and looking at it, though he was careful not to touch it, Bobby saw that it bore the imprint of Marsden, Carsley, and Marsden, Lincoln's Inn.

'That's the lawyer the Jennie girl is sweet on, I suppose,' Bobby commented to himself.

He crossed to the window and examining it carefully was able to detect what seemed to him recent scratches on the sill, as though someone had climbed in there recently. Unfortunately, the ground just beneath was flagged and showed no footprints. But bending out farther, though still with great caution, Bobby saw that just below the sill a piece of freshly-torn cloth fluttered on an old rusty nail that had at some time, for some reason, been driven in the wall, between the bricks. Cautiously he detached it, and placing it on paper on the writing-table, examined it closely.

'Bit of striped worsted, apparently,' he muttered. 'Well, I wonder what the C.I.D. will make of that? Got to look for someone wearing striped worsted trousers, I suppose.'

He heard motor cars arriving and concluded that the Yard people had come at last. He wished very keenly that he had been allowed to stay in the billiard-room. It would have been very interesting to see how the big men set to work. Mitchell would be there, no doubt, and other big wigs as well, perhaps even that semi-divinity, the Assistant Commissioner himself. For this was probably going to be a big case and rouse much public interest.

But a humble constable with only three years' service to his credit could not expect to be allowed to participate in the doings of the great, and so resignedly he took a slip of paper, timed himself very carefully, and copied out the brief report he had made of the incident of the caretaker and his apples and the escape of the intruder into the 'Elmhurst' garden.

He found that writing this out again took five minutes and a half and at that he rubbed his nose very hard indeed.

'More and more of a puzzle,' he thought. 'What was Dr Gregory doing for five and a half minutes?'

CHAPTER 6

Clues

MEANWHILE, in the billiard-room, the whole routine of
such investigations was in full process. Superintendent Mitchell himself was there, his natural loquacity a little checked,
but not much, by the presence of the Assistant Commissioner, for Bobby had been right in thinking the case was of
sufficient importance to draw even that potentate from the
Olympian heights whereon he usually dwelt. And there was
the Divisional Detective-Inspector, and one or two other
inspectors, all with their attendant sergeants, and an expert
photographer, and two finger-print experts, and various
other plain-clothes and uniform men till indeed the room
was so crowded it was a wonder anyone there could get
anything done at all.

Nevertheless a good deal of work was being accomplished
and gradually the crowd thinned as one or other departed
on this ground or on that, the photographer to develop his
plates, the finger-print experts after him, and everyone else
who had nothing more important to do, to search the garden
in the hope of finding footprints or any other clue. And the
unhappy Bobby, alone, hungry, apparently forgotten, sat
solitary in the study, and cursed the fate that had first
plunged him into the midst of what seemed likely to prove
the most sensational murder London had known for many
years, and then thrown him carelessly into the backwater of
a deserted study.

He had permitted himself to open the study door as wide
as possible, in the hope that one or other of the important-
looking people he saw bustling to and fro might notice him
as he sat within and watched them wistfully. The big man
with the pale, flat face and small sandy moustache was, he
knew, the famous Mitchell. At first sight it was difficult to

say why even the most desperate criminal dreaded this man's name and in his presence lost courage and self-possession; at least, it was till one noted how tightly the lips could close when they were not parted for speech, with what intensity of purpose the deep-set, grey eyes could glow at times. The tall, thin man in eye-glasses, who moved with so assured a step of authority and dignity, was probably, Bobby thought, the Assistant Commissioner, a person whose majestic path through life the humbler track pursued by Bobby had not yet approached. As a matter of fact the gentleman in eye-glasses was not the Assistant Commissioner, but the Assistant Commissioner's assistant private secretary. The Assistant Commissioner was a small, thin, harassed-looking man, who went in perpetual fear of superiors and subordinates alike, was bullied frightfully at home by wife and children and the domestic staff, and never opened a daily paper without a panic terror that it might be starting a campaign for his resignation. The Divisional Detective-Inspector Bobby knew, and there was also a detective-sergeant Bobby knew by sight from having seen him in short skirt, silk stockings with clocks, and a coquettish hat trimmed with cherries, leading the dancing girls' chorus at the last performance of the police minstrels. He still limped a little, though, from a bullet through the thigh he had received when arresting an Irish Communist at Liverpool, and there was some fear that this would interfere permanently with his dancing.

But no one took any notice of Bobby; his only visitor was Lewis, who came in and said he wanted to use the phone as Miss Jennie had told him to call up Peter Carsley and ask him to come at once.

'Can't get near the phone in the hall,' grumbled Lewis. 'There's generally one of your lot using it, and another telling him to hurry up because he wants to use it, too. Lucky they don't know about this one.'

But at last, when Bobby had almost resigned himself to stay there permanently, Mitchell himself strolled in, accompanied by another man to whom he was holding forth at great length on, apparently, the advantages of one special make of motor car over all others. His companion, whom Bobby did not recognize, tried to get in a word or two, but each time he opened his mouth was beaten down and silenced by the steady flood of the other's eloquence that finally swept him clean out of the room, though as he departed he did succeed in getting in one final shot when Mitchell at last paused for breath.

'I don't agree with you,' he said and vanished.

'There you are wrong,' said Mitchell with intense conviction.

Then he turned to Bobby, who was aware all at once of an odd conviction that the whole time Mitchell had been talking motoring, his attention had in fact been concentrated upon Bobby – and also that the concentration of Mitchell's attention was a formidable thing.

'Name?' Mitchell asked, suddenly brief.

'Owen, Robert Owen,' Bobby answered.

'Service?'

'Three years, a little more.'

'Age?'

'Twenty-five two months back,' answered Bobby, and thought to himself: 'You knew all that before.'

'Don't like night clubs, do you?' Mitchell fired at him next.

'No, sir.'

'Why not?'

'Some do, some don't,' said Bobby. 'I don't. That's all.'

'Wasn't it you gave Higgins April the Fifth for the Derby last year?'

'Yes, sir,' answered Bobby, just a trifle uneasily, for the regulations against gambling are severe.

'Jolly well Higgins did on it, too,' said Mitchell enviously. 'I suppose you did, too?'

Bobby shook a melancholy head.

44

'I put my ten bob on Orwell,' he confessed sadly.

'That's life, that is,' declared Mitchell profoundly. 'Know a good thing, pass it on to the other fellow, pass it by yourself. Next time you'll know better – perhaps. Got anything good for to-morrow?'

Bobby remembered suddenly the butler's double. He offered that.

'A long shot but it might come off,' he said.

Mitchell gravely made a note of it.

'I might risk half-a-crown, and I might not,' he observed. 'What's this about a fellow you saw cutting off through the garden next door?'

Bobby told his tale as briefly as he could; and he noticed that though Mitchell listened intently enough, he made no notes. This meant, Bobby felt sure, that Mitchell had already seen the caretaker of 'Elmhurst' and heard his story in full.

'Bad luck the caretaker smoothed those footprints the chap left under where he climbed the wall,' Mitchell observed. 'You didn't think to stop him?'

'No, sir,' said Bobby.

He made no attempt to offer any excuse, for he had an idea that Mitchell knew already everything he could say. And he thought also that Mitchell, talkative himself, was likely to prefer few words in others.

'You think there was blood on the glass on the top of the wall as if the chap had cut himself while climbing over?' Mitchell continued.

'Yes, sir. The left hand probably, judging from the position. Also I take it he must have been a young man and active from the way he got over the wall. And the caretaker says he threw a ripe tomato at him and hit him on the back, so his coat should show a stain.'

'Till he's cleaned it,' commented Mitchell. 'Still, it's something. So is the cut hand. Only was he the murderer, or was he only after apples, or was it something else altogether? What about this elderly man you say you saw?'

45

Bobby recounted how he had noticed him, noticed that he seemed interested in the house, and how his description tallied with that of the elderly man who had spoken to Sergeant Doran but had referred to the tragedy as to a case of suicide.

'Funny points about this case,' commented Mitchell. 'How did he know what had happened, and who is he, anyway? We shall have to try to find him, though, and that'll be a job unless he's willing to come forward.'

'At first,' Bobby ventured to remark, 'I thought it might be the man the butler here said Sir Christopher had warned him against. But the description's quite different.'

Secretly Bobby had hoped this might be fresh news to the great man, but apparently it wasn't, so that Lewis must have confided his suspicions to others as well as to Bobby.

'Have to look him up, too,' was all Mitchell said. 'There shouldn't be any trouble about identifying him, though. Most likely they'll know at Sir Christopher's office who it is. The description is all different, of course, but with most people if they describe a lame cow, it's odd they really mean a blind sheep – unless of course it's a woman describing another woman's hat. Hullo, hullo, what's that bit of cloth on the table there?'

Bobby was quite certain, in spite of these two 'hullos', that Mitchell had noticed it the moment he entered the room, for he had seen him look hard at it. Now Bobby told where and how he had found it, and by the light of his electric torch he showed Mitchell the scratches he had found on the window sill.

'This ought to have been reported before,' Mitchell said. 'Might be footprints in the garden.'

Bobby knew the garden had been searched, for from the window he had seen men busy at the task till darkness had made it impossible to continue. But he knew Mitchell knew that better than he did, so he said nothing again, and again

46

he had the idea that Mitchell approved this reticence. More mildly in a way and yet Bobby thought with more real meaning, Mitchell said:

'You should have left that bit of stuff where it was and let us know at once.'

'Sorry, sir,' said Bobby this time.

'Remember it another time,' Mitchell told him, 'that is if you are one who can learn from your mistakes. It's rare, most people only think of how to excuse them. How was this fellow you saw in the garden next door dressed?'

'I don't know, sir. I didn't see him.'

'You didn't ask the caretaker?'

'No, sir.'

'I did,' said Mitchell. 'He said he saw him clearly as he was running off, had only a glimpse of his face, thinks he was young and clean-shaven, and is certain he was wearing a grey tweed suit.'

Bobby said nothing, and Mitchell's eyes were on that fragment of striped worsted cloth as though he would tear its secret from it.

'Looks as though there were two of them,' he said. 'Burglars? But if that was one you saw escaping, what became of the other? How did they get the safe open? Must have had a key and known the combination, unless Sir Christopher left it like that – which isn't likely. Another point: looks as if a game of billiards had been going on. Now, if Sir Christopher was one of the players, who was the other? One of the burglars? No one seems to have seen anyone. There's the two young ladies, but there's evidence one of them was playing the piano the whole time, and the other was lying down. Anyhow, Sir Christopher was a dab at the game, and liked a strong opponent, and Lewis says he has never known either of the young ladies ever touch a cue. Can the old chap you saw, who spoke to Doran, have been in the house playing with Sir Christopher, shot him, and then walked away and spoken to Doran the way he did? You say he was looking at the house with a good deal of interest. If he had just shot someone in it, he might well be.'

'I had been standing there a good long time, sir,' Bobby said. 'I don't see how he could have got by without my seeing him – my recollection is he walked up from Rushden Road, like any passer-by. There's one point that struck me as a bit funny, if I may mention it,' he went on, a little nervously. 'After I had been in the "Elmhurst" garden I stood close to the entrance gate to this house, and made a note in my pocket-book. I didn't see Dr Gregory and I'm sure he didn't pass me. It took me at least five minutes and a half to write what I did. I've checked the time by copying it out again. Dr Gregory must have been in the billiard-room during that period, between five and ten minutes that is, with the murdered man on the floor. What was he doing all that time before he came out and called me?'

'Bear looking into,' admitted Mitchell. 'Bear looking into. Anything else you noticed?'

'No, sir.'

'I've offered the young ladies to leave a man here all night in case they feel nervous,' Mitchell said. 'Quite grateful they were, so that's all right. I think you had better take the duty. You can phone home that you are detained or your inspector will send a message round for you. They'll be back here soon to examine this room for finger-prints. Don't leave it till they come, but then you can go and get something to eat – the butler will give you something. I want you to sleep here. Miss Brenda's promised to provide some blankets, and you can make up a bed on the couch or somewhere. It's important to know if anything has been taken from the safe, or if it's been tampered with in any way, and I don't want it out of our sight till I'm sure. But we shall have to get that information from Sir Christopher's City staff, or his lawyers, and that'll have to wait till the morning.'

'Miss Jennie has sent for Mr Carsley already,' Bobby said. 'The butler came in here and rang him up. He is one of the firm that did Sir Christopher's legal work for him. I believe he and Miss Jennie wanted to be engaged but Sir Christopher wouldn't hear of it.'

'Possible motive there,' observed Mitchell, looking almost excited. 'Sounds interesting, anyhow. Nothing else to tell me, have you?'

'Only,' replied Bobby, remembering something that till now had escaped his mind, 'that Miss Brenda is engaged to a Mr Lester and thought she saw him near the drawing-room window about the time the murder was committed. But Lewis hadn't seen him or anyone else apparently.'

'Sir Christopher object to him, too?'

'I don't think so.'

'Might be him the game of billiards was being played with,' observed Mitchell. 'Bear looking into. I must go now, but I'm coming back, though I didn't mean to, and if Mr Carsley arrives while I'm away, don't say anything at first, but don't let him go till I've got back. Understand?'

'Yes, sir.'

'Suppose he won't stop, what'll you do?'

'Arrest him for obstructing a police officer in the execution of his duty,' answered Bobby.

'Young man,' said Mitchell, 'I almost think if you don't make a fool of yourself, which generally happens, you'll get on.'

He went away then and Bobby took care to be not far off when presently a ring at the door announced Peter's arrival. Lewis showed him into the drawing-room where Brenda and Jennie were waiting, and before very long Mitchell was back again.

'Our bird here?' he asked Bobby, who had admitted him.

'Yes, sir,' answered Bobby. 'He's in the drawing-room with the two young ladies. He's wearing a blue serge suit and his left hand is bandaged as if he had cut it recently.'

CHAPTER 7

An Oath Sworn

MITCHELL whistled softly.

'Bear looking into,' he said, 'that will . . . only if it's him did it, would he have the face to come back here like that? If he has, then he's the world's record holder for cheek and impudence. Gone in to talk to the two girls, has he? Well, we won't interrupt them just yet, though I would give a year's pay to hear what he's saying to them.'

'I think he and Miss Jennie are alone,' Bobby said. 'I saw Miss Brenda come out of the drawing-room and go upstairs soon after he went in.'

'Tactful young woman,' observed Mitchell. 'Makes me want to know still more what the other two are saying. A real sleuth, young man, would be hiding under the drawing-room table, noting down every word. I suppose you never thought of that?'

'No, sir,' said Bobby.

'Pity,' said Mitchell, 'not that listeners often hear anything that's much use – the really successful detective is the man who sits in his office waiting for people to come and tell him things. Hullo, who's that?' he added as there came a knock at the door. 'Some of our people again?'

'Shall I go?' Bobby said, and when he opened the door – Lewis, slumbering more or less profoundly on a chair in his pantry, had heard nothing – he saw a tall, thin, pale young man, with a high forehead, deep-set, eager eyes, a mouth of which the long, thin lips were twitching nervously. He had no hat, and his hair, which he wore rather long, hung over his forehead. He had a trick of frequently tossing his head to throw these loose locks back. Bobby noticed specially his hands, which were long and white, rather beautifully shaped and evidently very carefully tended. In his manner was something intense, or rather repressed, as if all the time he were holding his full energies in check, and when he spoke it was with a slight stammer, though whether that was habitual or the result of present excitement, Bobby could not tell.

'Oh, police,' he said now, staring at Bobby's uniform, 'police – it's true then?'

Bobby said nothing, but waited. The stranger went on:

'My name's Lester – Mark Lester. I'm a friend. We've heard Sir Christopher has been shot – is it true? I came at once. Is Miss Laing up still, do you know?'

'Mr Lester?' Bobby repeated, remembering the name at once. 'You had better come in. I think Mr Mitchell would like to see you – Mr Mitchell is in charge of the case at present.'

'Then it is true?' Mark exclaimed, following Bobby across the hall to the study. 'What a dreadful thing – I came as soon as I heard. It's Miss Laing I came to see.'

'Mr Mark Lester, is it?' asked Mitchell from the study where he had been listening to all this. 'The young gentleman who is engaged to Miss Laing? Come in here for one moment, Mr Lester,' and beckoning Mark into the study he let loose on him such a flood of talk and of comment on the terrible nature of all such events, and on the invincible determination of the force he had the honour to represent to bring those guilty to justice, that Mark, at first quite dazed, began soon to show impatience and restlessness. But Mitchell's flood of talk flowed on, and Bobby would have wondered at it, too, had he not by now begun to understand that with Mitchell, not only did his brain work faster and clearer when his tongue was wagging unrestrainedly, but that he used the spate of words always at his command to distract the attention of others, to soothe their suspicions or doubts and to lull them into a sense of security.

'Just so, just so,' Mark said, at last managing to get a

word in, and at the same time edging towards the door. 'I thought if I could see Miss Laing if she's still up . . .'

But Mitchell had him by the top button of his coat and now launched into a fresh exordium.

'Exactly,' said Mark, very firmly indeed, and with a jerk freed himself from Mitchell's detaining finger and thumb.

But when he turned towards the door, Bobby was there, filling it so that none could pass, and Mitchell said:

'So you see, Mr Lester, that's how it stands, and there's one point I would like you to clear up if you can, and that is, what brought you here at half past six this evening?'

'But I've not been here before to-day at all,' Mark answered impatiently.

'Not for a game of billiards with Sir Christopher?'

'Certainly not,' Mark answered. 'I've often had a game with him, of course, but not to-day.'

'There is evidence you were seen about half past six this evening near the drawing-room window here!' Mitchell snapped, his thin, loquacious lips set and hard now, his eyes intent and fierce and dominating.

But Mark only shook his head and looked puzzled.

'I've not been near here the whole day till now,' he asserted.

'What have you been doing this evening?' Mitchell demanded.

'I don't see why you want to know,' retorted Mark, a touch of excitement coming into his manner. 'What are you asking for?'

'A murder has been committed and I am an officer of police charged with the investigation,' Mitchell answered. 'As such, I have a right to expect the help and assistance of every respectable law-abiding citizen.'

'Oh, well,' Mark answered, his somewhat dramatic nature evidently impressed by this pronouncement – as Mitchell had meant he should be. 'I left the City about five as usual – I'm with Baily and Leyland, the discount house. I got home some time before six and till dinner I was busy with a lecture I'm to give in a week or two on Chaucer. We had dinner at eight.'

'We?'

'My mother and I – I live with my mother. After dinner I left mother with her wireless and I went back to my work till mother came in to say Mrs Boyd, the vicar's wife, had rung up to ask if it were true that Sir Christopher Clarke had been found shot. So I came here at once to see what had really happened.'

'Take you long?'

'I suppose about forty minutes or so. I had to walk as it's so late. It only takes about ten minutes by tube.'

'Ah, yes, I see,' murmured Mitchell, asking for Mark's address and making a note of it. 'What room do you use as a study?'

'It's the one that used to be the breakfast-room,' Mark answered, 'but I don't see – '

'No, no,' interrupted Mitchell, who did not specially wish that Mark should 'see' as he called it. 'On the ground floor, I suppose?'

'It's on the right of the front door as you go in,' Mark explained.

'Ah, yes, quite so,' murmured Mitchell, waving aside a point that was evidently for him quite without interest or importance. 'Anyone come in to see you while you were working?'

'I do not care to be interrupted,' Mark answered with simple dignity, 'when I am at work.'

'Very natural, too,' agreed Mitchell warmly. 'No one came in then? But I wonder how it is that when you were working in your study at home, you were seen in the garden here?'

'I wasn't,' said Mark. 'Who told you such rot?'

Bobby from his place at the door said:

'Miss Laing is coming downstairs, sir.'

53

'Ask her to come in here,' Mitchell said.

Bobby went across to her accordingly; and she followed him back into the room, a tall, dark, tragic figure, with, for all her superb composure, a strained look about her that showed how much she was feeling the recent tragedy. Bobby even noticed a faint trembling of the muscles of her strong, white hand. But that was all; and as she stood there it was odd how, by the mere force of her personality and her silence, she seemed to dominate them all. The big, experienced Superintendent, with his air of resolve and concentration; tall, thin, intense-looking Mark Lester with his manner of being held back by bonds that might break at any moment; Bobby Owen in all the vigour of his splendid young manhood, alert and strong in mind and body, too; all three of them seemed somehow smaller in her presence. Mitchell said to her:

'You know Mr Lester?'

She turned her grave and questioning eye from Mitchell to Mark and then back, and she bent slightly her stately head.

'I understand you are engaged to be married?'

'That is so,' she answered quietly, and then, looking at Mark, she added: 'I knew you would come as soon as you heard.'

The young man flushed and gave her a quick look of gratitude and devotion. It was odd, Bobby thought, that this look appeared slightly to trouble her, as if it had awakened an emotion deeper than she had expected.

'I think,' Mitchell continued, 'you told the butler here that you saw Mr Lester in the garden, near the drawing-room window, about half past six? Is that so?'

'I saw someone; I only had a glimpse,' she answered. 'Was it you, Mark?'

'No, I went straight home from the City and have been there ever since,' he answered.

'Then it must have been someone else,' she answered

54

tranquilly. 'I did see someone; I am sure of that.' She paused and something like a faint smile fluttered for a moment at the corners of her mouth. 'I suppose because I was thinking of Mr Lester, I thought it was him. I knew he wasn't coming to-night but I expect I hoped he might.'

Again Mark looked at her with the same manner of devotion and of delight at her having had such a hope; and again Bobby thought that he could see she was for a passing moment a trifle surprised or even troubled by the emotion that he showed. It was almost as if his feeling for her surprised her, and yet they were an engaged couple, still presumably under the influence of the mutual passion and attraction that had brought them together.

Whether Mitchell also had noticed this Bobby was not sure, but it was quite plain that the Superintendent was a little disconcerted. It was perhaps not altogether surprising that a young girl, just engaged, should jump to the conclusion that any young man she had a glimpse of near the house was her lover coming to visit her – hope, expectation, longing, these soon produce a 'wish-fantasy' easily taken for reality. All the same he was not satisfied. So he took refuge in his customary device of a flood of words that however dried up rather more quickly than usual under Brenda's calm and steady eyes.

Mark said:

'Well, it wasn't me Miss Laing saw, but it looks as if that gave you something to go on. If it was the murderer, then you know it was someone about my size and build.'

'Yes,' agreed Mitchell. 'Was the person you saw,' he added to Brenda, 'wearing a brown tweed lounge suit like this gentleman? Do you remember?'

'I think he had on a dark coat and striped trousers,' Brenda answered. 'You have a suit like that, Mark?'

'Yes, but I put it aside to send to the cleaners two or three days ago,' Mark answered. 'It's not gone yet.'

'Interesting,' murmured Mitchell, and glancing at

Bobby saw that he, too, was thinking of the morsel of striped trousering found outside the library window.

Only who was it who had left that behind him? And was it the murderer? And, if so, how had he been able to carry out a murder at one end of the house, a burglary at the other, and yet escape being seen except for this passing glimpse Miss Laing reported? Mitchell shook his head; it seemed impossible to him and yet he did not know what to make of it.

Mark turned abruptly to Brenda. It was a little as if something that had been holding him back had been suddenly slackened, so that for the moment he was freer, as if for the instant his real self was showing. He said with a kind of fierce, almost dramatic intensity:

'Your father's murderer shan't go unpunished. If the police can't find who did it, by God in his Heaven, I will.'

It was a sudden and unexpected outburst that startled them all.

'I hope we shall succeed,' Mitchell said drily, 'but if we fail, Mr Lester, you've taken a great oath there.'

'Mark,' Brenda exclaimed, and for once even her superb tranquillity seemed troubled. 'Mark, you should not have said that. Mark, what made you?'

Mark himself was looking a little surprised.

'I don't know,' he muttered. 'It came into my mind; it just came into my mind somehow and I had to say it.'

Brenda turned and walked away and Mark followed her. Mitchell did not try to stop them, but he had a very worried air as he watched them cross the hall and disappear into the drawing-room where Peter Carsley and Jennie were still together, unaware till now, presumably, of Mark's arrival.

'I've a feeling,' Mitchell said slowly, 'that there's more in this case than in any I've ever handled – and a whole lot more than any of us has any idea of at present. If it wasn't that young fellow Miss Laing saw, who was it? Struck me she accepted his denial rather easily. Was that because she believed him at once – or because she didn't believe him at all? But then again, why should he want to murder the father – stepfather – of the girl he's going to marry. Though he does seem one of the high-strung, half-loony, artistic, literary type, that's always liable to go in off the deep end any time almost. Unstable as water, and ready to run in a flood like water any way you give 'em a tilt. Now, if Sir Christopher had objected to their engagement, same as you say he squashed that between Mr Carsley and the other girl – one could see a bit clearer. Bear looking into, though.'

'Yes, sir,' agreed Bobby. 'Here is Mr Carsley,' he added as the drawing-room door opened and Peter came out and walked quickly towards them.

CHAPTER 8

The Heiress

NOT without a certain emotion, for it seemed to them both it might be the solution of the mystery that was approaching them, the veteran Superintendent, the youthful constable, watched as Peter came quickly across the hall.

'Good-looking enough for the pictures pretty near,' Mitchell muttered to himself, noting the classic regularity of the young man's features; 'but all the same that mouth looks as if it would take a lot to stop it,' and indeed the look of almost fierce resolve stamped upon the young man's features, the firm lines about his mouth, something as it were of fire shining in his eyes, gave him an air like that he had worn when he had run almost the whole length of the field at Cardiff, clean through the opposing fifteen, to score at last for his side. 'Made up his mind to something and nothing's going to stop him. Only what?'

'It's the Carsley, sir,' Bobby said in his ear excitedly; 'he played for the University when I was there – jolly good man, ought to have been capped for England.'

Mitchell nodded, and was about to follow his usual plan of launching into a long harangue on the subject of sport in general, and Rugby football in particular, when there came a fresh knock at the door. Bobby went to answer it, for by this time Lewis's slumber was profound. It proved to be the finger-print experts come back to examine the study. So that room had to be left to them, while the other three sat in the hall, and Peter, who had been waiting in a kind of heavy brooding silence, said to Mitchell:

'There are some things I want to tell you. My name's Carsley, Peter Carsley. My firm's acted for Sir Christopher in legal affairs. Before I say anything else, I want to examine his safe. I believe it was found open. I have reason to believe it should contain a bundle of securities and bonds worth about twenty thousand pounds, mostly payable to bearer, all easily disposable of, and also diamonds worth a very large sum.'

'Then,' said Mitchell with decision, 'you may be pretty sure there's neither securities nor bonds nor diamonds there now. Only if there's been a burglary to that extent here, why was there murder at the other end of the house? How do you know all this, Mr Carsley?'

'The securities form part of a trust – the Belfort Trust,' Peter answered. 'There has been a change of trustees, owing to a death, and the new trustee, a Mr Belfort, is anxious to assure himself everything is in order. It was arranged he was to examine the papers here to-night. He was to dine here, and Sir Christopher was to go through the papers with him afterwards. It would be a long job, and Sir Christopher thought he could spare the time more easily here in the evening, than during the day in the City. Sir Christopher removed the securities from our care this afternoon – of course, we have his receipt – and he told Mr Marsden, my partner, that he would keep them all night and return them to-morrow.'

'Did anyone else know of this arrangement?'

'I suppose so,' answered Peter. 'It wasn't a secret. Our staff would know, and some of Sir Christopher's very likely, and Mr Belfort himself, of course, and anyone he mentioned it to.'

'Mr Belfort doesn't seem to have arrived,' Mitchell observed. 'Did Sir Christopher tell Mr Marsden about the diamonds you speak of?'

'Yes. Marsden asked if it wasn't rather dangerous to keep such a large sum in securities anyone could dispose of anywhere at any time almost. Sir Christopher said he had had diamonds worth as much in the safe for the last three months, and he thought the Belfort bonds would be all right for a single night.'

'Did Sir Christopher deal in diamonds?'

'Sometimes, as a sort of side line, when he saw a chance of a profitable deal. I believe he put through some fairly big deals at times. And I think he liked to have them as a sort of reserve for days when you never know what's going to happen to stocks and shares, or even to banknotes. He used to say diamonds and gold were always worth their value, but you could carry a fortune in diamonds in your pocket while you wanted a steam lorry to deal with any really big sum in gold.'

'Prudent gentleman, Sir Christopher,' Mitchell mused, 'even though it's always the prudent that seem let down the worst in the end, and now neither diamonds nor gold will help him much. I could see Mr Marsden in the morning at your office?'

'I don't know,' said Peter grimly. 'I don't know what he'll do; he may be there for all I know or he may – bolt.'

'Why bolt?' asked Mitchell, and Peter said:

'He told me this afternoon that he had embezzled the money of our clients to a very large amount and that the firm was bankrupt – fraudulently bankrupt.'

'He did, did he?' said Mitchell, blinking both eyes, and for once quite taken aback by this abrupt declaration. 'Well, that's – well, what did you do?'

'I don't think I quite remember,' Peter answered. 'It was rather a knock-out – I had never dreamed of such a thing. I didn't believe it at first, I thought he was just joking. Afterwards I went out and walked about the streets a bit. Then I went to see Sir Arnold Ameson, the K.C. He advised me to ring up the Public Prosecutor and ask for an appointment in the morning. I think he didn't quite believe it either; he said perhaps Marsden was only trying to frighten me. Then he said I had better go straight to Scotland Yard but I ought to see Marsden first to make sure he meant it. So I started off to do that, and then I thought it was silly, because I was jolly sure Marsden meant it all right enough.

I didn't know what to do, and I walked about a long time, and then I made up my mind to go to Scotland Yard. So I went home to get a wash and change, and something to eat first, because I felt such a wreck, and I found a message asking me to come here. So I did.'

Mitchell looked and felt rather helpless. Here was another big case, superimposing itself, as it were, upon a mystery that already seemed as puzzling as any he had ever dealt with. Before he could say anything, one of the finger-print experts put his head round the study door.

'You're wanted on the phone, sir,' he said to Mitchell.

'Ah,' said Mitchell, almost with relief, and went off. He was absent some minutes, and when he came back, he said:

'They've finished in there so we can go back. No luck with finger-prints so far, but then it's not often they're much good now – I believe these days when a six-year-old sets out to raid the strawberry jam in his mother's pantry, he puts on gloves first. It's what the papers call the spread of popular education. No trace of anything of value in the safe, either, Mr Carsley – no securities, no bonds, and no diamonds.'

He led the way into the study again, and as he settled himself comfortably, waving Peter to one chair and Bobby to another, he added carelessly:

'I see you've hurt your hand, Mr Carsley – how did that happen?'

Peter looked straight at his questioner; and now it was in challenge and in counter challenge, in defiance and in dreadful menace, that their gaze met.

'I cut it sharpening a pencil,' Peter said slowly, his eyes still staring straight into Mitchell's. 'When I pretty well ran out of the office after what Marsden told me, I was very upset and excited. I was off my head almost. It meant ruin at the best, it might mean public disgrace and prison if I couldn't clear myself of complicity. I remember thinking I must make some notes of what Marsden had said and pulling a pencil out. It wanted sharpening and my knife slipped and

I cut myself. I expect I was a bit shaky. I flung the pencil away and never made any notes after all.'

'I see,' said Mitchell slowly, 'I thought perhaps you might have done it while you were climbing a wall with glass on the top?'

'I don't know what you mean,' Peter answered, his eyes still quiet and steady. 'What wall? What glass? Why should I climb a wall with glass on it? I have told you how it happened.'

'I notice you are wearing a blue serge suit,' Mitchell said. 'Have you had that on all day?'

'No. I told you I felt so dirty and untidy and hungry, I went home for a wash and change before going on to Scotland Yard.'

'Not all our visitors are so particular,' said Mitchell dryly. 'I suggest you had another reason for changing your clothes.'

'What?' asked Peter.

'The coat you were wearing showed a stain where it had been hit by a tomato thrown at the man seen climbing the wall next door.'

'I don't know what you are talking about,' Peter answered steadily. 'If you care to send to my rooms, you can look for yourself. So far as I know, though my grey tweed suit is old enough, it shows no stain of any kind on the coat – and certainly no sign of having been cleaned recently.'

'It doesn't,' agreed Mitchell. 'When I was rung up just now, it was to receive a report from one of my men that a grey tweed suit found in your rooms had been examined and no stain or sign of recent cleaning found.'

'As I told you,' said Peter quietly. 'But does that mean you have had my rooms searched?'

'It does.'

'Had you a search warrant?'

'Oh, come, Mr Carsley, sir, and you a lawyer,' Mitchell protested gently. 'It's a service flat you occupy, isn't it?

Our men only called and asked permission to have a look through your rooms. There were three of them – one in plain clothes and a sergeant and constable in uniform. Numbers always impress, and it's a funny thing, too, but a uniform counts for a lot with most people – why, most of 'em would think more of a recruit in uniform than of the Commissioner himself in plain clothes. Your housekeeper lady did hum and ha a bit, but there were three men, and two of them in uniform, and people beginning to look already, and then of course it was explained to her that it was all entirely in your interest, and surely she knew enough of your standing and reputation to realize that everything was exactly as it ought to be, only it just happened certain steps were necessary. I don't know what she thought all that meant, but she agreed to our men having a look round – and if they had found signs of a recent stain on the back of the jacket of your grey tweed suit, Mr Carsley, I am inclined to think it would have been my duty to arrest you.'

'After which,' retorted Peter, 'it would have been my pleasure as a lawyer to try to make things hot for you.'

'Ah, we shouldn't have been afraid of that,' commented Mitchell pleasantly, 'not as if you were a charming young lady with big eyes and a look of innocence itself – the very devil that sort, have us permanently scared. Another thing. Your housekeeper – she looks after your clothing for you, doesn't she?'

'Yes.'

'She says you had two suits of grey tweed but only one was found.'

'I have only one,' Peter answered. 'I had two but the other – the newest one – I gave away to a fellow who said he had been at school with me. I didn't remember him, but he seemed to know fellows I knew, and as he said he had a chance of a job in Birmingham, if he could raise the fare and get there looking decent, I gave him a pound note and a suit of clothes. I daresay he was a fraud.'

'Very likely,' agreed Mitchell. 'When was this?'

'Two or three days ago.'

'Then it wouldn't help us,' sighed Mitchell, 'if we found him, and he was still wearing that suit, and it showed a stain on the back of the jacket. Could we find him, do you think?'

'I'm afraid not,' Peter answered. 'I was too glad to be quit of the poor devil to ask for his address or anything, and I don't remember his name – Hicks or Hickson or something like. that. He said he would write and tell me if he got the Birmingham job. He hasn't so far.'

'Would anyone remember him?' Mitchell asked. 'Anyone see him, I mean?'

'I don't suppose so. He spoke to me in the street outside my flat and I took him in myself and let him out again. Very likely no one else saw him.'

'Very likely,' agreed Mitchell softly. 'I think that's very likely indeed.'

'I'm afraid you don't believe me,' Peter said calmly. 'Well, I'm very sorry, but I can't help that. But I should like to know what all this means and what you're talking about?'

'A strange man,' explained Mitchell, 'presumably the murderer of Sir Christopher, though that's not certain, was seen escaping over the wall of the next door garden. A tomato was thrown at him, hit him on the back, and would presumably stain his coat. He is also believed to have cut his hand on the glass on the top of the wall. He is described as young, active, clean-shaven, and wearing a grey tweed suit. There was no attempt at pursuit because then what had happened was not known.'

'A pity,' observed Peter, 'but doesn't it occur to you that a good many people are young, active, clean-shaven, and wear grey tweed suits?'

'That's our difficulty,' admitted Mitchell, 'that's why we can hardly proceed to immediate arrest. You tell us also that your firm is bankrupt and that large sums, formerly in your charge, are now missing from Sir Christopher's safe over there?'

'I may remind you,' Peter pointed out, 'that I consulted Sir Arnold Ameson about five o'clock, some time, I suppose, before all this happened. I think it is fairly obvious that if I had contemplated burglary and murder, I shouldn't have been to see Sir Arnold first.'

'It's a point to remember,' agreed Mitchell. 'I understand you and Sir Christopher were on bad terms – you wished to be engaged to his daughter and he objected. Is that so?'

'Yes,' answered Peter. 'So we got married three weeks ago.'

'Eh, what? What's that?' exclaimed Mitchell, once again fairly startled. 'You mean that?'

'Of course I mean it,' answered Peter. 'You can ask my wife if you like, Mrs Carsley, Miss Jennie Clarke till our marriage.'

'Did Sir Christopher know?'

'I think he had some suspicion or some idea we didn't mean to give each other up because he disapproved. My wife is of age and was a free agent. But I think he was suspicious, for when he was at our office to-day he gave us instructions for two things. One was for settling forty thousand pounds on Miss Laing – that's his stepdaughter, Jennie's half-sister – on her marriage to Mark Lester next month.'

'That's a lot of money; that was generous of him,' Mitchell commented.

'A great deal of money and very generous of him indeed,' Peter said. 'I could hardly believe it, I didn't think he was that sort at all. There it is, though. His instructions were quite definite. He also destroyed his will, and gave instructions for drawing up a new one, leaving all the rest of his money to his daughter, Jennie, now my wife – if she were unmarried at his death.'

'Everything to her?'

'Exactly.'

'But she isn't unmarried – she's married to you.'

'Exactly.'

'Well, then, she gets nothing? Is that it?'

'She gets everything,' Peter replied. 'Neither the deed of settlement for Miss Laing's benefit, nor the new will, was completed or signed. Consequently the projected settlement is null and void and as Sir Christopher died intestate, owing to the new will not having been signed, his one surviving relative takes everything. Miss Brenda Laing being only a stepdaughter, the child of his wife by her first husband, is a stranger in blood, and has no claim whatever on the estate. Everything goes to the sole surviving child, his daughter, Jennie. She is sole heir.'

'And she is your wife and now she takes everything?' Mitchell repeated.

'Exactly,' answered Peter once again.

CHAPTER 9

Wakening Love

THE Superintendent's reaction to these revelations was un-expected. He took out his watch, looked at it, and pursed his lips for a low whistle.

'Ought all to have been in bed long ago,' he said. 'I'm never fit for anything next day if I don't get a proper rest. Good night, Mr Carsley, see you again soon I expect. By the way, while our man was looking round your flat he found your passport, so he's taken charge of it. You don't mind, do you?'

'Yes,' said Peter.

'I thought you would,' said Mitchell, amiably, taking Peter's arm in friendly fashion and drawing him out of the study into the hall. 'Take my advice and try to get some sleep yourself. Good night.'

'Good night,' said Peter.

The front door closed behind Mitchell's burly figure. Peter stood still and silent, staring after him, evidently engrossed in many thoughts. In the drawing-room they heard the front door close – Mitchell had not shut it silently – and Brenda opened the door of that room and stood on the threshold, waiting, without coming forward. One had the idea somehow that she was of the few who know how to wait – to wait till the moment comes. Behind her, Bobby, from his place within the study, could see the small, troubled face of Jennie, fluttering doubtfully there as if she wished to pass her stepsister and yet did not dare. The light from the hall lamp shone on her features and showed that she had been crying. It occurred to Bobby that Mitchell had gone as he had done, without a word or sign, partly because he did not wish to remind Peter or the others of Bobby's presence in the study, and that it was also for that reason that he had so gently led Peter into the hall. The study door had been left wide open, but, in the large comfortable arm-chair he was occupying, Bobby was not conspicuous. He shrank still farther back into it and he heard Jennie call:

'Peter, have they gone? Peter, what did they say?'

'Asked a lot of questions,' Peter answered, frowning and troubled, 'and then just cleared out.'

Jennie pushed by her sister and ran to Peter's side. Brenda followed slowly and after her came Mark Lester. Plainly they had all either forgotten Bobby or assumed that he had departed with his chief. Bobby did not think it necessary to remind them of his presence, he was fully prepared to listen to anything they chose to say among themselves before him, and he thought that so he might easily gain valuable information if not about the facts, at any rate about their beliefs, their characters, and their intentions.

'What sort of questions?' Jennie was asking. 'Was he horrid?'

'They've been nosing about my rooms,' Peter said. 'Like their cheek. I suppose you can't blame them, though. Apparently some chap, wearing a suit like the one I had on all day, was seen climbing the wall next door, and of course they think that was me.'

'How silly,' said Jennie, with intense conviction.

'The man I saw wasn't dressed like you,' Brenda remarked. 'He was wearing dark things and striped trousers – I'm quite sure of that, it's why I thought it was Mark at first, I suppose. Do you think there were two men?'

'It's the will that's making them suspicious,' Peter said. 'Jennie, if your father had had time to sign his new will, you would have had nothing. The money would all have gone to charity. That means, my wife would have had nothing. But he died before signing it, and you get everything. That means, my wife's a rich woman. I've married a rich woman because your father died to-night. I think it's plain they draw the obvious conclusion.'

68

'I never thought of that,' Brenda said in her deep, slow tones. 'There's such a lot you never think about.'

'We won't take the money, we won't touch it,' Jennie said simply. 'That'll make them understand. It must be just as father wanted. Of course, Brenda must have hers.'

'No,' said Brenda, almost with violence. 'No.'

'I don't think that would make any difference so far as I'm concerned,' Peter said moodily. 'People would only say you had done it trying to save me.'

Mark, who had not spoken before, said from behind, with great emphasis:

'That's all rot. Jennie mustn't give up her money. Why should she? It's perfectly obvious the will was only a dodge to try to stop you two marrying. But you had got married already, so that doesn't count for anything. And I think Brenda ought to have the money meant for her. I suppose she is entitled to some share anyhow, isn't she?'

'A stepdaughter is a stranger in blood,' Peter said. 'In law, Brenda is not entitled to anything. No one will accuse you, Lester,' he added bitterly, 'of committing murder to make your wife rich.'

'Anyhow, she ought to have what was clearly meant for her,' Mark repeated.

'Yes, of course,' agreed Jennie.

'No,' said Brenda. 'No.'

'I think I know how you feel,' Mark declared. 'I know exactly how you feel,' he repeated, 'but I've got to consider your future, your happiness.'

'Happiness?' she said with a strange accent. 'Happiness?'

'Well, of course,' Mark said, 'you don't feel like that now; it's natural to feel after such an awful thing happening you'll never be the same again.'

'Never,' Brenda said. 'Never.'

'You'll feel differently in time,' he told her tenderly.

'You don't think so now, but you will – when the murder's been cleared up and the murderer punished.'

'When,' said Brenda, 'when ... ' She added: 'Was it murder?'

'Must have been,' declared Mark. 'It can't have been suicide or accident because of two shots having been fired. So it must have been murder?'

'Must it?' said Brenda.

'Oh, I see what you mean,' he said, staring at her. 'Yes, there's that. Anyway, I'll find out. I'm going to work on my own lines. The police are never any good in a case like this, all red tape, no intuition; intuition working on reason is what you want. And once we know what's really happened, there'll be no need for Jennie to do anything silly about the money. First thing is to find out who the revolver belonged to. I've an idea about that.'

'Oh, don't let's talk about it any more,' Jennie cried suddenly, 'it's all too horrible. Brenda, Peter's going to stay here to-night.'

'But the spare room,' began Brenda, becoming the careful housewife again, and then when Jennie gave a little nervous laugh: 'Oh,' she said, 'I forgot you two are married. I can't realize it.'

'Three weeks,' Jennie said, and took Peter's hand.

They went away up the stairs together, he still looking very gloomy and troubled and she trying to cheer him. From the hall the other two watched them go and Mark slipped an arm round Brenda and said to her softly:

'It won't be long before we are married, too, and then I shall never have to leave you.'

'Oh, Mark, don't,' she cried with a sudden burst of emotion, releasing herself from his clasp almost with violence, 'not now, not while he's lying there ... it's awful.'

For a moment her strong self-control seemed on the point of breaking down, but Mark caught her hands and held them in his.

'Dearest, my own,' he said, 'it's a dreadful thing to have happened but you can't help it ... Brenda, it's not upsetting you so much because you think it was Peter did it?'

'Oh, no,' she answered, 'I know he didn't, I never thought that, I never thought any one could.'

'I don't either,' Mark told her. 'I'm afraid some people will, but that'll be all right when we get at the truth. I must make that my business – to get at the truth.'

'Must you?' she said, looking at him intently. 'Must you, Mark? Why?'

'We've got to know it,' he declared. 'Oh, there'll be all sorts of talk always going on. There'll be hints about you – '

'About – me? About me?' she stammered.

'Yes, and about Jennie, too. About Peter, of course. About me, too, very likely.'

'Oh, Mark, no, no one could – Mark,' she exclaimed.

'My dear,' he said, 'you don't know what people are capable of saying or how quickly gossip can spread.'

'There was a burglar in the house,' she reminded him. 'Why don't people think ...?'

'Looks,' Mark said, 'as if the burglary took place some time before the murder. And you can hardly imagine a burglar emptying a safe and then going right to the other end of the house to commit a murder – if it was murder, as you said.'

'It's all so dreadful,' Brenda said again.

'I think,' he said, softly, 'you feel it more than Jennie does, though he was her own father and only your stepfather.'

'I think I do,' she agreed. 'Poor Jennie's so taken up with Peter she can hardly realize it all. He was always rather harsh to her, too, they were never like some fathers and daughters are. Well, that's all the better now. Peter's very fond of her, I suppose.'

'Not in the way I am of you,' Mark said as softly as before.

He tried to take her hands again as he spoke but she drew back. She held him at arm's length and did not answer. A little troubled, he said:

'Why do you look at me like that?'

'Do you care for me?' she asked intensely. 'I never thought you did – I mean not like that. Why do you care for me?'

'I always have,' he told her. 'The first time I saw you it was like that. Didn't you know?'

'No,' she answered, shaking her head slowly, 'and it is very strange. If I had known before – perhaps it would have been different.'

'What?' he asked. 'What would have been different?'

She had a vague gesture he did not understand.

'I knew there was life,' she said, 'I knew there was death – but I never knew love was – like this ... real.'

'It's more real than life or death,' he said. 'Life doesn't last so long and death's soon over, but I think that love goes on.'

'It's strange talking like this,' she mused, 'when ... when he's lying there ... he's dead and we are talking like this,' she repeated.

'We're both a bit worked up,' he said, 'that's all ... you can't have things happening and not feel it.'

'I suppose that's it,' she agreed.

'I want you to feel I love you more than anything else in the world,' he told her.

'It's hard to understand,' she answered, watching him gravely. 'I always thought people liked each other ... I thought a girl liked to have a nice man to do things for her ... that's nature ... I thought a man liked to have a pretty girl to show off ... that's nature ... but you make me feel to-night it's all so different from that.'

'Of course it is,' he declared, 'just as different as it can be.'

'Do you love me?' she asked, but when he made a step towards her, once more she drew back.

'No, no, not now, not here,' she said, almost wildly.

'Dearest, dearest,' he protested, 'you're getting morbid.'

'Perhaps I am,' she agreed.

'You want a rest,' he told her, 'you want quiet. Brenda, you don't feel you love me yet, do you?'

'I don't think so. I don't think I understand what love is,' she answered. 'I think I could hate more easily. I think I know what hate is.'

'I'll teach you love instead,' he said smilingly.

'I think you are already,' she murmured, half to herself, and at that he kissed her with sudden passion.

But again she held him away, though this time very gently.

'Not to-night,' she said. 'You must go, it's very late.'

In a little while he did go, and Brenda went upstairs to her own room, having evidently entirely forgotten all about Bobby and her promise to supply him with blankets.

'They're all a bit hysterical, no wonder either, but hysterical, that's what they are,' Bobby told himself; and presently went to find Lewis and to wake him up, though that was no easy task. But finally from him he was able to extract some cold meat and bread and a couple of rugs.

Then Lewis retired sleepily to his bed, and Bobby settled down to snatch an hour or two's rest.

'Funny thing,' he thought as he dozed off, 'seems as though it had needed the murder to make those two find out they were in love – wonder what being in love's like,' he mused and slept profoundly.

CHAPTER 10

Uncertain Deductions

DEEPLY though Bobby slept, his slumber was as light as it was profound, and the first sound of movement in the house next morning brought him to his feet.

Lewis was not up yet, but in the eyes alike of the cook, of the parlourmaid, of the housemaid, of the 'tweenie', Bobby found favour. He was shown to a bathroom, Lewis was wakened in order to provide a razor, he was presently installed before an excellent and copious breakfast, and the least he could do he felt in return for so much goodwill was not only to be willing to talk himself but also to listen to the opinions and the comments of the cook, the parlourmaid, the housemaid, and the 'tweenie', to say nothing of those dignified observations which Lewis, when presently he made a yawning appearance, felt disposed to contribute to the discussion.

But presently bells upstairs began to ring, there were cups of tea to be prepared, breakfast to be got ready, rooms to be dusted; and, with the domestic staff getting busy over the day's routine, Bobby decided to take a stroll through the gardens and see what he could find there, and as he did so he felt he knew nearly as much about the household as if he had lived there for years.

'More,' he told himself, 'for then I should only have my own ideas and they would be all wrong, but now I've the ideas of four women and one man, all wrong, too, of course, but adding five all wrongs together should get one somewhere near the truth – and that's the difference,' he mused, 'between life and mathematics, in which five all wrongs only add up to a still bigger all wrong.'

Early as it was, there was already a constable posted at the gate where Bobby had waited in vain for Sergeant Doran the previous evening, for experience had taught the authorities that, as the news of what had happened spread abroad, crowds would assemble to stare and gossip, and would need to be kept continually on the move.

So far the newspaper men had been comparatively calm, for Mitchell had been careful to let them imagine that the murder was a result of the robbery of the safe, and 'Millionaire Murdered by Burglars' was the legend appearing in various forms on every newspaper placard. The most acute 'crime specialist' in all Fleet Street had not as yet guessed that anything else lay behind what appeared a plain straightforward tale of bandits murdering to effect their escape when interrupted in committing a robbery. Even the efforts of two of the more popular and enterprising of the Sunday press to obtain from Jennie an article, to be written with tears in her eyes, on 'How you feel when your Daddy's shot' (exclusive), and from Brenda on 'Home life of murdered millionaire' (exclusive), had met with no success, and had indeed been pressed with less than usual energy, and but few promises of exceeding rich reward.

So far, therefore, the reporters had been quite well behaved, and except for an article in a leading journal, advocating passionately the use of the 'cat' in all such cases, the papers were not giving the affair any very great attention. It was too early yet also for crowds to have assembled, so, after a short chat with the man on duty, Bobby strolled on round the garden, making a very careful examination of the ground and drawing a sketch map in his pocket-book on the chance that it might be useful. With very special attention he examined also a solitary footprint that had been found in the soft mould of a flower bed at the angle where two gravel paths joined. It had already been measured, photographed, treated in fact in all ways as issued instructions demand that footprints found in such circumstances should be treated, and now it was protected by a careful arrangement of twine, upright sticks, and a waterproof cover. One felt that if attention to a footprint could catch a criminal, this man was as good as under arrest already.

'Interesting, eh?' a voice said behind him, and Bobby, turning sharply, jumped to the salute as he recognized Mitchell.

'Yes, sir,' he said. 'Very narrow footprint for its length, too, sir.'

'What about it?'

'The elderly man I reported as appearing interested in the house yesterday evening, shortly before the murder, had very long narrow feet,' Bobby answered. 'I noticed them particularly.'

Mitchell regarded Bobby with a very pained expression.

'Sort of Hoodoo you are, aren't you?' he complained. 'As soon as I get a working theory going, you turn up with some new fact and knock it endways.'

'Sorry, sir,' said Bobby.

'Anything happen last night after I left?'

'The two young ladies and Mr Mark Lester came out and joined Mr Carsley in the hall. They talked a little.'

'Did you hear what they said?'

'Yes, sir. The study door was open and I think they forgot I was there.'

'I thought they might,' Mitchell remarked. 'Anything interesting in what they said?'

'Mr Carsley said he was suspected and it was natural enough. Miss Jennie – Mrs Carsley that is – said they must refuse to take her father's money, it must go to charity as if he had had time to sign the new will. Mr Lester said that would be silly and at any rate Miss Brenda ought to have what had been meant for her. Miss Brenda said she wouldn't touch it. They were all very excited and a bit hysterical, I thought. If any of them knew anything, there was nothing to show it in what they said. Mr Carsley stayed the night here with his wife. Mr Lester said the police were no good, that he would find the murderer himself, and the first thing was to find out who the revolver belonged to. He talked as if he really thought he had some private information. I thought he rather frightened Miss Brenda. She seemed nervous, and as if she were afraid something might happen to him, too. After Mr and Mrs Carsley went upstairs, Mr Lester and Miss Brenda talked about their private affairs.'

'Go on,' said Mitchell. 'There are no private affairs in a murder case.'

'No, sir,' agreed Bobby. 'I thought they both seemed in a very emotional state, very highly strung and over-wrought. They talked in an excited sort of way, not the way people generally talk. It seemed as if Miss Brenda had got engaged to him without meaning it very much, just because he was there and her stepfather wanted it. The servants in the house here say the same, they say it was Sir Christopher did it all.'

'I wonder why,' mused Mitchell; 'generally it's the women are the matchmakers. Seems as if he wanted to get rid of her.'

'That's what the servants think,' Bobby answered. 'They all seem to be a little afraid of her, they don't seem to know why themselves, just a vague general feeling. I've noticed myself she has a sort of way of imposing herself, when she's there you're half the time wondering what she's thinking and what she'll do. Anyhow, they say Sir Christopher wanted to get rid of her and practically put the engagement through himself.'

'Doesn't seem consistent,' observed Mitchell, 'bad psychology somewhere – on one hand, she's such a determined, strong-minded young lady that everyone goes in awe of her. She only has to stand there to make you feel her force. On the other hand, she's a meek, obedient, little thing who lets her stepfather choose a husband for her, and does just what she is told. Picture don't fit.'

'No, sir,' agreed Bobby. 'But from what they say in the house, it seems Mr Lester has always been pretty keen and perhaps that accounts for it. And last night, hearing her talk, both of them, it was as if the murder had made her realize her own feelings, that really she had cared for Mr Lester all the time but was only just beginning to understand it.'

'Let loose her emotions in a way,' Mitchell remarked, 'let them loose on both sides perhaps. That might explain it.'

'I made a shorthand note of their talk as well as I could,' Bobby added. 'I have not transcribed it yet.'

'Do that,' said Mitchell; 'then change into plain clothes and bring the longhand note to me personally.'

'Yes, sir,' said Bobby, and Mitchell noticed with approval that the young man did not ask for instructions how and where he was to find his Superintendent – he was evidently prepared to manage that part of it for himself, and Mitchell had a preference for young men who did not want too much dry nursing.

'You could identify the elderly man you reported seeing and think made that footstep, if you were to see him again?' he asked.

'Yes, sir,' said Bobby.

'Good. Did Mr Lester strike you as meaning it when he said he was going to have a try on his own account to find the murderer?'

'Yes, sir.'

'Then he'll have to be watched,' said Mitchell with decision. 'We don't want any amateurs mucking about, upsetting things, especially one who may himself be the man we want.'

Bobby offered no comment on this, and Mitchell, who had expected one, went on after he had waited a little:

'Did you hear anything else of interest while you were talking to the servants?'

'They are all quite sure,' Bobby answered, 'that Miss Brenda was playing the piano in the drawing-room all the time and therefore can't have left the room. They all say they heard the playing going on all the time without a stop. One of the maids seems to know quite a lot about music and she says she knows quite well the piece Miss Brenda was playing, and is sure there was no break in it.'

'What about Miss Jennie?'

'She was lying down in her room. She can hardly have come downstairs without being seen by Lewis, who was in his pantry, except once when he came out to post a letter. But that was about six and the cook says she heard Miss Jennie moving about in her room after that.'

'She gains a fortune and Miss Brenda loses one by Sir Christopher's death,' Mitchell mused, 'but apparently the Jennie girl knew nothing about the will then, and anyhow it would need pretty strong evidence to convict a young girl like her of parricide.'

'Very strong indeed, sir,' agreed Bobby. 'They all say she is a very gentle, quiet girl.'

'Sometimes they're the worst when they kick over the ropes,' Mitchell remarked. 'Anything else?'

'The cook says she doesn't believe Sir Christopher had a revolver at all, and so the one found near his body can't have been his. Apparently, if he had one, no one has ever seen it. It was supposed to be kept in a locked drawer in his room and he talked about it sometimes. But both the cook and Lewis seem to have an idea that it was bluff on his part.'

'I wish we knew,' Mitchell said. 'They told us that, too, but the two young ladies seem always to have taken it for granted he really had one. But we found the drawer in which it was supposed to be kept still locked, there's no sign of its having been opened, there's no sign of a revolver having been kept there or anywhere else, no ammunition or anything. And he certainly had no licence, though that doesn't go for much. Half the people with pistols haven't got a licence, and don't know they're liable to heavy penalties if they are found out. If Sir Christopher had it in his pocket, why was that? and how did his murderer get hold of it? If we can clear up that part of it, we should be a long way to clearing up the whole. Any more information?'

'Sir Christopher went to the billiard-room about six. One of the maids saw him go. He was still there at a quarter past six because he rang for something he wanted and she brought it him. He was alone. He had a cue in his hand and was apparently practising strokes. Lewis says he often did that and that he used to say he cleared his mind and solved his business worries and problems like that, just as some people say a game of patience helps them to think things out. The maid says that going back from the billiard-room she heard someone moving in the study and wondered who it could be, but did not go in. She says she never thought of burglars in broad daylight. She thought it wasn't her business and went on. If what she really heard was the thief at work, then that's when the robbery took place, about six fifteen. I think it's believed the murder took place at six thirty?'

'That's when you saw – or didn't see, when the caretaker next door saw – a man in a grey tweed suit running away. Also Sir Christopher's watch stopped at two minutes past the half hour. He is said to have been particular to keep it right.'

'Seems to suggest, sir,' said Bobby, 'that the theft in the study and the murder in the billiard-room are not connected – can't imagine a man robbing a safe and then waiting a quarter of an hour to commit a murder at the other end of the house.'

'And it was about a quarter past six apparently,' commented Mitchell, 'when Miss Laing saw some man she's quite sure now was not Mr Lester go past the drawing-room window. At least she thinks that was the time, but by now she's not too sure of that either.'

'The safe was opened with a key,' Bobby went on, 'and apparently by someone who had some knowledge of the house and of Sir Christopher's habits. There is a large sum missing apparently. Mr Carsley says his partner has embezzled money and has run for it. Mr Marsden, as Sir Christopher's lawyer, would know his habits, and might have provided himself with a key of the safe some time or another.'

'We've thought of that,' said Mitchell. 'Marsden was seen in Piccadilly Circus soon after half past six. That gives him a good alibi for the murder but not for the robbery – you can get to Piccadilly from here in a quarter of an hour easily by tube. He didn't go home last night. We are looking for him. Better get those shorthand notes of yours written out as quickly as you can and then bring them to me.'

'Yes, sir,' said Bobby, saluting and went off to carry out the instructions given to him.

CHAPTER II

Marsden Returns

I T was still fairly early when Bobby presented himself at the Lincoln's Inn office of Marsden, Carsley, and Marsden, where this morning not much work was being done.

Neither partner had yet arrived and even the managing clerk, who was so much the managing clerk that he was a trifle inclined to think he was the firm as well, was not undisposed this morning to permit and even to share in conversation on the thrilling topic of the murder of one of the firm's principal clients.

'What you want to stop this sort of thing,' he declared, 'is the "cat"; a good dose of the "cat" all round and we shouldn't hear so much about bandits and burglars.'

And in this sentiment all cordially agreed, for they had all read the same thing in the paper that morning and naturally therefore they all believed it. Indeed, the managing clerk waxed quite eloquent on the merits and virtues of the "cat"; and if anyone had told him that what really roused his enthusiasm for flogging was a primeval love of cruelty lurking in his sub-consciousness he would have been most indignant. For indeed he did not know himself that what moved him was the pleasure and excitement it gave him to think of a naked back, its flesh torn and bloody and scarred with the strokes of a whip.

On the virtues, merits, and advantages of flogging, as a kind of universal Pink Pill for all moral ailments, the managing clerk was still holding forth to a thrilled and sympathetic audience when Bobby made his appearance. At Scotland Yard they had told him that the Superintendent would probably be found or heard of at Mr Carsley's office, and he had therefore come along with the transcript of his shorthand notes. But he was informed that Mr Mitchell had not been there, and that nothing was known about him, and a little puzzled and not quite sure what to do next, Bobby was going away again when he saw Peter approaching.

'Shaved badly,' Bobby thought to himself, 'eyes bloodshot, hasn't slept much, bit of a wreck altogether – can't wonder, I suppose.'

Peter evidently recognized him, too, though he had not seemed to notice him much the night before, and though Bobby had then been in uniform, and was now in plain clothes. Stopping, Peter said harshly:

'This is what you call shadowing a suspect, I suppose, is it?'

'I have had no instructions of the kind,' Bobby answered.

'Got my passport anyhow,' growled Peter. 'I suppose suspects are always shadowed – part of the routine. But you aren't very clever about it, I think.'

'I don't even know if you are a suspect, as you call it,' retorted Bobby. 'I've not been put in charge of the case yet and I don't know much about it. I'm looking for Mr Mitchell, that's all.'

'Well, he's not here,' Peter said, 'but there's something I want to tell you people, and as you're here I may as well tell you. I don't know that it amounts to much; I had almost forgotten all about it till now.'

He led the way into the office and Bobby followed.

'Mr Marsden not here, I suppose,' Peter said to the managing clerk as he entered with Bobby close behind. 'I thought not. You must just carry on as usual at present, God knows what's going to happen, but get on with the work the best way you can.'

He beckoned to Bobby to follow him into his private room and there said to him:

'I want you to tell your Mr Mitchell this. Somebody or another left two stalls here for the Regency Theatre for Sir Christopher yesterday.'

'Yes?' said Bobby, supposing there was more to come, for that fact in itself didn't seem to him to be of much interest.

'That's all,' said Peter.

'Well,' said Bobby, 'I'll tell Mr Mitchell if you wish me to, but I expect he'll rather wonder why.'

'Well, there's this as well,' Peter said, 'but it's only an idea, not fact like the other. Sir Christopher seemed a good deal upset and worried to receive them – I don't know that frightened would be too strong a word.'

'Frightened?' repeated Bobby. 'What at?'

'It's because I don't know and can't imagine that I'm telling you,' snapped Peter. 'Also it seems two tickets for the same theatre were left at his City office the day before and two more tickets at his house the day before that.'

'For the same theatre still – the Regency?'

'Yes.'

'That's where they always put on classical things, isn't it?' Bobby asked. 'Shakespeare and so on.'

'I believe that's the idea at present,' Peter answered, 'and it's taking very well just now. The "Silver and Grey" production they call it, and I've heard people say it's the best *Hamlet* that's been seen for years.'

'Two stalls left for him here yesterday,' Bobby repeated, 'two more in the City the day before and two more at his house. Doesn't seem any sense to it, unless there's someone very keen on the production and keen on his seeing it, too.'

'Three nights running,' Peter said. 'Why should they be?'

'It might be someone wanting to meet him privately,' Bobby remarked. 'If his murder had been planned before, it might be that the theatre was thought a good place to get him, and only because he wouldn't go was the murder carried out where it was. But that seems a bit far-fetched. Possibly it was only that someone wanted to talk to him privately. It's a trick played sometimes when people want to see each other without attracting attention. Both go to the same theatre and then they get a chance to talk during the intervals. It may have been something like that.'

'If so, it was someone Sir Christopher had no wish to

meet,' Peter said. 'He didn't go, he seemed upset at the idea, worried, indeed. In any case, he wouldn't have gone for pleasure, his taste in the theatre didn't run to Shakespeare, he always said he liked something tuney and leggy, or a good farce. But not Shakespeare.'

'It does seem a bit rummy,' Bobby agreed. 'I'll report to Mr Mitchell, but I can't see myself that it can have anything to do with what's happened. Of course, you can never tell, any trifle may give the clue you're looking for and clear up everything, only there are so many trifles and only one that hides the clue.'

The managing clerk himself put his head in at the door, though that was a little below his dignity. But, though a managing clerk, he was also human, and was burning with curiosity.

'Gentleman from Scotland Yard wants to see you, Mr Peter,' he said. 'Says his name is Mitchell.'

'Ask him to come in,' said Peter, and Mitchell accordingly appeared, and lifted his eyebrows at the sight of Bobby.

'I was told you might be here, sir,' Bobby explained, 'and so I came with the transcript of the shorthand notes you said you wished to see. Mr Carsley said he wished to give some information for me to report to you.'

'What information?' Mitchell asked.

Peter repeated his story whereto Mitchell listened with interest.

'Bear looking into,' Mitchell decided when Peter had finished. 'Don't see any sense to it, don't see what it can mean, but it'll bear looking into. May I use your phone?'

He picked it up as he spoke, and, calling Scotland Yard, gave instructions for inquiries to be made at the Regency to find out if possible who had bought the tickets, if they had been used, and if Sir Christopher's name had been mentioned.

'Another long report that'll mean,' he sighed. 'Nearly a foot high in this case already. I don't know how many men we haven't working on it and they all send in reports and I have to read them all – what a life. Well, Mr Carsley, heard anything about your partner – Mr Marsden's the name, isn't it? Any fresh developments?'

'Only that I went round to the Public Prosecutor's office before I came here,' Peter answered. 'They are sending round two men to go through the books and find out how things stand. I shan't touch a thing myself. Excuse me.'

The phone had just rung. He answered it, listened, and then said:

'That's all nonsense. I can't say any more at present, except that we hold Sir Christopher Clarke's receipt for all papers connected with the Belfort Trust as handed over to him in good order yesterday. You can tell your client that from me, but he'll have to be a bit patient for the present. Scotland Yard has the case in hand. Of course, you will be informed of anything fresh. Mr Belfort was to have dined with Sir Christopher last night. Did he go? ... oh, I see. Well, he needn't worry, but I can't say anything more at present.'

He rang off and turning to Mitchell said:

'That was Mayne and Mayne, who are acting for Mr Belfort, the new trustee. He seems to have got it into his head that there's something wrong with the Trust. Whatever's wrong anywhere else, Belfort's all right. Sir Christopher's estate will be responsible and there won't be any attempt to dodge responsibility either.'

'Did they say why Mr Belfort did not keep his dinner engagement?' Mitchell asked. 'I heard you ask.'

'They say he did keep it, but when he arrived he found police in charge and was told Sir Christopher had been found shot dead. So not unnaturally he went away again – apparently convinced it was a case of suicide and that the Trust money had all been embezzled. I am inclined to think now,' Peter went on, 'that there must have been rumours in circulation about Marsden – about us, the firm, I should say.

What the real situation is we shan't know till they've been here from the Public Prosecutor's office – no one knows at present but Marsden, and he's cleared out for good, I suppose.'

The door opened and Marsden himself came in. Neither Mitchell nor Bobby had any idea who he was, but Peter jumped up with an astonished cry:

'Good Lord, Marsden, you – you, after what you told me last night?'

'Is this gentleman Mr Marsden?' Mitchell asked, and added in an undertone: 'Bear looking into.'

'My name is Marsden,' that gentleman agreed. 'I suppose you are from Scotland Yard from what they tell me in the office? Sorry you've been troubled. It's what comes of having the biggest fool in the country for a partner. Carsley, what cursed piece of idiocy have you been up to?'

'You told me last night,' said Peter, 'you had embezzled moneys belonging to our clients. The Public Prosecutor is sending two of his staff round to investigate things at once.'

'Well, they can trot away back again,' said Marsden, 'and you can trot off with them if you like. I rather gathered you had been making an even more priceless fool of yourself than usual. Of course, this is the end of our connexion. You've ruined the firm nearly as thoroughly as I thought you had last night by offending old Clarke. Now he's dead, and that doesn't matter, and so you make yourself even a more disgusting fool in another way. What I told you, you blighted young idiot, was that in making Sir Christopher our enemy you had ruined the firm as thoroughly as embezzling clients' money would have done. It was only afterwards I realized that you are the kind of thick-headed young Pharisee who might have misunderstood what I meant.'

CHAPTER 12

Marsden Explains

MITCHELL was the first to break the silence that followed, for Peter was far too bewildered, first by Marsden's unexpected return, and then by this astonishing announcement, to be able to get out a word. Following on the strain of recent events, it was too much for him altogether, and one could almost see him struggling to get his mind adjusted to this new development and to make out what it meant. Marsden was watching him with a kind of fury of contempt and rage he made no effort to conceal, that it seemed probable might find fresh vent at any moment. Bobby, looking on with interest, absorbed in the drama of the scene, imagined too that he could detect a strain of uneasiness, of terror, perhaps, in Marsden's manner, and he supposed this was not unnatural in such circumstances. But none of the three of them spoke till Mitchell murmured, half to himself apparently:

'Bear looking into, bear looking into.'

Then Peter said, looking straight and hard at Marsden:

'There was no misunderstanding. I know what you said.'

'You mean you know what you think I said,' retorted Marsden. He turned to Mitchell, 'You are from Scotland Yard, you are Mr Mitchell, aren't you? I've seen you in the courts, I think.'

'Marsden,' Peter burst out suddenly, 'do you mean that all clients' money is all right?'

'I mean this,' Marsden snarled, his sharp, dark eyes small points of blazing anger. 'I'm not going to have anything more to do with you. You're not only a fool, you're a mischievous fool. I would sooner have a mad dog for a partner than you. I've done with you for good and all. Our partnership's dissolved; if I have to bring an action for damages for malicious slander or something like that to get rid of you, I'll do it. Any communication I have to make to you for the future will be in writing or before witnesses.' He turned to Mitchell. 'This is what happened,' he said. 'Sir Christopher Clarke was our most important and influential client. He has a daughter. My precious partner here started making love to the girl; not a bad idea for a penniless young lawyer to make up to the only daughter of an extremely rich man. Naturally, Sir Christopher objected. Any man in his position would. Carsley's no standing, no brains, no money, nothing except impudence. Most men in Sir Christopher's position would have done what Sir Christopher did – kicked him out and told the girl to have more sense. Of course, it was obvious the money was the attraction, and Sir Christopher took steps to settle that part of it. He instructed me to draw up a new will by which his daughter was to get nothing if she married Carsley. Well, that was a good idea all right, and I've no doubt Carsley would have dropped the girl like a hot potato –'

'Marsden,' said Peter quietly, 'try not to be more offensive than you can help or I shall probably throw you out of the window.'

'Now, now, Mr Carsley,' interposed Mitchell mildly.

'Only unfortunately,' Marsden went on, giving Peter a look that meant he would be more offensive still if and when and as he got the chance, 'like a prudent young man, Carsley had got round the girl and they were married already. Sir Christopher had instructed me to let Carsley know. I did so and in his rage and disappointment Carsley let out about the marriage having taken place. Well, of course, I saw at once that meant the end of everything for the firm, absolute and complete ruin. Sir Christopher wasn't the sort of man to sit down to that kind of thing. He would hit back, hard, and he wouldn't believe I hadn't known anything about it – wouldn't care either. So there was our most important client turned into our mortal enemy, with both the power and the will to smash us like a rotten tomato. It was a bit of a facer. I daresay I rather lost my self-control. I admit I talked a bit wildly. When a man comes and says to you: "Oh, I've just done something that ruins you absolutely and completely, you're done in for good and all", you do get a bit excited.'

'You said,' repeated Peter stubbornly, 'you had embezzled clients' money, you talked about bankruptcy, fraud and bankruptcy.'

'What I actually said,' explained Marsden, speaking to Mitchell again, 'was that what he had done had ruined the firm as completely as if it had been found out that I had embezzled clients' money.'

'I shall know what to believe,' Peter said, 'when they've been here from the Public Prosecutor's office and carried out their investigation.'

'Who cares what you believe?' retorted Marsden, 'and no one, either the Public Prosecutor or anyone else, is going to be allowed to investigate our affairs, not likely.'

'Don't you think,' suggested Mitchell, 'I'm only making the suggestion, just a suggestion in a friendly way, because what has been said is pretty serious and would bear looking into – don't you think it would be as well to let anyone who comes from the Public Prosecutor have all the information they want, let them see everything. That would put an end to any chance of any gossip or talk.'

'Just what it wouldn't do,' retorted Marsden, 'it would only set every tongue wagging all round here. It would finish the firm's last chance of surviving if it were known we had had the Public Prosecutor sending to investigate our affairs. That's not going to happen. If any client, as a result of Carsley's incredible folly and mischief-making, doesn't care to trust us with the charge of his interests any longer, and that's pretty sure to happen in some cases at least, his connexion with us will be wound up at once and in every case, in every case, everything will be found in order. I answer for that. But,' he went on, speaking still directly to

Mitchell, 'I don't deny there are some transactions I've carried out – oh, quite proper, ordinary deals, the sort of thing every firm of even the highest standing does in the way of routine every day – that all the same I don't specially want to explain to people like members of the Public Prosecutor's staff. They have to take a very stiff, pedantic view of everything. Quite right for them. But you can't carry on business always like that. A little while ago I took a largish sum from one client's account and used it for another account. Quite all right. It was to save investments having to be sold out at a serious loss – the security was there all the time, you understand. I could have borrowed on that security from a bank, but you know the scandalous interest they charge. I didn't choose to pay it, not with the bank-rate down to one and a half. I could justify that transaction in any court, but Carsley here would be quite sure that I had put the money in my pocket – lost it going to the dogs, probably. There's going to be no investigation of this firm, except by clients, by agreement, or on behalf of clients whose claims we haven't met. And there won't be any of them. So long as we can meet all claims there's going to be no investigation of the affairs of this firm. I want to make that quite clear.'

'Quite a reasonable attitude,' agreed Mitchell, 'assuming of course – I don't suggest for a moment you can't – that you can satisfy all clients.'

'We can, of course we can,' declared Marsden, bringing down his hand heavily on the table. 'The firm will have a hard job to pull through, but no client will be a penny short. Carsley's all right of course. Sir Christopher hadn't signed his new will he had instructed us to draw up – Carsley has the draft still, I suppose – and so through his wife Carsley takes every penny Sir Christopher leaves.'

'The police are already fully awake to that fact, Marsden,' Peter said. 'It was quite unnecessary to remind them – and not very clever. I'm already suspected of the murder though I didn't commit it.'

'You don't really mean they suspect you?' Marsden asked with an air of surprise that Bobby at least was inclined to think was only assumed. 'You're a priceless fool ... but murder ... the first thing I said was: "Hullo, Carsley's done the old man in for his money", but of course I didn't mean it and besides the paper talked about burglars.'

'You're taking a lot of trouble,' Peter remarked, 'to try to give the police an idea that was the first that occurred to them.'

'Oh, well,' said Marsden and looked at Mitchell. 'Is that so?' he asked.

'I take it everyone is more or less under suspicion in cases like this,' Mitchell remarked mildly.

'Well, I suppose you can prove where you were at the time of the murder?' Marsden remarked, turning to Peter.

Peter did not answer. He was looking straight in front of him, his face pale and worn, his expression very intent, his eyes with an odd strained look to them; to Bobby's fancy it was of an almost complete despair that his looks and attitude spoke.

Mitchell said:

'By the way, Mr Marsden, you weren't at home last night. We had occasion to ring you up, as Sir Christopher's lawyer, and we were told you weren't there.'

'No, I went to Paris,' Marsden answered.

'As a result of arrangements already made, I suppose?' Mitchell asked indifferently.

'No,' answered Marsden, 'it was totally unexpected. I got word of a piece of business that might be picked up there and off I went.'

'I suppose,' suggested Mitchell, 'you let someone know ... ?'

'I'm afraid I didn't,' Marsden answered. 'I was still excited and upset and this chance of new business turning up – well, I thought of nothing else but going after it. I thought it might mean salvation after all, drowning man snatching at a straw.'

'Any objection,' asked Mitchell, but not as if he really cared, 'to tell us what hotel you stayed at and what the business was – confidential, of course.'

'I didn't stay at an hotel,' Marsden explained. 'I went to the private flat of the friend who put me up – he gave me his key. And I can't tell you his name, partly because I've promised not to, partly because, if I did, you would know at once what the business was. It's a rather important amalgamation of two big firms, and if I am lucky I might get the legal business connected with it. But I can't say anything more, it would be a betrayal of confidence; it might, if it got about, ruin the very delicate negotiations that are going on, and of course if the indiscretion were traced to me –'

'At Scotland Yard, we're used to keeping secrets,' Mitchell hinted mildly, but Marsden shook his head again.

'Not my secret,' he said.

'You got the business?' Mitchell asked.

Once more Marsden shook his head, lifting at the same time his white, well-kept hands with a gesture of resignation.

'No luck,' he said. 'I found I was weeks ahead, nothing settled yet, there had been a bad hitch my friend had not known about. I still hope of course, but the whole thing's put off for the present. Then this morning I read in the papers about Sir Christopher, and I thought I had better get back as quick as I could, so I hired a private plane and flew over. My first idea was that it would be all right again – now old Sir Christopher was dead. I know that sounds a bit brutal, but what I mean is, I felt we had nothing to be afraid of from him any more, now he was dead – he couldn't smash the firm now just to get at Carsley. So – well, in a way his death seemed good luck for us, and then when I got here I found that that unimaginable idiot of a Carsley had put us in the soup again, dished the firm for good and all: the oldest, best-established firm going couldn't survive one of the partners trotting off to the Public Prosecutor and asking for an investigation. You must excuse me,' he added, 'if I talk a bit wildly; it's rather trying, first to have your partner ruin you by playing the fool with your biggest client's daughter, then to be saved by that same client getting himself murdered, then to be faced with ruin again by a new piece of idiocy on your partner's part. I hardly know where I am or what I'm doing or saying – the only thing I feel I want to do is to tell Carsley what I think of him, and good Lord, what's the use?'

'I see, I see,' said Mitchell, 'Well, I thought it would bear looking into. The fact is, there's rather a curious complication in this case. Sir Christopher's safe was robbed last evening and apparently a large sum of money in bearer bonds, and a number of diamonds of unknown but probably considerable value are supposed to have been stolen.'

'Bonds? Not the Belfort bonds?' Marsden asked quickly.

'Yes,' said Peter.

Marsden whistled softly.

'Sellable anywhere, anyhow, by anyone,' he commented. 'Well, at any rate, we're all right there. We hold Sir Christopher's receipt; he's responsible, his estate rather, we're not. A big haul for the thieves; but then if it was thieves, it wasn't –'

He paused and glanced at Peter, a little as if he were sorry that thus his innocence seemed to be proved.

'The murder probably happened some time after the robbery,' Mitchell explained. 'There doesn't seem any connexion, but it's a curious coincidence and it'll bear looking into.'

'So I should think,' Marsden agreed. 'Those thieves, whoever they were, had some luck – they can't have known there was all that money there in bearer bonds or dreamed what a haul they were going to make.'

'Depends on who the thieves were, what they knew,' observed Mitchell. 'If I mention certain facts, it is only because they are there and can't be overlooked. It is reported that last night you made a statement, since denied, that your firm was ruined and bankrupt, and that certain frauds had taken place. You had reason to be aware that a large sum was in Sir Christopher's safe. The safe was not forced, it was opened with a key. Obviously Sir Christopher's legal adviser would have had every opportunity to provide himself with an impression from which a key could have been made. You did not return home as usual, but left hurriedly and unexpectedly for the Continent on a business errand which you cannot explain, as it is confidential.'

'I returned,' Marsden said quickly, 'the quickest way I could.'

'On the news of Sir Christopher's murder reaching you, you return,' Mitchell agreed, 'and you now declare yourself in possession of sufficient funds to meet all liabilities, though, for the reasons you have explained, you decline all independent investigation of your books. I think it my duty to mention these facts but I am at present drawing no conclusion of any kind. If you wish to make any statement, at any time, you can always let me know at Scotland Yard.'

'Well, that puts the hat on it,' Marsden said, 'just about settles our chances of pulling through – one partner suspected of burglary and the other of murder.'

CHAPTER 13

Mark Lester Takes a Hand

AFTER Marsden had said this there was a silence in the room for a moment or two. Bobby, watching the Superintendent, who appeared plunged in deep thought, had the idea that this silence pleased him, that he wished it to sink, as it were, into the minds and consciousness of the two partners. Of them, Marsden looked scowling and defiant; but Peter was staring gloomily before him, as if there was something very strange showing in his intent gaze, something that looked like horror or despair or some other such deep emotion, yet his mouth and lips were set in lines that seemed to show a resolute determination not to let it get the better of him. Still neither of them spoke and presently Mitchell got to his feet.

'A little early to talk about suspicion yet, gentlemen,' he said gently. 'At present we are only concerned with the facts. When we have them sorted out, then it'll be time enough to talk about suspicions. Are you thinking of going abroad again just now, Mr Marsden?'

'I shall have all my work cut out for me here,' Marsden answered with another angry glare at Peter. 'What I've got to do now is to try to keep what clients we have left, if that's possible. Trying to get more is rather a forlorn hope at present.'

'Then,' suggested Mitchell, 'I daresay you wouldn't have any objection to our taking care of your passport for you for the present. Mr Carsley has already trusted us with his.'

'No, I haven't,' said Peter. 'You took it. You never asked, you took it.'

'Only because you weren't there at the moment,' Mitchell pointed out in quite a pained voice. 'Anyhow, we're asking Mr Marsden.'

Marsden looked more scowling and defiant than ever, and Bobby almost thought for a moment that there was going to be an outburst. But then with a sort of hard laugh Marsden produced his pocket-book, took out the passport, and flung it angrily on the table.

'There it is if you want it,' he said angrily. 'Perhaps you would like to take our finger-prints as well.'

'Ah, finger-prints,' said Mitchell, slipping the passport into his pocket, 'finger-prints – oh, it's only small fry we catch with finger-prints nowadays, and it's not small fry we are up against in this case. Of course, if we should need them I know we can rely on both you gentlemen. Good morning, gentlemen, good morning.'

Neither of them made him any answer. Leaving them sitting there facing each other with dark and angry looks, Mitchell left the room, and Bobby, since he did not know what else to do, followed.

Outside, Mitchell beckoned to a taxi he saw at a distance. He had not seemed to be aware of Bobby, hovering humbly just behind, but now he remarked to him over his shoulder:

'Taxis for supers., buses and trams for sergeants and inspectors, and constables can foot it. That,' said Mitchell with deep appreciation, 'is discipline.'

'Yes, sir,' said Bobby respectfully.

Watching the slow approach of his taxi, held up by the manoeuvres of a leading K.C.'s car that seemed nearly as big as the surrounding houses, Mitchell asked:

'Well, what do you think of all that?'

'Don't know, sir,' said Bobby, who indeed felt completely bewildered by what he had heard.

'Has Marsden been embezzling his clients' cash?' Mitchell went on; 'is that why he bolted? If so, why did he come back? Was it because he heard of the murder and thought it was safe to return with Sir Christopher out of the way? Then where does Carsley come in? He can't account for his movements at the time of the murder, says he was walking

97

about the streets. Feeble sort of story, but it might be true, feeble stories sometimes are, most likely because truth's a feeble growth in this world. But the murder meant a fortune for him and his wife. Adequate motive there, and we know no other. Marsden, according to Carsley, said last night the firm was bankrupt, and now says every claim can be met – is that because he has the missing bonds and diamonds in his pocket? Did he come back because he thought the bigger crime, the murder, would cover the smaller one, the theft? And, anyhow, there wasn't Sir Christopher to be afraid of any longer. Then there's the doctor – if the murdered man was dead when he entered the billiard-room, why was he as long giving the alarm as you say he was? Was it to let some-one escape? Who was the man seen escaping over the next door garden wall and is it only a coincidence that Carsley's hand was cut? Who was the man Miss Laing says she saw and why did she think it was Mark Lester at first? Can you make sense of all that, young man?'

'No, sir,' said Bobby.

Mitchell surveyed him with a benevolent eye.

'What I like about you,' he said, 'is the way you encourage conversation, always some apt remark to make, some interesting comment to pass.'

'Thank you, sir,' said Bobby.

'If you want a man to talk, and he don't,' Mitchell continued, 'then, if you keep it up long enough, about the weather and what'll win, and what possessed the Arsenal directors to pick the team they did last Saturday, or, if it's a woman, about how well she's looking and how wonderfully her hat suits her and isn't Greta Garbo just lovely and is it true Ronald Colman's eyelashes are artificial – then in the end they'll start talking, too. Talk, my boy, has loosened more tongues than anything else, except, perhaps, champagne, and do you think you could get champagne for suspects through an expenses list?'

'I don't, sir,' said Bobby.

'Then you talk and they'll talk and so it all comes out. Of course, you have to have a kind of natural gift for talk. I have,' added the Superintendent modestly.

'Yes, sir,' agreed Bobby.

Mitchell looked at him suspiciously.

'I suppose someone told you,' he remarked. 'After all, there's only one way to get to know things and that is to wait till someone who knows already comes and tells you. That's the first maxim in my forthcoming book, *The Complete Detective and How to Be It*, which will be one of the world's lost masterpieces because I'll never write it. But remember that – talk and it shall be talked unto you.'

'Yes, sir,' said Bobby.

'And in this case, what we want above all,' continued Mitchell as his taxi at last drew up, having finally succeeded in evading the famous K.C.'s fifty (there or thereabouts) cylinder chariot, 'is to find out who the revolver belonged to. Keep your eyes and ears open, and if you hear anything new, come along and tell me personally – personally, mind. That is,' added the great man, chuckling pleasantly, 'if they'll let a constable of three years' service get anywhere within a mile of a superintendent, which it isn't likely they will, is it?'

'No, sir,' agreed Bobby.

'Not if I know 'em at the Yard,' said Mitchell with conviction, and climbing into his taxi was driven away, leaving Bobby standing on the kerb.

It was still early, and Bobby had the rest of the day before him; for, partly owing to the fact that he was officially recorded as having been on all-night duty – though part of it had been spent wrapt in comfortable slumber – and partly because his inspector was willing to be amiable to a young man reported engaged in long conversations with the great Mitchell, Bobby had been excused his next turn of duty. He was therefore not due to report again till two p.m. next day.

He felt a little disappointed that the Superintendent had not assigned him to any duty in connexion with the case, for he had entertained a wild and presumptuous hope that that might happen, and that he might find himself transferred to the C.I.D., if only temporarily. But evidently that was not to be, nor had it ever been likely, and he now decided that the excellent breakfast he had been treated to by the favourably-disposed cook at 'The Cedars' was worthy of being followed by an equally excellent luncheon.

So he chose a restaurant that looked as if even K.C.s themselves might patronize it – and everyone knows that counsel learned in the law acquire their knowledge by a prolonged course of dinners, thus becoming experts therein – and having there passed an agreeable but slightly expensive hour, set off to walk home, partly that he might not have to face a wasted opportunity at teatime, partly because he thought that a long quiet walk might give him an opportunity to reduce to some sort of logical order the chaos of disconnected facts that seemed to surround the murder of Sir Christopher Clarke.

'But it wants brains,' he decided humbly, 'not my sort, but the kind of brains people like double firsts and bankers and politicians must have.'

He went a little out of his way to pass by 'The Cedars', for it was in his mind that he would try to cultivate the further acquaintance of the butler, Lewis, who might, he thought, know more than he had yet told.

Before the house a small crowd was still assembled, in spite of all the efforts of one of Bobby's comrades, bored but assiduous, to make them move on. Bobby stopped for a moment to chat to this man, learnt that though there had been plenty of coming and going, including several reporters from each and all of the various newspapers in the world – at least, so the constable said – it did not appear that anything new had happened. Nor was Bobby's soul so lofty but that during this brief conversation he managed to let it be known that he had just come from reporting to Superintendent Mitchell in person, and had orders that, in certain circumstances, he was again to make a personal report. Aware that this news would fly through the whole division as swiftly as ever did the news through any country village that Jack and Jill had been seen kissing down the lane, Bobby nodded a farewell and strolled away. He would, he thought, wait a more favourable opportunity for meeting Lewis. Judicious inquiry at the different public houses in the neighbourhood would soon reveal which one he 'used', and then it would be easy to meet him there. Just before turning the corner into the next street he glanced back with some vague idea that he might see Lewis coming out of the house on some errand or another, and saw instead Mark Lester walking down the drive and then turning along the road to where Bobby was standing.

Vaguely interested, Bobby waited, busying himself with a pretence of lighting a cigarette. Coming nearer, Lester saw him and evidently recognized him. He hesitated and then came up and Bobby said:

'Oh, good day. Mr Lester, isn't it?'

'Yes,' Mark answered. 'I saw you yesterday, I think.'

'Yes,' agreed Bobby. 'I happened to be on duty when Dr Gregory found the body.'

'I wanted to ask you,' Mark said. 'I heard you had been at the gate of the drive for some time so that no one could have passed without your seeing them. Is that true?'

'Well, not exactly,' Bobby answered. 'I had to meet my sergeant there so I had been waiting some time. But I was in the next door garden once for a few minutes, and then anyhow it doesn't amount to much. Anyone who wanted to could easily get into the garden, and up to the house, either through the hedge, or over the wall, or from the next door garden for that matter.'

'There's nothing new turned up, I suppose?' Mark asked.

'Not that I know of,' Bobby answered, 'but I'm not engaged on the case. It's the C.I.D. people who take these cases in hand, you know.'

'Do they know Dr Gregory owed Sir Christopher a good deal of money?'

'I can't say for certain,' answered Bobby cautiously. 'I understand that's not so, though,' he added, knowing well that a contradiction of a fact is generally the best way to get it confirmed, as happened now.

'Well, it is so,' Mark retorted with emphasis. 'I heard Sir Christopher myself bullying Gregory like anything, threatening to sell him up and so on.'

'Did you?' said Bobby, not as if he were much interested. 'Do you know if it was a really large sum or if it had been owing long?'

'No, Sir Christopher didn't say, but he was in a temper because it hadn't been paid. You know, what you people want to do is to find out who that revolver belonged to.'

'Ye-es,' agreed Bobby, as though not quite sure about it. 'They may be trying to.'

Mark looked very contemptuous.

'Trying?' he repeated. 'They don't want to try, they want to do. You know all this isn't very jolly for us – people are saying already it must have been someone who knew the house, and everyone's heard it's been said I was hanging about here myself at the time of the murder. Nice for me, isn't it?'

Mark was evidently a good deal excited. Trying to soothe him, Bobby said:

'Everything possible will be done to find out the truth, you may be sure of that.'

'I'm going to have a shot at it myself,' Mark retorted. 'I'm not going to trust to you people. I've just been telling Miss Laing I'll find out the truth for myself. Did you know there was someone who had been uttering threats against Sir Christopher? I suppose you don't, but I do, and I mean to find out who it was.'

CHAPTER 14

An Offer of Help

'You mean a little old man, rather shabby, boots down at heel, thin face, long nose, grey whiskers?' Bobby asked, remembering what Lewis had told him and the description given.

'You know him?' Mark asked eagerly, and with evident surprise, and Bobby hesitated.

'Look here, Mr Lester,' he said gravely, 'this is a police matter and a serious one. If you have any information you ought to give it at once to the officers in charge of the case. If you try to take action yourself you may do a great deal of harm; you may be helping the guilty man to escape.'

But Mark only shrugged his shoulders with a very contemptuous air.

'I did try to talk to one of your men,' he said, 'but he wouldn't listen. Told me if I knew any actual facts to put them down in writing, but they didn't want theories – ideas, that is. To the official mind, ideas never have any value, all it wants is facts.'

Bobby understood that all this meant simply that there had been some sort of passage of arms between Mark and one or other of the officers engaged on the case. It was fairly plain however that Mark was very much in earnest and Bobby began to think harder and quicker than ever he had done before, and much more clearly than ever he had been able to do in any examination room, where a sort of creeping miasma had always seemed to come over his spirit the moment he entered it. It seemed to him that it would be very desirable to keep some kind of watch on Mark's activities that might easily become embarrassing to those in charge of the case and yet might at the same time, for detective work is fifty per cent luck and forty-nine per cent chance, lead to valuable results. Bobby had to decide, too, whether the information about Dr Gregory was of sufficient value to justify him in undertaking the formidable task of seeking admittance to Mr Mitchell's presence. But the fact itself was one it was probable was already known to the investigators, and Bobby decided to wait for something more important and less likely to be known before attempting to force his way through to the Superintendent. He had an idea his welcome would be but chilly unless he brought information of real value. He determined, therefore, to make his report this time through the ordinary channels, and all this had passed so swiftly through his mind that Mark was hardly conscious of more than the very slightest hesitation before Bobby said:

'If you could put your hand on anyone who had really been threatening Sir Christopher, it might mean a lot. If you think you can really manage that, I should think it my duty to carry out any suggestions you make.'

Mark, who had been looking not too good-tempered before, greeted this remark with a very pleased and gratified smile. Evidently, the idea of a police officer placing himself, so to say, under his orders, tickled his vanity a good deal, and Bobby, who had already perceived that Mark had rather more than his full share of that by no means uncommon quality, felt he had gone a long way towards gaining the other's confidence. It seemed to him Mark was one of those who, if only they are called leaders, are prepared to follow dutifully in the path pointed out to them, and he felt sure that now, at any rate, he could be certain that Mark would get into no mischief and do nothing to hamper the official investigation. For Bobby, too, was young and full of self-confidence, and a little too much inclined to trust entirely in his own abilities and powers.

'Of course,' Bobby went on, 'I'm an officer of police and I must retain my right to inform my superiors any time I feel that's my duty. But I would promise to consult you before doing so.'

'That'll be all right,' said Mark, quite satisfied with this somewhat vague undertaking.

'Quite possible,' Bobby continued, 'that working on your own lines you may hit on something important. You would have one advantage – if police make an inquiry, that sets everyone talking for miles, and as like as not the guilty man takes alarm at once. Whereas no one takes any notice of any ordinary person asking a question or two. And besides,' added Bobby carelessly, 'you might find it useful to have a police-officer following up behind you, ready to come in at once any time you thought fit.'

Mark was evidently impressed by this picture of himself, leading the inquiry with the police waiting in the background, waiting his directions and command. Bobby clinched the business by letting out casually that he was a St George's College man. Once again Mark was impressed and Bobby felt that the conquest of his confidence was complete.

'I take it,' he said, 'what you mean to do, Mr Lester, is to try to identify this man and assure yourself whether his threats amounted to anything. You've no idea who he is?'

'I know nothing at all about him,' Mark answered, 'except that I saw him once, talking to Sir Christopher. He was evidently very excited. It was just outside "The Cedars", and apparently he had been waiting there for a chance to get hold of Sir Christopher. All I heard was Sir Christopher telling him to clear out, and quick about it, if he didn't want the police sent for, and the old fellow shaking his fist in a fury and spluttering out something I couldn't catch. Sir Christopher said he had been trying to get money out of him.'

'Did Sir Christopher seem disturbed or alarmed in any way?'

'Oh, no, just annoyed, as anyone would be naturally at such a scene. I don't suppose I should have thought of it again, only Lewis told me the same man had been to the house afterwards and used threats of a vague sort, and I know also that he had turned up at Sir Christopher's City office and tried to see him there.'

'Do they know anything about him at the office?'

'They think his name is Harris or Harrison or something like that, but they aren't sure, no one took much notice of him. He was just told to clear out unless he wanted to get into trouble. They thought he had been drinking. He seems to have talked in a vague sort of way about making Sir Christopher sorry one day, and getting his own back and so on. There's no trace of any correspondence in the office with anyone of any name like Harris or Harrison or of any business transaction either.'

'Going to be a bit difficult to trace him,' Bobby mused. 'Not much to go on – a name that may be something like Harris and a fairly vague general description and all London to search.'

Mark looked rather helpless and had nothing to say.

'We could keep a look out here,' Bobby suggested, 'in the hope that he might turn up again some time – could you spare the time? I have to go on duty at two each afternoon at present. Only it would have to be a continuous watch. It's no good going on for an hour or two and then taking a rest. Turn your back for five minutes and your man is dead sure to have come and gone again.'

Mark was plainly not much attracted by this notion of keeping a long steady watch outside 'The Cedars'. His idea of detective work was a swift and brilliant following-up of clues that led by one inevitable deduction after another to a dramatic climax. The suggestion that instead it largely consisted of a patient, interminable, inexorable watch for something you knew it was a thousand to one would never occur, was an idea as novel to him as it was unwelcome. He pointed out with some asperity that if the man they were looking for were guilty, he would not be likely to return there, and if he were innocent, then it was no good finding him. Bobby agreed, and having made Mark realize that a detective's job was neither so easy nor so exciting as it is sometimes believed to be, made another suggestion.

'You said they told you at Sir Christopher's office that they thought he had been drinking, didn't you?' he asked.

Mark nodded.

'But how's that going to help us to find him?' he asked doubtfully.

'It's only a chance,' Bobby said, 'but it looks to me as if our friend had needed a little bit of Dutch courage to nerve him up to face Sir Christopher, who was a pretty formidable old boy, by all accounts. And if he had needed a drink that day to buck him up, then the day he came here he might have visited one of the pubs near so as to work up his courage to tackle Sir Christopher again at his house.'

'Even if he did, he wouldn't have left his name and address,' Mark pointed out.

'Only a chance,' Bobby agreed, 'but they might remember him and they might have something to tell us – you never know. Also, they might be asked to let us know if he came again. It would mean spending the whole of the rest of the day going from one pub to another and having a drink at each,' he added resignedly.

Mark expressed the opinion that this was a disgusting prospect, and Bobby said he thought so, too, but added that, owing to the licensing laws, most of the drink they would thus have to consume would be of the variety known as 'soft'. But this was a consideration that seemed to cheer them only to a very limited degree, so that they both looked almost as depressed as before.

Conscientiously, therefore, they worked their way from 'The Crown and Sceptre' to 'The Golden Lion', and from 'The Golden Lion' to 'The George and Dragon', and from 'The George and Dragon' to 'The Green Man', where at last their luck turned. For entering into amiable conversation with the young lady behind the bar, they learned that a customer, answering the description of the man they sought, had been there once or twice, the last occasion being on the night of the murder of Sir Christopher Clarke, an event the young lady remembered well because of the 'turn' it had given her. It seemed, moreover, that this customer had been the first to bring the news, long before the evening papers had got hold of it. That he was the bearer of such startling and exciting intelligence had naturally attracted a good deal of attention to him, and was the principal reason why the barmaid remembered him so well among the thousand and one customers she served every week or two. She remembered, too, how he said more than once: 'Mark my words, it's not murder, it's not murder at all.' But in that he had been proved quite wrong, for the papers all said the dead man had been shot twice, which made any idea of suicide or accident quite untenable.

Bobby remembered that, oddly enough, the same words, 'It is not murder,' had been used by Brenda Laing, though the coincidence did not strike him as of importance, since both suicide and accident had been ruled out. He thought that probably in these defaulting days, as soon as anything happened to any well-known City man, it was at once put down as suicide.

The barmaid added that the customer had seemed very excited, and had further expressed with some fervour the general opinion that Sir Christopher had come to the end he deserved, and this opinion no one had controverted, for the dead man had won but little popularity from his neighbours.

Questioned further, the barmaid said she had no idea of who this customer was. Nor did she think anyone else had. It was the news he brought that had interested people, not his identity. Nor had he said much about himself. And he had not been there since, so far as she knew. Only at the very last one little fact came out in response to Bobby's persistent questioning.

'He did say,' the barmaid told them, 'that we had good beer here, and so we have, too, none better, and I remember he said it was always good beer at a "Green Man", and that was the sign of the house he used, where there was good beer, too.'

'Didn't say where it was, did he?' asked Bobby. 'If it's anywhere near, I'll go along and see what their beer's really like and if it's as good as this.'

But the barmaid knew nothing about that, and Bobby and Mark retired.

'I wonder how many "Green Man" pubs there are,' Bobby sighed. 'We shall have to get a list of the lot.'

'How are we to do that?' demanded Mark.

'We'll start by ringing up all the big brewers,' Bobby said, and accordingly he and Mark each took possession of a telephone kiosk, where each spent considerable time and innumerable twopences in ringing up every brewer in the telephone directory, Mark starting from the top of the list and Bobby from the bottom till they reached an agreed name in the middle.

Fortunately 'The Green Man' is not too common a sign, and the two lists with which they emerged from their respective kiosks were not too long. Hurriedly they plotted a route to follow, and then Mark got out the little two-seater he owned, and they started off. Their luck was in, for at the second house they visited, the moment they entered it they saw, sitting in a corner with a glass of beer before him, a man answering very well to the description of the one they sought.

CHAPTER 15

Mark Lester Keeps a Secret

STUPENDOUS luck, Bobby thought to himself, and with great satisfaction he saw that their quarry seemed too absorbed in his own thoughts to have noticed their arrival. Quickly Bobby made up his mind that it would be better not to risk rousing his suspicions in any way by the two of them, Mark and himself, accosting him together. It would be easier to get him to talk, and less likely to make him take alarm, if first one of them sat down near and began to chat, and then the other strolled up as if recognizing an acquaintance. But to persuade Mark, all trembling with excitement as he was, to remain in the background for even a minute or two would be, Bobby felt, somewhat difficult. Moreover no one could possibly suspect Mark of being a policeman, while Bobby was by no means sure that his own appearance – tall, the carriage of a drilled man – might not rouse such a suspicion in an uneasy conscience. It seemed better, therefore, that Mark should make the opening move, and Bobby said to him:

'I think it would be just as well if it didn't look as if we had come here together. If you go and sit near, and try to get him talking, I'll come up and join you in a few minutes, as if you were someone I knew and I had just noticed you. Only be careful, talk about anything at first, don't risk alarming him – cricket or racing or football.'

'Good idea,' approved Mark. 'Not that I know much about cricket or football or racing,' he added, as one might say, 'not that I know much about slums, or sewage, or lice,' and, provided with the liquid refreshment he had ordered, he strolled across to where their quarry was seated, still apparently deep in thought.

'Hope he won't make a mess of it,' Bobby thought,

'but anyhow no one could ever take him for one of our fellows,' and he observed with relief and a touch of amusement that Mark sitting down close by their quarry had at once lapsed into apparently equally deep meditation, and was not taking the least notice of his neighbour.

'Lester has some idea how to set about it,' Bobby told himself, and, noticing a vacant seat that gave him a good view of the pair of them, sat down there.

He had some slight natural talent for drawing, though of course this sign of individuality had been severely repressed at the public school he had attended. He still liked to practise it, however, and had even found it useful on occasion. Now, getting out his pocket-book, he proceeded to make a sketch of Mark's neighbour, with whom Mark was beginning to exchange a few words.

The task interested him, he spent more time over it than he had intended, and when it was finished he regarded it with the frank admiration our own handiwork usually arouses in ourselves. Even if its artistic merit was smaller than Bobby was inclined to think, it was at any rate a recognizable likeness, and a man who was sitting near and had been looking on with much interest, remarked:

'Artist, sir, I presume?'

'Oh, no,' said Bobby, flattered. 'Only a little sketch for my own amusement.'

'A remarkably good likeness all the same,' declared the stranger. 'My brother-in-law is a porter at the Royal Academy,' he explained, 'so naturally I'm interested in art.'

'Indeed,' said Bobby. 'Well, I'm glad you like it – I suppose you don't know the gentleman?'

'Only from seeing him here,' answered the other; 'we've just said "how do" sometimes, that's all.'

'Interesting face,' observed Bobby. 'I wonder what he does?'

'Something to do with the theatre,' the other answered;

'seems to have free tickets to give away sometimes – the other day he had tickets for four stalls he was showing round.'

'Oh, indeed,' said Bobby, interested.

There came into his mind the odd story of the free tickets for the Regency Theatre sent to Sir Christopher Clarke three times running before his murder. A curious coincidence, it seemed to him, and yet he could see no meaning in it. Taken up with this idea, he forgot to watch Mark and his companion as closely as he had been doing until now. He saw they were talking together and that satisfied him. Turning to his own new acquaintance, he said to him:

'I suppose you don't know which theatre?'

The other shook his head. All he knew was that the man they were talking of had boasted of having theatre tickets to give away and had shown tickets for four stalls in proof. Two of these stalls he had in fact given to someone. Bobby's friend did not know to whom, but he had seen them handed over, and effusive thanks and a round of drinks had followed. Bobby's interest seemed to amuse him a good deal, and he told Bobby chaffingly that it was no good trying to cadge tickets off the old gentleman, who knew very well how to keep hold of them.

'Keeps them for extra special friends,' he said.

'Have to see what I can do, all the same,' Bobby answered laughing; 'I'm always open to free theatre tickets, and in fact I rather think the man he's talking to now is a friend of mine. I'll go over and get an introduction, I think, and see what I can do.'

'Bit too late,' replied the other. 'He's gone.'

Startled, Bobby looked, just in time to see his quarry disappearing swiftly through the doors, while Mark watched him go and then turned and began to come in Bobby's direction.

'Near closing time, you know,' Bobby's new friend

said, a little astonished at the air of dismay with which Bobby had witnessed this swift disappearance.

But Bobby did not hear. He was watching Mark now, and he saw that in him there had occurred an extraordinary change. He stumbled as he walked, as though he could not see clearly where he put his feet, his cheeks had grown thin and pinched, and had taken on a dull grey leaden tint, his eyes were fixed and staring, his whole air was that of one who had suddenly been called to gaze upon a horror almost beyond human bearing. He seemed even to be breathing with difficulty; and not only Bobby, but his new friend too, saw that something was wrong. He said:

'Your friend's ill.'

Bobby jumped up and went to meet him.

'What's the matter? What is it?' he asked anxiously.

'God –' Mark muttered in a kind of hoarse, half-strangled whisper; 'God in Heaven –'

'What is it? What's happened?' Bobby repeated. 'Pull yourself together,' he said sharply. 'Everyone's looking.'

Everyone in fact was looking. They were the centre of all eyes. Mark's appearance was in itself enough to attract attention, and that hoarse, half-strangled whisper of his had penetrated to every corner of the room.

'I never dreamed of that,' he said again with the same air of almost insupportable horror. 'My God, I never dreamed of that.'

'Of what? Of what?' Bobby asked with angry impatience. 'Pull yourself together,' he repeated. 'Here, you had better have some brandy.'

As he spoke he turned to the barmaid and gave the order, but that damsel shook her head with great firmness.

'If you ask me,' she said, 'he's had enough already and he don't get no more, not here.'

'Nonsense,' exclaimed Bobby, irritated almost beyond

bearing by this new difficulty, 'it's not drink, he's had none.'

But the barmaid, who knew her duties and her responsibilities, remained unmoved.

'If it's not drink, what is it?' she asked. She added: 'I've seen the horrors before to-day.'

The question was one Bobby could not answer, and the girl's last words struck him, for Mark had indeed very much the air of one who had seen 'horrors'. He turned to Mark and Mark muttered:

'I'm going . . . no good stopping here . . . not now.'

'That's right,' agreed the barmaid, relieved.

Mark made for the door almost at a run, brushing by Bobby abruptly enough and without taking any notice of him. Puzzled and angry, Bobby followed. Mark's little car was drawn up outside, in the court used by the customers as a parking place. Mark was already climbing in and Bobby followed, only just in time, for in another minute Mark would have been off.

'It's no good your coming, no good now your coming,' Mark said to him, wildly, almost with the manner of wanting to push him out again.

'Well, I am,' Bobby said. 'What the devil's the matter with you, Lester? Have you gone quite cracked?'

'I wish I had,' Mark whispered. 'I wish I had.' More loudly he said: 'I'm going straight home, it's not your way, you had better get out, take a taxi, I'll pay for it.'

'Wait till you're asked,' Bobby snapped. 'I want to know what's happened? What did he say to you? Why did you let him get away from you like that?'

Mark made no answer. But though they were already travelling at a high rate of speed he crashed his foot on the accelerator and sent the car flying down a fortunately straight and empty road at a speed that fairly scared Bobby.

'Are you mad?' he shouted. 'Do you want to get us both killed? Slow up, slow up, I tell you.'

Mark looked at him, hesitated, and then obeyed, but unwillingly enough. Bobby said:

'Next time you feel like committing suicide, wait till you're alone.'

'Why, that's good advice,' Mark answered, 'so I will.'

Bobby looked at him sharply, for there was a tone in his pronunciation of these last words that Bobby did not like. He said:

'Tell me what's happened.'

'Nothing,' said Mark.

'Nonsense,' Bobby roared, raging, 'tell me what he said to you.'

'Nothing,' answered Mark stubbornly.

Bobby nearly choked.

'Then what made you look like that?' he demanded.

'Like what?' Mark returned, and then: 'I didn't,' he added comprehensively.

'You did,' said Bobby with emphasis, 'you jolly well did ... look here, Mr Lester, what's the good of playing the fool? It's quite evident he told you something, something important, unexpected. What was it?'

'He told me nothing,' said Mark. 'It wasn't the right man.'

'That's a lie,' retorted Bobby, 'a barefaced lie.'

'It wasn't the right man,' Mark repeated.

'It was,' Bobby fairly shouted, 'you know it was, and he told you ... what did he tell you?'

'Nothing,' said Mark again, 'nothing at all.'

'You little rat,' Bobby growled and laid hold of him. 'For two pins, I'd take you by the throat and shake the life out of you.'

'Go ahead,' said Mark.

Bobby stared at him, trying to make out his expression in the dim light within the car. Bobby's arm fell to his side, his anger abated, he began to understand that more had passed between Mark and the man in the public house than he had dreamed of, that there had been that between them which had taken from Mark Lester all hope, all strength.

But what it was, Bobby could not even imagine.

'Mr Lester,' he said as gently as he could, 'won't you tell me the truth?'

'No,' said Mark.

Bobby sank into silence, baffled and uneasy. He recognized he was faced with a determination it would not be easy to break down, a settled resolve that would not soon change.

'If you don't,' he said presently, 'it may very likely mean that the murderer will escape.'

'Brenda – Miss Laing –' Mark answered slowly, 'told me once that murderers never escape. Perhaps that's true.'

Bobby thought to himself that the records of the C.I.D. did not support that belief and then he thought again that perhaps those are records in which all things are not recorded.

'Mr Lester,' he said once more, despairingly this time but making a last appeal, 'I only want you to tell me what has happened to disturb you so much.'

'Nothing,' answered Mark inflexibly. 'There is nothing to tell you. The man I spoke to was not the right man. He had nothing to do with it. He knew nothing. That's all.'

'All lies, you mean,' Bobby answered.

'As you like,' Mark answered indifferently, and then his voice changed and all the indifference faded from it as he exclaimed: 'Look, look where we are, where we've come to.'

Bobby saw then that they were passing the Regency Theatre.

'The Regency,' he said, 'why, what about it?'

'Nothing, I didn't know we had come this way,' Mark mumbled. 'We've come miles out of our way.'

He increased speed again.

'I meant to go straight back,' he said, 'and we've come round here instead.'

They shot through a press of traffic, and the Regency Theatre with its great flaring sign 'Shakespeare' was left behind.

CHAPTER 16

A Warning

I т was in silence that they drove on, and Bobby was still deep in troubled thought when presently the car stopped, this time just outside 'The Cedars'.

'I'm going in here,' Mark said to him. 'You can do what you like. I shall be some time.'

'I'm coming in with you,' Bobby said.

'No, you aren't,' Mark retorted violently; 'not you, you aren't.'

He got out of the car, and, leaving it standing there, walked up the drive to the house. Bobby did not attempt to follow. He had no authority to insist on accompanying Mark, and in Mark's present mood he was not likely in any case to learn anything from him. It would be better to wait, he thought, till Mark reappeared, when he might be more communicative. At any rate it was necessary to wait to make sure that no developments took place as a result of Mark's visit.

Inside the little car it was hot and stuffy, nor was there much room for Bobby's long legs, twist and curl them as he might. He got out accordingly, and began to walk up and down, occasionally pacing the length of the drive. But in the house nothing seemed to be happening, all was quiet, and only the glimmer of a light here and there showed that the inmates had not retired for the night.

As he walked up and down, Bobby racked his brains in vain to imagine some explanation of these bizarre happenings. What could it be, he asked himself again and again, that Mark had learned at 'The Green Man' which seemed to have filled him with such horror, and why had he come on to 'The Cedars' at this late hour? Was it to communicate to those in the house what he had learned at

'The Green Man'? Was it something he felt he must tell them of at once? But, if so, why had he so obstinately refused to breathe a word of it to Bobby?

One hypothesis did indeed come into Bobby's mind, but it seemed to him so improbable that he put it aside at once.

But still the problem teased and worried him till at last, when it was not far from midnight, the front door opened, and there appeared, plainly visible in the light from the hall behind, first Mark himself, and then the tall form of Peter Carsley.

They came a little way down the drive together towards where Bobby was waiting, and Peter said in a troubled and uneasy voice:

'You know ... well, it's ... well, we had never thought of such a thing.'

'No,' agreed Mark. 'No.'

'Don't you think ... well, wouldn't it be better ... I mean, it does seem like rushing things, doesn't it?'

Mark answered, pausing to light a cigarette:

'That's my affair and Brenda's ... if Brenda agrees, it's no one else's business.'

'No, in a way, no,' agreed Peter, 'only things are a bit exceptional just now, aren't they?'

'It's because they are that I think it would be better to get married at once,' Mark said, and in the darkness, at a little distance, Bobby fairly jumped as he asked himself, with increased bewilderment, if it was to hurry on the date of his marriage that Mark had driven here with such speed, and if this necessity to hasten the ceremony was a result of what he had been told at 'The Green Man'.

'All this is getting madder and madder,' Bobby said to himself resignedly.

Peter was talking again now. He said:

'You'll need a special licence.'

'There won't be any difficulty about that, will there?' Mark asked. 'I can say we have to go abroad or something like that.'

'No, I expect that will be all right,' Peter agreed. 'Well, I hope you'll be happy.'

'Happy?' Mark repeated with a startled accent, as if that were the first time such an idea had occurred to him. 'Oh, happy,' he said again, with an accent stranger still. He went on slowly: 'When I saw Brenda first, the very first time, I knew I had to marry her ... or no one. I knew she was meant for me. It's funny to feel like that, why do you? Is there something makes you? I didn't know till then that people did, but then it somehow came over me ... did you feel like that?' he asked abruptly.

'Oh, I don't know,' answered Peter, awkwardly. 'I suppose I just thought Jennie was a jolly fine girl and I went on thinking so till I thought it would be a jolly fine thing if we got married. That's all.'

'Would you have let anything come between you?'

'We jolly well didn't,' Peter answered. 'We knew her father would never consent ... we knew he might never forgive us ... we knew it might mean he would try to smash my firm and I should have to get out ... and we didn't care ... if it had been all that ten times over, we should have done just the same.'

'I don't mean like that,' Mark said in a low voice. 'I mean ... all that's nothing at all ... lots of people get married against their people's wishes ... I mean if ...'

He paused and Bobby leaned forward in sudden, swift excitement, for the idea had come to him very vividly that in what Mark was about to say would be exposed his secret. But Mark was silent still, and Peter said:

'What do you mean? If ... if what? ...'

'Nothing,' Mark answered in changed tones, and Bobby understood that now the secret, whatever it was, would not be told. 'Only nothing would keep me away from

Brenda ... neither heaven nor hell,' he said with a kind of restrained vehemence.

'Well, I don't suppose they'll try, will they?' Peter asked. 'So long as Brenda's willing and neither of you mind making people talk a bit ... that's all there is to it.'

'That's all there's to it,' Mark repeated, but again with an odd accent in his voice.

Peter was silent for a moment or two. There seemed to be something he wanted to say that he didn't quite know how to express. He said at last, rather hurriedly:

'Look here, old man ... there's just one thing ... I don't want to meddle ... but now you're going to get married ...'

'Go on,' Mark said.

'It's about trying to find out who shot Sir Christopher,' Peter explained. 'You said you meant to have a try ... I should give that up now if I were you ... I think you ought to ...'

'Do you? Why?'

'I think you ought,' Peter repeated. 'Lester, I wish you would promise me you would ... give that up, I mean ... for God's sake, man,' he broke out passionately, as though he could no longer quite control himself, 'for God's sake, stop that.'

'I will,' Mark said quietly. 'I promise you that.'

'Good,' said Peter very heartily. 'Good,' he repeated, in tones of an immense incomprehensible relief. 'Besides, you may have a chance to investigate another murder soon.'

'What do you mean?' Mark asked sharply, and Peter laughed a little.

'Well,' he said, 'if you had seen the way my dear partner looked at me to-day ...'

'Oh, Marsden?'

'Nothing he would like better than to cut my throat ... rather slowly, by preference. I'm not sure he won't have a try.'

They had begun to walk on again now, and had come to where Bobby was standing waiting in the shadow of the trees lining the drive. Mark was the first to see him and apparently remembered him then for the first time.

'Oh, you,' he said, 'you're there still.'

'I thought I would wait for you,' Bobby answered quietly.

'It's that policeman,' Mark explained to Peter. 'You know.'

'Oh, yes,' agreed Peter, recognizing him. To Bobby he said: 'Did you hear what I was saying?'

'I heard what you were saying just now,' Bobby answered, without thinking it necessary to emphasize that he had heard the rest of the conversation as well. 'I don't know if you meant it or if you were joking, but it's rather serious to say someone wants to murder you.'

'Well, he does all right,' Peter retorted, 'and what's more, I told him I would tell you people so, so that you would know where to start looking if I were found some day with a knife in my back or my head bashed in.'

'Do you mean that there has been a quarrel and he has used threats?' Bobby asked cautiously.

'Quarrel?' repeated Peter. 'Depends what you call a quarrel – when you were at the office this morning, when you went away, didn't you see how you left us? glaring at each other across the table and only not going for each other because we knew the clerks would call in the police. If we had been alone somewhere ... not but that I could tackle Marsden with one hand tied behind me, and he knows it, too.'

'But you don't suggest ...' began Bobby and paused.

'I very much suggest,' Peter retorted. 'Marsden wanted to buy me out. Under the deeds of partnership he has the right to do that. But there's a little clause that if we can't agree as to the figure it is to be settled by arbitration, after an independent examination of the books of the firm.'

'Well, that's all right, isn't it?' asked Bobby.

'Depends on what you call all right,' Peter answered again, 'but I'm inclined to think Marsden has very good reason for objecting to an independent examination. He has offered me better terms than there's any need to. I've refused them. If there's anything wrong, it's going to come out. I think that's only fair to clients for one thing. And if anything comes out, I'm not going to have people saying that I knew all the time, but cleared off while I could, with my share of the swag.'

'Have you any reason to think there's anything wrong?' Bobby asked.

'Well, again, that depends on what you call reason,' replied Peter. 'One night Marsden told me there was a big deficiency and clients had been swindled wholesale, the next morning he said I had misunderstood him, there was nothing wrong at all, all accounts were perfectly straight. But he won't let the books be seen, he's trying to keep them even from me, though of course I've a right to see everything when I'm supposed to be a partner. And between that afternoon and the next morning he had been to Paris for some unknown reason and come straight back, and meanwhile there had been the big robbery here.'

'Are you suggesting he may have murdered Sir Christopher?' Bobby asked.

'No,' Peter answered slowly and heavily, 'no, I am quite certain he didn't do that ... quite certain, more certain than I am that Sir Christopher was murdered at all. Besides, I thought you people said he had an alibi, that he had been seen in Piccadilly or somewhere.'

'You can't always be sure of an alibi,' Bobby remarked. 'When you are sure of it, it's conclusive. But alibis are often faked and always have been, from Dick Turpin on.'

'Well, anyhow,' said Peter, still in the same heavy and sombre tone, 'it wasn't Marsden shot Sir Christopher, you may be sure of that. But I'm not sure Marsden didn't do the job with the safe. Of course, I know I oughtn't to say that, it's libellous, I suppose ... anyhow I mean to make sure about our clients' money. I'm more or less responsible there. My father made the firm, it was nothing when he joined it and he made it, and I'm not going to quit till I've made sure everything's all right – or isn't. I told Marsden so quite plainly when I turned down what he offered me to quit then and there, and if anyone ever looked murder, he did. So I told him I would give you people a hint where to begin to look, if anything happened to me.'

'I see,' said Bobby, though not quite certain yet whether Peter were in earnest. 'Only I hope he won't, because we've got one murder on our hands already, and it's quite enough. I take it, Mr Carsley, you've no actual information you can give us to connect Mr Marsden with the robbery here.'

'I know no more than you do,' Peter told him.

'Which isn't much,' Bobby remarked. 'You said just now you weren't quite certain Sir Christopher was murdered? What did you mean?'

'Oh, nothing,' Peter answered.

'Mr Carsley,' said Bobby, 'both you and Mr Lester are a little too fond, in such a serious affair as murder, of saying things that then you say mean – nothing.'

'Well, it's all such a fog,' protested Peter, rather more meekly than Bobby had quite anticipated. 'What actually happened isn't known for certain yet, and till it is, I'm lawyer enough to want to take nothing for granted. That's all.'

'Not even a dead man with two bullets in him?'

'Above all, not a dead man with two bullets in him,' replied Peter, very gravely.

'I'm going. Good night,' Mark interrupted abruptly.

He walked away quickly, and a moment or two later they heard his car departing. Peter said:

'Good example. I'll follow it, it's late.'

'One moment,' Bobby said. 'What you've told me about Mr Marsden is serious. I shall have to report it.'

'I suppose I meant you to,' Peter agreed. 'It looks to me as if he's got to stop me or ... or it's got to come out if he has been playing tricks with clients' money. And there's no way of stopping me – except one.'

Bobby made no comment, but he was inclined to be of the same opinion, as he remembered Peter's square chin and jaw and the hard lines his mouth could set into.

'That's all,' said Peter. 'Good night.'

He went back into the house and after a pause for reflection Bobby went round to the back. Seeing there was still a light, he knocked gently. He had made a half promise that morning to the favourably disposed cook that he would do his best to watch over them and the house, so as to protect them against any more robberies or murders. His fulfilment of this promise as evinced by his appearance even at this hour was therefore warmly welcomed. Lewis was more than cordial, and produced an excellent whisky, after recommending an old port that during his master's life he would never have dared to dream of laying a finger upon. Bobby, however, preferred the whisky. The cook, the parlourmaid, the housemaid, and the 'tweenie', all assured him in turn that now they would be able to sleep in peace, after this proof of watchful guardianship, which had, as the cook said, relieved them all from the fear of waking up in the morning with their throats cut. Also Bobby learnt that already the domestic staff knew that the marriage between Brenda and Mark was now to take place as soon as possible.

On the whole, it seemed the domestic staff approved, though admitting that it did not seem quite respectful to the memory of 'poor Sir Christopher, and him not in his grave yet, and them talking of marrying already'.

'But it's not as if it was her own father,' the cook pointed out; and they all agreed that Miss Brenda, who had almost frightened them before by the stillness and so to say 'intensity' of her manner, had seemed much better and more normal recently.

'I heard her laugh, almost natural like,' said the parlour-maid.

'Uplift somehow, if you know what I mean,' said the housemaid. 'I didn't use to think she cared for Mr Lester much, but the way she looked at him to-night . . .'

'Beautiful,' said the 'tweenie' rapturously, and though 'tweenies' are only there to be seen and not heard, her remark touched such responsive chords in the bosoms of the others that she escaped all rebuke.

CHAPTER 17

Difficult Points

IT was with no very welcoming expression that Superintendent Mitchell looked up when Bobby was shown next morning into his room at Scotland Yard. His desk was piled high with papers, before him were different sets of reports on three different cases, all requiring immediate attention and all needing to be read through and digested before the daily routine interview with the Assistant Commissioner. His air was formidable as he said:

'What do you want? Do you think I've nothing better to do than waste my time with every three-year man who thinks he would like a chat?'

'Orders were to report personally, sir,' answered Bobby, facing the storm bravely, without betraying any sign that his heart was in his boots.

'If you had anything new and important to say,' growled Mitchell. 'How the dickens did you manage to get them to send your name in?'

'I told them I wanted to see the Assistant Commissioner,' explained Bobby.

'You did ... what?' gasped Mitchell. 'The Assistant Commissioner,' he repeated on a rising scale. 'Oh, you did ... and what did they say to that?'

'Oh, a lot of things,' answered Bobby. 'All different,' he added.

'Suppose they had taken you to him?'

'Well, sir, I risked that, one has to risk something,' Bobby answered. 'So when they wouldn't, I told them a superintendent would do.'

Mitchell fairly bounded in his chair.

'You told them a superintendent would do?' he repeated

faintly. 'Young man, is that what they taught you at Oxford?'

'Oh, no, sir,' answered Bobby, shocked.

'What do they teach you at Oxford?' demanded Mitchell.

'I'm told it's where,' Bobby explained, 'they teach an English gentleman to be an English gentleman.'

'Well, now, is that it?' said Mitchell, much interested. 'Well, I've often wondered and now I know.' With a sudden change of manner he added: 'Now, Owen, out with it, and unless it's something to justify your infernal cheek, you're for it.'

'Mr Lester informed me yesterday,' said Bobby, 'that Dr Gregory owed Sir Christopher money and was being pressed for payment.'

Mitchell flung an expert and practised hand into the thick of one of the paper jungles before him, extracted a paper, and looked at it.

'Two hundred and twenty-five pounds,' he said. 'Stated by Dr Gregory to have been repaid. No trace of this alleged repayment can be traced in Sir Christopher's accounts either private or at the office, but his private accounts seem only rough notes. Dr Gregory produced an I.O.U., torn in half and with pen drawn through. States same was returned to him when payment was made. States same was cash payment.' He put the paper back and looked at Bobby. 'Any information to add to that?' he demanded ominously.

'No, sir,' said Bobby, and before Mitchell could hurl the thunderbolt he evidently had in readiness, Bobby proceeded with a brief account of his expedition in Mark's company to 'The Green Man' the night before and of the results.

Mitchell put his thunderbolt by, listened attentively enough, and when Bobby had finished said:

'Go away. Write out a full report. Come back with it.'

Bobby took a document from his pocket and laid it on the table.

'The report, sir,' he said.

Mitchell took it up and looked at it.

'When you've been a bit longer than three years in the Force,' he observed, 'you'll know better than to forget the red ink ruling – this has none at all.'

'Sorry, sir,' said Bobby, a trifle dashed.

'You'll never get on in the Force,' Mitchell told him, 'if you forget your red ink. Is this sketch the one you say you made of the man Mr Lester talked to?'

'Yes, sir.'

'Have to get it reproduced,' said Mitchell. 'Been more useful if it had been a photograph, though. Still, have to do the best with what we've got – important to trace him. Got any idea what it all means?' And then as Bobby hesitated, he added: 'Out with it, never mind how silly it is.'

Thus encouraged, Bobby obeyed.

'It did just occur to me as possible,' he said, 'that it was Lester himself who shot Sir Christopher. Miss Laing's first story was that she saw him outside the drawing-room window just before the murder was committed, and though she denies it now, it may be true all the same. Lester seemed extraordinarily keen on discovering the murderer and it struck me that might be merely an attempt to mislead us. If that's so, and it's really Lester himself who's guilty, is it possible that the man in "The Green Man" knows, and told Lester so, and that's why he was so frightfully upset – at finding his guilt was known. If so, that would be why he got the man away before I had a chance to speak to him.'

'It's possible,' agreed Mitchell, 'but doesn't seem very likely. I don't know, though. At any rate, it's clear this man knew something that Lester had no idea he knew. We've got to find him somehow and find out what it is he does know. But if that's the way of it, why should that make Lester rush off to get Miss Laing to marry him immediately?'

'I heard Lester say something about going abroad. He might think the marriage would be an excuse for getting out of the country. Or he might think it would help to divert suspicion if he married the dead man's daughter.'

'Stepdaughter,' corrected Mitchell. 'What motive could he have if he's guilty? Sir Christopher's death apparently means that Miss Laing gets nothing instead of the very large sum she would have been entitled to, if he had lived long enough to complete the settlement he intended. One doesn't murder in order to deprive the girl one's going to marry of a fortune – at least, I never heard of a case.'

'Would Lester realize that, sir?' Bobby asked. 'Is it possible he thought he would take a bigger share of the estate if Sir Christopher died intestate?'

'Most people would know better,' Mitchell remarked. 'Most people know stepchildren aren't blood relatives.' He dived again into the piled-up papers before him and successfully extracted the one he wanted. 'Miss Laing was aware of her stepfather's intentions,' he said. 'She knew that in the case of his death intestate, she would not be entitled to anything. Miss Laing has shown documents proving that she knew all that. Presumably if the girl knew, Lester would know, too. Are you quite sure Lester was really as disturbed and troubled last night as you say?'

'Yes, sir,' answered Bobby with conviction. 'I can't describe it. Whatever it was he found out ... it wasn't that he seemed afraid exactly or just surprised or anything like that ... the barmaid said he had the "horrors" and so he had – but not from drink. It was what he had been told had given him the "horrors", and he looked it, too. The "horrors", that was it.'

'And yet he wouldn't tell you what it was,' Mitchell mused, 'and denied there was anything at all and went off full tilt to persuade the girl to marry him as soon as possible? Can't see much sense to it. Most likely the explanation is simple enough, but what is it? Bear looking into, anyhow.'

'Yes, sir,' said Bobby.

'Pity,' Mitchell remarked, 'you let "The Green Man" fellow get away. Once you had traced him you ought to have stuck to him.'

'Yes, sir,' said Bobby.

'Suppose you think you couldn't guess Lester would behave like he did, getting the fellow away on the quiet after being so keen on asking you to help him, and so it's no fault of yours?'

'Well, sir,' Bobby answered, considering, 'it wouldn't happen like that again, and so I suppose it oughtn't to have happened like that then.'

'But it did,' Mitchell pointed out severely. 'The fact is, you made a bloomer, young man.'

'Yes, sir,' said Bobby meekly.

'When I find one of my men who doesn't make bloomers,' declared Mitchell, 'I'll put him in a glass case, along with a harp and crown, and leave him there. I believe I've read somewhere that it's the general who makes the fewest mistakes who wins the war. Well, it's the detective who makes the most bloomers who gets to the superintendent's chair – "believe the man who knows". Because why? Because the man who makes the most bloomers makes the most successes as well, the two being naturally twins.'

'Yes, sir,' said Bobby.

'I suppose you didn't notice what size feet he had?'

'Short, broad, and rather on the small side,' answered Bobby. 'He couldn't possibly have made the footprint in "The Cedars" garden.'

'Anyhow, I suppose you would have recognized him, if he had been identical with the man who spoke to Doran; I forgot for the moment you saw him, too. But who was that old boy and where does he come in? And if that was his footprint, what was he doing in "The Cedars" garden? Possibly he had nothing to do with it, only then why did he tell Doran it was suicide? Then you say your "Green Man" chap said it wasn't murder and that Carsley said the same thing? What's that mean?'

'It must be murder,' Bobby pointed out, 'a man can't shoot himself twice through the heart, either by accident or on purpose.'

'I know that,' retorted Mitchell. 'The point that's worrying me is why so many of them seem to want to go out of their way to say it wasn't murder. You say that Lester, after being told whatever he was told in "The Green Man", went straight to find Miss Laing? Is it possible there's something she knows? Does he want to marry her with the idea of preventing her from giving evidence against him? I wonder if that can be it. Only what can she know? There's fairly strong evidence she was playing the piano the whole of the time. It's just possible there was a break nobody noticed, but her stepsister says there wasn't, and the parlourmaid girl seems quite sure – says she'll take an oath there was no break and that she was listening the whole time. Then there's Gregory. He owed Sir Christopher money, but Sir Christopher was a valuable patient – a hundred or more every year. You report he was a long time before giving the alarm. That might be to give someone a chance of escape, only why should he? Then there's Peter Carsley. With him, we always come back to the fact that he had a good solid reason for wanting the old man out of the way. That Sir Christopher was shot that day meant to Carsley he had married a rich woman instead of a pauper. Do you think there's anything in this talk of his about his partner being likely to murder him?'

'Haven't an idea, sir,' Bobby answered. 'Doesn't seem likely and yet somehow I thought he meant it.'

'Nasty for us if it happens after we've been warned and practically asked for protection,' mused Mitchell. 'I must send Gibbons or someone to have a chat with him and report. Or I wonder if it means that he intends to murder Marsden and that's the first step.'

'But why should he?' Bobby asked, startled, for this was an idea quite novel to him.

'Why should anyone?' retorted Mitchell. 'People commit murders for all kinds of reasons, but never for a really adequate reason, because there is no adequate reason for committing a murder. But in this case, it is possible Marsden may know something; apparently he has been dropping hints like that to some of our men, only with the usual addition that he can't say anything till he's sure. But if he does, Carsley may mean to do him in and then claim it was self-defence and call us to prove he had asked for protection. When are you for duty next?'

'Two p.m. to-day, sir.'

'I'll ring up your inspector and ask him to put another man on in your place. You can spend your time hanging round "The Green Man", trying to see if you can find the man you saw last night or anything about him. It's important to know what he really said to Lester. I'll circulate your sketch but you will have the best chance to identify him as you've seen him. Keep up your connexion with the servants at "The Cedars" too. It may be useful. Report to-morrow to Inspector Gibbons. I've had enough,' said Mitchell, sighing gently, as he regarded the neglected piles of paper on his desk, 'of telling you to report to me personally.'

CHAPTER 18

Gossip of the Past

So the rest of the day Bobby spent hanging about 'The Green Man'; flirting with the barmaid, who brought to that operation a mechanical dexterity that would have enabled her, one felt, to flirt with the Albert Memorial had professional exigencies required it; in chatting with other customers on such matters of current interest as the last football season, the coming football season, and the newest rumour of the latest attempt to dope the most recent greyhound favourite; and in drinking beer till he was reduced to the incredible condition of actually loathing the sight of the stuff!

His persistent efforts, however, met with no success. The barmaid confirmed the statement that the customer Bobby seemed to think might be the dear old friend he had not met for years had been occasionally in possession of complimentary theatre tickets, but for what theatre she did not know. For her part, she preferred the pictures – Constance Bennett, now, and for a moment the barmaid almost forgot her professional poise and dignity in a touching human enthusiasm. One or two of the other customers had also chatted with him occasionally, and could report that he was rather fond of muttering vague threats against someone against whom apparently he cherished a grievance, but as there is nothing on earth so absolutely devoid of all interest as other people's grievances no one had paid him any attention or had any idea to what or to whom he referred. Nor did it seem that here he had ever spoken of, or made any reference to, that murder of Sir Christopher Clarke, about which on the night it happened he had shown himself so excited and so interested at the other 'Green Man'. Bobby thought it barely possible this silence was not without its significance.

But no one knew anything else about him, or had any idea of either his name, his address, or his occupation.

It was therefore with the knowledge that he would have little to report to Inspector Gibbons in the morning that Bobby, after closing time, made a somewhat depressed way to the nearest tube station.

'They'll pack me off straight back to my beat, I expect,' he decided, and then he wondered if he could get permission to make inquiries at the different theatres in the hope that if the man he was looking for was really connected with the stage, he might be traced that way. 'Wonder,' he thought, 'if it could be this old boy who bolted over the garden wall next door the day of the murder – if he did it, the excitement might have made him young and active again for the time. Only then would he have quietly gone off to get a drink and tell everyone it wasn't a murder? – and what the dickens can they all mean by talking about it's not being a murder when it's perfectly certain it was?'

Absorbed in these thoughts Bobby nearly forgot to alight at the station he had booked to, the one nearest to 'The Cedars'. It was thither he made his way and when he tapped at the back door of the house, he received his usual warm welcome. Evidently they had been expecting him, in spite of the lateness of the hour, and the cook said it made them all feel so safe to know he was always there and always watching. 'Always there and always watching' seemed to Bobby somewhat to exaggerate the case, but he made no attempt to correct her.

Then Lewis produced his excellent whisky, the cook consented to join them in a thimbleful, not more – discipline and decorum alike forbade that the parlourmaid, the housemaid or the 'tweenie' should be offered any such opportunity – and, on the conversation becoming general, and even animated, Bobby learnt it was now settled that Miss Brenda's wedding was to take place almost immediately, that it was to be a very quiet affair, that a perfect whirl of preparation was already in full progress. All the household agreed that the difference in Miss Brenda was wonderful. She seemed so much more natural, more human in every way. It was, all the women agreed, a kind of wakening, as though her love for Mark Lester had brought to her a new life, leaving all the old existence behind.

'Changed her it has,' Lewis agreed, 'so you wouldn't hardly think it was the same girl. You could almost say it was as if she had just come alive, if you know what I mean.'

'A week ago,' declared the cook, 'I thought she was only taking Mr Lester because the master said so, and of course she had to do what he said, not having nothing of her own like, and her only a stepdaughter he could have turned into the street any minute. But now –'

She paused, and the 'tweenie' said ecstatically:

'Now she worships the ground he treads on.'

'Don't you go for to take the words out of my mouth, my girl,' said the cook crossly, and if only there had been any household task the cook could have thought of that wanted doing, the 'tweenie' would have been dispatched then and there to attend to it.

'But why,' interposed Bobby, 'why should he be so keen on Miss Brenda marrying?'

The general opinion seemed to be that Miss Brenda, with her quiet, sombre ways, her trick of remaining still and silent and yet somehow supremely vital and aware, had, as people are fond of saying without quite knowing what they mean, 'got on Sir Christopher's nerves'. And Lewis was also of opinion that he felt his own daughter, Miss Jennie, was rather put in the shade by Brenda's quiet intensity of manner.

'There was something about her,' Lewis said, 'that made you always know she was there and yet she wasn't either, if you know what I mean.'

Bobby confessed that he didn't altogether, and Lewis tried again.

'In the house where I began my career,' he said, 'the lady had a daughter what turned into a nun finally, poor soul. But before we knew what was wrong, we used to notice she had that same way of standing very still, of seeming to be there and yet not there, as if there was something so much on her mind there was nothing else that mattered.'

'Do you mean Miss Brenda is religious?' Bobby asked.

'Oh, no,' said Lewis, and he and the others all smiled a little at the suggestion. 'Never goes near a church, she don't. It used to worry Miss Jennie quite a lot. She got the clergy once or twice to come and talk to Miss Brenda, and Miss Brenda would just sit and listen, and never say one word, but just look, and you could see the poor man get more and more hot and red and uncomfortable, and then he would say: "Could they pray together?" and she wouldn't say a word, but just look and look, and off he'd go, wiping his forehead most like. I heard one of 'em say once she was the sort they burned for a witch in the old days, and you could tell he was thinking it wasn't such a bad idea, neither.'

'You mean she's a bit absent-minded?' Bobby asked, doing his best to understand.

But at that they all laughed outright.

'There's never a pin dropped but she knows it,' Lewis declared, 'and what's more, you always know she knows.'

'But always as nice and pleasant a lady as you could want in a house,' the cook added, 'a lady as is a lady, which is what some isn't.'

'I've nothing against either young lady,' declared Lewis, 'only with Miss Jennie, you know where you are, you know all about her, but Miss Brenda – somehow you don't notice the other one if she's there. What I say is, poor Sir Christopher noticed it, too, and didn't like it, thought his own girl was being put in the background, if you know what I mean.'

'But Miss Brenda had no claim on him,' Bobby remarked;

'if he felt like that, he could have sent her away any time he wanted to?'

'He thought too much of her ma to do that,' asserted the cook.

'It wasn't that at all,' insisted Lewis, whom a third sampling of that excellent whisky was making both talkative and dogmatic, 'he was afraid of her, that's what it was. God knows why, but it's a fact. I've seen him pretending to read the paper and watching her all the time, and her sitting there as still and silent as ever, so you felt he could have screamed and run. We were all afraid of her, as far as that goes, if you know what I mean. But not like him.'

'I should hardly have thought from what I've heard,' Bobby observed, 'that Sir Christopher was a man likely to be afraid of anyone.'

'No more he wasn't,' declared the cook stoutly, 'not him, nor us neither, only what is true about him, poor gentleman, is that he wasn't ever the same after his wife died. That was when Miss Jennie was quite a tiny tot, you know.'

It seemed the cook was the only one of them who had been there in the lifetime of the late Lady Clarke. Sir Christopher had married her very soon after the death of her first husband, Brenda's father. Sir Christopher had been in New York at the time, but had at once left important interests there to return home to do what he could to help the widow and also presumably to urge his suit with her.

'Fixed it all up, so I heard tell,' remarked Lewis, 'before her first husband was cold in his grave.'

'The master was always like that,' declared the cook; 'never let anything stand between him and what he wanted, small or big. A hard man, too, but it was only after her death he went quite the way he was these last years. Changed him somehow.' She lowered her voice. 'The night she was buried,' she said, 'I heard him myself, crying over her coffin like a child, so you could hear him right outside on the stairs, so you would have thought it was tearing him in half. You wouldn't never have thought that of him, would you now?'

'You wouldn't,' agreed Lewis. 'It just shows.' He said: 'Even him as granite and iron was butter to, he had his soft spot once. But after that it must have gone hard as the rest of him, for I never saw sign or trace of it.'

'All the same it was there,' the cook insisted. 'He was always a little different with me, along of my having known her, and every year you could tell when the day came round when she died.'

'If he was so fond of her mother,' Bobby observed, 'that must have been a great bond between him and Miss Brenda.'

'Ah, no one ever knew what that one thought,' Lewis said. 'She was always quiet and still, thinking her own thoughts and never telling.'

'It was her ma's death changed her,' the cook went on. 'Until then she was always merry and bright, like any other young thing before their troubles come. But afterwards she went the way she's always been since, silent and still. Even when she was moving about the house seeing to things, she seemed the same somehow, still and quiet – waiting, I used to think sometimes, waiting for her mother to come back to her.'

'Quite different now,' said Lewis benevolently, helping himself to the whisky for the fourth time, 'and I can't say I'm sorry for it, neither. But it's a wonder how different she is, now it's fixed up with Mr Lester.'

'That's because,' explained the 'tweenie' in a whispered aside, 'she worships the ground he treads on.'

'I suppose it's because he thought so much of her mother he was going to settle such a large sum on Miss Brenda,' Bobby remarked. 'She loses that now.'

'Done in, according to law,' said Lewis, 'same as our legacies – we was all down for a year's wages, "if still in testator's employ" same as we are.'

'Two hundred extra for me he put down,' added the cook. 'That was along of my being here when his poor wife died.'

'Miss Jennie says it'll all be paid just the same,' the parlourmaid interposed. 'It's only right.'

'Then Miss Brenda will get her forty thousand, too?' Bobby asked.

'Well, now, that's what's funny,' the cook replied. 'Miss Brenda don't seem to want to have it, and Mr Carsley doesn't want her to, neither, though quite agreeable to us having ours.'

'Nothing funny about that,' Lewis pointed out. 'Our little bits of legacies don't amount to nothing much, but forty thousand pounds, same as she was to have, that's money.'

'There's been words about it,' confirmed the parlourmaid. 'Miss Jennie thinks Miss Brenda won't have the money along of what Mr Carsley said, and it's worrying 'em both. Like a ghost he looks and never sleeps a wink, for you can hear him all night long walking up and down.'

'What's worrying him,' pronounced Lewis, 'is that he knows there's some as thinks it's him that did it, along of it putting all that money in their pockets and saving Miss Jennie that's Mrs Carsley now from being cut off without a penny. Not that I believe it myself,' added Lewis generously, 'but it's the gossip round here.'

Evidently this observation was intended to elicit Bobby's opinion. But Bobby was careful to express none and as it was now very late he got up to go. Before he was allowed to depart, however, he was obliged to renew his promise to continue the watch he was believed to be keeping over the safety of the house and its inmates, and to look in again the following evening to make sure, as cook said, they were all still alive and had not been murdered in their beds, a fate she appeared to anticipate with patient resignation.

As he came round from the back of the house into the drive, Bobby saw that the front door was open and that two people were standing there, clearly outlined in the light from the hall behind, so that he could recognize immediately both Brenda and Mark Lester. Apparently, Mark was just going and in Brenda's tone and accent, as she bade him good night, there was more than enough to prove the household staff had not been wrong in the estimate they had formed of her sentiments.

Not that what she said was much in itself, and indeed Bobby did not quite catch the actual words. But in her voice, in every curve and line of her body as she leaned towards him, as in that of his as he strained upwards from the lower step on which he stood to her upon the threshold, there was enough to tell the same story of the same utter and complete abandonment, so strange a contrast to her former cold, complete restraint.

But now that was forgotten, gone as if it had never existed, gone as if now there was nothing she had either the wish or the power to hold back. For just one moment Mark responded in an embrace into which it seemed that both of them threw their very souls. The next instant he was hurrying down the drive, as though afraid lest the memory of that divine instant should pass before he had time to carry it away with him, and Brenda whispered after him a 'Goodbye, my dearest,' that was still vibrant with the passion of their brief embrace. Then she went back into the house, closing the door behind her.

Unwilling to follow Mark too closely, a little ashamed of having been the witness, even involuntarily, of a moment of such high passion, Bobby lingered in the drive, waiting till Mark should be quite away.

'No doubt how those two feel,' he told himself, and he remembered that he had wondered when he knew how readily Brenda had fallen in with Mark's desires, whether her consent was due to her love for him or whether it had just seemed to her a way of escape.

But now there could be no doubt of her feelings, and yet

it seemed to Bobby that in their embrace, in the passion they had seemed to show, there had been a hurry, an abandonment, that had about it something ominous and threatening, as though they knew their hour was short and that what they felt for each other they must express while there was still time.

It came into his mind that they had been like two people upon whom a doom had been pronounced and who knew that at any moment it might be put into execution.

And then it seemed to him this was absurd, and that it was the night that was making him fanciful, that and the way in which he had concentrated all the faculties of his mind upon recent events.

'Two lovers kissing each other good night, that was all,' he told himself crossly, but without conviction.

Walking slowly down the drive, Bobby reached the gate. There he turned to look back at the big house behind, huge and formless in the night, with behind it driven clouds that threatened storm. The chatter of the servants that he had listened to so long began to form itself in his mind as the chorus of some dark tragedy that was still hastening to a destined end he could do nothing to avert. The death of Sir Christopher now seemed to him as but one incident in a greater drama, some immense and tangled tragedy of the human soul, some long-drawn tale of wrong and sin and suffering of which the end was not yet, wherein that murder was but one incident, that threatened more and worse to come before the full tale was told, the last debt paid.

A few drops were falling from those threatening clouds above when at last he turned and made his way homewards.

CHAPTER 19

More Theatre Tickets

BUT of all these fancies and imaginings Bobby felt a little ashamed when next morning he awoke in the clear daylight, with the early sunshine streaming into his room.

After all, what had they been founded on but the commonplace and ordinary incidents of two lovers bidding each other good night, of a story of a man grieving for the loss of his wife, of a young child growing silent and self-contained when left alone among strangers, of a preference given to a child in blood over an alien, and of a natural wish and disposition to be honourably disembarrassed of that alien's presence.

'No sign of any ill will,' Bobby reflected, 'or any grudge against the stepdaughter when arrangements were being made to settle forty thousand on her.'

Bobby was careful to be early at the Yard, but even so found that Superintendent Mitchell had already been there and at work for more than an hour. Inspector Gibbons was a later arrival, and when presently he sent for Bobby and heard his report, he seemed less disappointed at Bobby's failure to find the man he had been sent to look for than Bobby had feared. But then, detectives are as well used to the most promising and hopeful inquiries turning out only a fresh chase of the illusive wild goose, as are youthful poets to receiving back their manuscripts from the editors and publishers to whom they offer them.

Encouraged by the fact that his failure brought down on his head no official rebuke, and seemed rather to be accepted as a matter of routine, Bobby ventured to suggest that he might prove more successful if he were allowed to pursue his inquiries at the theatres, since it seemed, he thought, there might be some connexion. The Inspector smiled wearily.

'Suppose you think that wouldn't ever occur to us?' he observed. 'You young fellows are always the same, always wanting to teach your grandmothers how to suck eggs. A copy of that sketch you made was shown to every theatrical manager and every theatre agent in town yesterday. None of them recognized it. To-day it'll go the rounds of the provincial theatres.'

Bobby looked suitably abashed; and the Inspector added a few more details of the steps that had been taken to solve the mystery, giving Bobby a fascinating glimpse of a huge organization, slowly, patiently revolving without either haste or pause. He began to realize that in sober fact the detection of crime is not a matter of individual genius, of brilliant and dramatic improvisations on a given theme, but rather the slow collecting and feeding of facts into a great machine that in the end slowly and ponderously churns out the legal proof required. And he saw that this process is often as dull and tedious a job as that of sitting all day on an office stool, adding up figures – or as he had found his own evening at 'The Green Man', drinking beer he didn't want and exchanging commonplaces on subjects that didn't interest him with people who interested him still less.

There was Mitchell, for instance, one of the most famous and successful detectives of the day. And like any other successful business man, he spent nearly all his time at his desk, struggling with masses of correspondence and reports. Glancing at a pile of cigarette ash and deducing therefrom the age, income, and political opinions of the smoker, was a feat entirely beyond his powers. As for false moustaches and cunning masquerades, they were as alien to his habits as they are to those of a suburban vicar. Indeed, to-day, such delights are privileges apparently reserved solely for grave financial magnates and responsible heads of national banks.

Continuing, Bobby gave a brief account of his conversation with the servants at 'The Cedars', and Inspector

Gibbons said it was interesting, but he didn't see it had much to do with the case they had under investigation.

'Lots of men are fond of their wives just the same as lots aren't,' observed the Inspector, 'and anyhow, all that happened twenty years ago, and even if Sir Christopher wanted to get rid of the stepdaughter he evidently meant to do what was right by her – a good many rich men wouldn't want to settle forty thousand on their own daughters, let alone on a stepdaughter that had no claim on them at all. Got your report ready?'

Bobby produced it, a little proudly, and he was disappointed to see that the Inspector regarded it without enthusiasm.

'What's all the fancy work for?' he demanded.

Bobby, much hurt, realized that this disparaging reference was to the beautiful and elaborate red ink ruling with which he had taken such pains. He tried to explain the Superintendent had seemed to think red ink ruling essential and Gibbons indulged in a faint chuckle.

'Had you on proper,' he said, 'you can take it from me, red ink to Mitchell is much what a red rag is to a bull. Too late to alter it now,' he added as Bobby showed signs of wishing to resume possession of the unlucky document, 'it'll have to go in as it is, red ink and all. Now you can clear out and mooch round the theatres. Mitchell said if you asked permission you were to have it – but not unless you did. It's his way of encouraging initiative. He says most likely you'll only be wasting the taxpayers' money, but that don't matter so much now the budget's balanced. You're to make inquiries of the attendants only. Mitchell says most likely they know things managers and stars never dream of, and you might get to know something useful. In the evening you can mooch around about "The Green Man" again, but don't make yourself conspicuous asking too many questions. Finish up at "The Cedars". Mitchell says we must watch developments there. He's worried about Carsley and

Marsden, he thinks there's trouble brewing. They're both being trailed, but then they both know it, so that's not much good, except by way of a check. Bad for us,' Gibbons added, shaking his head, 'if one of 'em goes and does the other in and it came out at the inquest we had been warned and hadn't managed to stop it. Leading articles in all the papers about gross incompetence most likely.'

So the rest of that morning Bobby employed in wandering from one theatre to another, showing the copy of his own sketch he had been provided with to the various attendants and learning with monotonous regularity that none of them could recognize it; though, with a kindly wish to oblige, one commissionaire thought he remembered someone like that he had served with in Mesopotamia during the War, and a stage doorkeeper was sure there was a strong resemblance to an American actor who had been dead some years, and at one box office the sketch was definitely recognized as that of a former backer of musical plays, now in gaol through an unfortunate devotion to business that had induced him to sign rather more share certificates than there was strict authority for issuing.

None of these clues seeming promising, Bobby pursued his quest and was preparing to accost the magnificent six-foot-sixer who stands superbly outside the Regency Theatre, between Shaftesbury Avenue and St Martin's Lane, when he saw Mitchell himself alighting from a taxi near by. As Bobby was not in uniform he took no notice, for it might well be that Mitchell had no desire to be recognized. But he watched closely; and when Mitchell crooked a finger and then disappeared into a teashop near, Bobby followed him. Mitchell was settling himself at a table near the window. He nodded to Bobby and pointed to a chair at the same table.

'Coffee for two,' he said to the waitress and added to Bobby: 'Your country pays, but if you want a sausage roll as well, that comes out of your own pocket.'

'The coffee will do me, sir, thank you,' Bobby answered.

'Any luck?' demanded Mitchell.

'No, sir.'

'Been reading your report,' Mitchell went on. 'Glad to see you remembered about that red ink. What's a report without red ink?'

Bobby did not answer but he was aware of a faint twitching at the corner of Mitchell's mouth that made him hastily decide no future report of his should show so much as a sign of red ink.

'Seems you think,' Mitchell continued, 'there's more to come?'

'I don't know what I do think, sir,' Bobby answered, 'but I feel certain whatever it is didn't begin with Sir Christopher's death and hasn't ended with it, either.'

'Mr Lester,' observed Mitchell, looking thoughtfully out of the window at the theatre opposite where a certain bustle of people entering and leaving witnessed to a busy box office and the success of at least one Shakespearian revival, 'went on to the "Butterfly" night club after you saw him last night. He was there till nearly three this morning; and when he left he was fairly soused, but some pals saw him home, so there was no chance to run him in.'

Bobby both looked and was very much bewildered. He felt it utterly incredible that after that 'good night' scene, touched with a real and high emotion, Mark should have gone straight to a night club and got drunk there. He was almost inclined to think there was some mistake and Mitchell said:

'Surprised to hear that, eh?'

'I can hardly believe it,' said Bobby.

'Bear looking into,' agreed Mitchell. 'A young fool in love is generally sufficiently drunk all the time not to bother about getting drunk at night clubs as well.'

'I suppose,' asked Bobby hesitatingly, 'I suppose, sir, it's quite certain it was really Mr Lester?'

'Report from the man I put to trail him,' answered Mitchell.

Bobby still looked very bewildered. It seemed to him a psychological impossibility that after experiencing that moment of high emotion, Mark should have felt the need for the vulgar stimulus of drink. It was like supposing that a man who had just escaped a violent and sudden death by some mere chance would seek the thrill of a 'fun fair', or that the winner of a fortune on the Stock Exchange would want at once to go to play at darts for halfpennies. Mitchell seemed to understand what Bobby felt, for he said:

'Bit of a puzzle, eh? The fact is, we are badly up against it in this case. We're at a complete standstill with the facts. We don't know who it was escaped over the next door's garden wall or what he had to do with it. We don't know who it was Miss Laing said she saw by the drawing-room window, or whether it was Lester as she said at first, or Marsden, if it was him robbed the safe, or someone else altogether. We don't know why three times in succession stalls for the theatre were sent to Sir Christopher, or who sent them, or whether that means anything or not. We don't know why Dr Gregory took so long giving the alarm or if he ever really paid the money he says he did and has the torn I.O.U. to show for it. We don't know who it is Lester saw at "The Green Man", and why first he was anxious to find the fellow and then when he did, denied his identity. We don't know what Lester was told or why whatever it was should make him both want to get married and get drunk. We don't know who the old boy was who told Sergeant Doran it was suicide or why they all keep saying it wasn't murder when it's perfectly plain it was nothing else. We don't know if Miss Laing was really at the piano when the murder was committed, and we can't trace the revolver that was used, or find out whether Sir Christopher meant it when he said he had one in his possession that can't be traced either and that he certainly had no licence for. And now we don't know whether Carsley and Marsden are working together to fool us or are planning to do each other in. About all we do know is that the murder put a fortune into the pocket of Carsley's wife, and took another out of Brenda Laing's pocket, and that Carsley's hand was cut as was that of the man who climbed the garden wall in such a hurry; and what's the good of knowing so little when there's so much we don't know and can't find out? We're at a complete standstill with the facts and the psychology of the case is beyond us altogether.'

'Yes, sir,' agreed Bobby.

Mitchell was playing with his coffee spoon and staring at the same time at the busy theatre entrance opposite.

'Doing good business over there,' he remarked. 'Do you know, I'm not sure, after reading your report, that the solution of the whole thing is not, quite literally, staring us in the face at this very minute.'

'Sir?' said Bobby, startled, looking vaguely round the tea-shop, as if searching for the solution referred to that Mitchell apparently thought was visible.

'Have to wait,' Mitchell mused, 'and see if things go on pointing to the same conclusion – or if it strikes anyone else the same way.'

He looked sharply at Bobby as he spoke, and Bobby knew well that he was being tested. He felt there was something Mitchell hoped and expected him to say, but as he had not the least idea what it could be, he had to remain silent. Mitchell looked a little disappointed, as if Bobby had failed in some way, and Bobby remarked rather hurriedly, partly perhaps in order to prevent Mitchell from dwelling on this disappointment whatever it might be:

'Mr Lester is being trailed then, sir?'

'Of course,' answered Mitchell, 'they all are and most of them know it, though I'm not sure Lester does. He doesn't seem as if he were noticing much just now. You hadn't known about the trailing? One up to the other fellow if you didn't spot him. He reported Lester's saying good night to Miss Laing, too, only he put it rather differently. How he put it was: "Said good night to girl on doorstep and kissed same." Left us to guess whether it was girl or doorstep got the kiss, but likely enough we should have guessed right even without your report. What have you been doing this morning?'

Bobby ran over the names of the theatres he had visited and Mitchell said:

'You haven't been to the Regency yet, then?'

'No, sir, I was just going when I saw you.'

'Shakespeare they are playing there, isn't it?' Mitchell asked. 'Any good, do you know?'

'The papers say it's a very fine and novel reading of *Hamlet*,' Bobby answered. 'I've not seen it myself.'

Mitchell produced some money.

'When you're over there,' he said, 'get me two stalls for to-night. Leave the tickets at the Yard, will you? I promised my old woman a show to-night, only I wanted something jolly with lots of legs and music and she wanted Shakespeare, so we've decided to compromise on *Hamlet*. When you're married, always compromise with your wife when you can, Owen.'

'Yes, sir,' said Bobby. 'What shall I do if there are no seats left for to-night?'

'If there are no seats left for a Shakespearian production in the West End of London,' said Mitchell benevolently, 'you needn't do anything, because the end of the world will have arrived. Afterwards you can go on to Lincoln's Inn, and try to get Peter Carsley, or Mr Marsden, or both if you can, to have lunch with you. You can make it a good lunch. After all, if one has Oxford graduates in the Force one may as well make use of them, and I daresay lunch was one of the things you studied at the 'Varsity – the Assistant Commissioner always squirms when I say "'Varsity" to him, I don't know why.'

'To squirm at that word, sir,' explained Bobby, 'is one of the more important points of the U-ni-versity curriculum.'

'Is it, indeed?' said Mitchell, 'now that's interesting. Before you send your lunch bill in to Expenses, give it to me to initial, and then perhaps they'll let it through, if you've luck. But I don't say it'll run to champagne, mind.'

'No, sir,' said Bobby.

'Talk to 'em,' said Mitchell as he rose to depart, 'talk to 'em good and long and then they'll talk back again. Champagne might make 'em suspicious but talk won't, and it's not in human nature to listen long to another fellow without wanting to get your own word in. Remember what I told you before – talk and it shall be talked unto you. Oh, and if you like, you can tell them both about Lester getting drunk at the night club.'

He nodded and departed, leaving Bobby quite convinced that in these last words lay the cause and reason of the instructions given him.

CHAPTER 20

A Second Warning

THAT Mitchell had some obscure motive in wanting those tickets for that night's performance at the Regency, and that in his choice of an evening's entertainment Mrs Mitchell's alleged preferences had but small part, Bobby was also well assured. Yet what that motive might be, he could not even begin to guess. Had he not been under definite orders to spend his evening at 'The Green Man', he felt he would have been tempted to visit the theatre himself, even though it was only a Shakespearian revival, in the hope of getting some hint as to what was in the Superintendent's mind.

But perhaps that would have been a breach of discipline. It was Mitchell who was playing the game, it was he at whose will the pieces moved, Bobby himself was but a pawn whose business was merely to proceed modestly from square to square at the player's will.

Most likely there would be someone at the theatre Mitchell wished to watch, and as there was not too much time to spare, if he were to be in Lincoln's Inn by lunch time, Bobby hurried across the road straight to the box office. There he bought the two stalls Mitchell required and at the same time showed his sketch. But though it seemed to rouse a certain interest, and was looked at long and carefully, complete ignorance of the original was protested.

'No one I've ever seen, I'm sure of that,' decided the box office, and as all this had taken time, and it was now later than ever, Bobby had to hurry away as fast as he could back to Scotland Yard with the tickets and then on to Lincoln's Inn, where he arrived just in time to come face to face with Peter as that young gentleman emerged from the office of his firm.

Peter knew him again at once.

'Come to relieve the other fellow who's been trotting after me all day like a pet dog?' Peter asked him harshly.

Bobby for a moment did not answer but looked at Peter curiously, for the other's appearance startled, almost shocked him. In the bloodshot eyes of the young man there was a look as of a strain too great to be borne much longer; the whole expression of the pale, drawn face was that of a man not far from collapse, and yet at the same time the mouth was still as firmly set as ever, the square chin had still its defiant, upward tilt. It was as if in the contest between the red-rimmed, nervous eyes and the grim-set chin and mouth, the latter still had the upper hand and would not yield it easily.

'You don't look well, Mr Carsley,' Bobby said.

'A murder in the family is a trying experience, especially when you know you are suspected and have a chap hanging after you all day long,' Peter retorted, and would have passed on, but Bobby stopped him with a gesture.

'I wanted to ask you,' he said. 'Have you seen Mr Lester this morning?'

'Lester? No. Why?'

'He visited a night club last night and got very drunk,' Bobby explained. 'I was wondering how he was this morning.'

'He did what?' Peter asked, and it was evident that for some reason this information disturbed him. 'Lester? Are you sure?'

'Our information is that Mr Lester, after visiting Miss Laing last night and persuading her to agree to their getting married immediately, went on to a night club and got very drunk. He would probably have been run in by some of our people, only that friends saw him home.'

Peter made no comment, but stood silent and moody, evidently considering this news that for some hidden reason so much troubled him. Was it danger, Bobby wondered, that the other sensed in Lester's indiscretion, or was it something that cut deeper still?

'Mr Carsley,' Bobby said, 'I don't think you are being frank with us. Wouldn't it be better if you were? That is, if you want your father-in-law's murderer brought to justice?'

Peter looked at him but made no answer. None was required, the look was enough. It very clearly meant that whatever Peter knew, nothing would ever make him tell. Whether he were guilty himself, or knew something that pointed to another's guilt, or whether in fact he only entertained some possibly ill-founded suspicions, it was certain he would never speak. But after a time he said slowly:

'How do you know there is a murderer? How do you know it was – a – murder?'

'If it wasn't murder, what was it?' Bobby asked sharply, more than a little startled to find this same idea put forward once again. 'Isn't the doctor's evidence good enough?' he demanded.

'I forgot the doctor,' Peter answered. He added: 'You are following Lester about, too, are you?'

'We're following, as you call it, everyone who shows unwillingness to help us get at the truth,' Bobby answered tartly, 'or who seems to be trying to shelter the murderer. A suspicious attitude, you know.'

'Oh, I know you suspect me,' Peter answered quietly. 'It's rather a wonder you haven't made up your mind to arrest me. There's that – coincidence – of my having cut my hand just as the fellow must have done you say you saw climbing the garden wall next door. And it's a fact I can't say whereabouts exactly I was at the time it happened; and it's another fact that because of it my wife gets all her father's money, instead of nothing. Only does one murder one's father-in-law to get his money for one's wife? Matter of taste, I suppose, but I don't think I ever wanted to marry a rich wife.'

'Perhaps that's why you've not been arrested,' Bobby

suggested. 'Mr Carsley, there's a lot I should like to talk over with you and it's getting near lunch time. If you will come and have something to eat with me somewhere, we could talk more comfortably.'

'Is this the new technique of – shadowing, do you call it?' Peter asked suspiciously.

'Of course not,' Bobby said impatiently. 'In your case you must remember you've given us double reason for wanting to keep you under observation. You've thrown a heavy responsibility on us by telling us you consider yourself threatened by Mr Marsden. If that came to anything, we should be blamed for not having stopped it.'

'Oh, well,' Peter answered, 'you can wash that out now. I expect I was a bit far gone when I told you that, and anyhow Marsden is not so crude as all that. What he's hoping now is to see me hanged; and until he finally gives up hope of that coming off, I think I'm fairly safe from more direct methods. He told me as much quite plainly last night, and any help he can give you to getting me put on trial, you won't have to ask for twice. In the interval he's playing for time, very successfully, too. He's got a perfect genius for holding things up, but I'll get through in the end. Meanwhile, the office is like Bedlam, with the poor devils of clerks not knowing which of us to stand in with, whether he's an embezzler or I'm a murderer as he's fond of hinting, or whether we're both – both. To do him justice, I believe half the time he thinks I really did do it.'

He began to walk away, and when Bobby repeated his invitation to lunch, he once more shook his head.

'There's a lot we could talk over,' Bobby insisted.

'I daresay, but we aren't going to,' Peter answered and walked off.

'Obstinate beggar,' Bobby reflected, watching him go. 'One thing, if it's true there's anything wrong about their clients' money, he'll find it out sooner or later. Not the sort you turn off easily, once he's got an idea in his head.'

He waited a little longer and presently Marsden appeared, evidently also on his way to lunch. He, too, recognized Bobby at once and greeted him quite amiably.

'Making any progress?' he asked. 'Your people are still shadowing me, but I suppose I mustn't complain, though it's rather a bore. Still, you chaps know your job, I must say that. I don't think anyone else has noticed it. Do you know I've been nearly coming round to ask for a talk with some of you people?'

'If you've information you think you can give us,' Bobby said, 'it will be very welcome. We aren't making much headway at the moment, though there are a number of clues being followed up. Have you seen Mr Lester lately?'

'Lester? The man that's engaged to Miss Laing?' Marsden asked. 'No, I hardly know him. Why?'

'He got badly drunk at a night club last night,' Bobby answered.

Marsden appeared rather amused.

'Saying farewell to his bachelor ways, I suppose,' he remarked. 'By the way, the papers say the revolver Sir Christopher was shot with has not been identified and it's not certain whether he actually possessed one or not.'

'One of our difficulties,' agreed Bobby. 'It is known that he used to talk about having a pistol but no one seems ever to have seen the thing. If he possessed one and it's the one that was used to shoot him, obviously that would be a very important fact indeed.'

'Well, I can tell you of someone he told me himself he had shown it to,' Marsden said. 'It was someone who thought he had a grievance and who used threats. Sir Christopher told me he showed this fellow a pistol he had, and warned him that if he tried to play any tricks he would get the contents.'

Bobby thought this piece of information sounded promising. He suggested their having lunch together and pressed Marsden for further details. But Marsden, though he accepted the invitation to lunch readily enough, knew no more. He could give no hint of the identity of the person concerned. All he knew was what Sir Christopher had told him, but it seemed fairly good evidence that Sir Christopher had actually possessed the weapon of which he had talked, though hitherto no proof of that had been found. To Bobby all this seemed important, the implications to be drawn from it more important still. Forgetting Mitchell's instructions to talk continually, he lapsed into a worried silence. And more and more did it seem to him certain that this unknown was the centre of the whole mystery, and was also identical with the unknown of 'The Green Man' to whom Mark Lester had spoken and who after that had disappeared.

'This man you speak of,' he said finally, 'we've got to get hold of him somehow or another.'

'I don't see how that would help you,' Marsden answered. 'You can be pretty sure he doesn't know anything about it. There's an old saying. When you want to know who is responsible for anything, find out who profits.'

'We want more than that to show Treasury Counsel,' Bobby remarked, 'before he would be willing to order a prosecution.'

'You won't get it,' declared Marsden. 'The man who finished old Sir Christopher left no evidence. If I'm right in what I think, he had every advantage and every means for doing what he did without leaving any traces, and he made use of them all very cleverly. I should say you had better give up trying only – only – '

'Only what?' Bobby asked.

'Only for this,' Marsden answered, 'it's my idea there's worse coming.'

'In what way?' Bobby asked cautiously.

'I'm speaking in confidence,' Marsden said, 'only it seems to me – what happened to the father might happen to the daughter next.'

'You don't mean . . . ?' Bobby stammered, staring.

'I don't mean anything,' Marsden answered, 'except that I think you're altogether likely to have a second murder on your hands before long. A wife with money is good but money of one's own is better still. So if I were you I should try to keep an eye on Miss Jennie that's Mrs Carsley now.'

CHAPTER 21

A Step Forward

NOTHING more could Marsden be induced to say, but this that he had said, Bobby thought of sufficient importance to make of it a special report to headquarters.

Not that he was there allowed to see Mitchell. Special instructions seemed to have been issued on that point.

'Old man,' explained the sergeant to whom Bobby spoke, 'says if he wants to see you, he'll send for you, and meanwhile you're to be kept out, handcuffs and violence to be used if necessary.'

'I shouldn't think of making it necessary,' protested Bobby, quite hurt, and went away to write a brief report, perceiving however from the large bottle of red ink ostentatiously brought for his use by one of the officers on duty that the tale of the superb adornment he had given his last report was already a current jest – for, possibly because its duties are seldom humorous, nowhere is even the tiniest, feeblest joke more keenly appreciated than at 'The Yard'.

The report duly written and sent in, Bobby went on to spend the rest of the afternoon pursuing without success his inquiries at the different theatres, of which there seemed to him so many that when, in an evening paper he bought, he read the customary weekly article they all publish explaining that the theatre is slowly dying, he could not help wondering how many would be open if the theatre were in rude health.

His evening he spent at 'The Green Man', equally without success, and then went on to 'The Cedars' to assure the household there that protection was still being extended to them, to consume some more of Lewis's excellent whisky, and to listen for an hour or so to gossip and chatter from which he learned little, except that a marriage licence had been procured, that the wedding was fixed for the coming Saturday, and that Miss Laing seemed very happy about it.

'Different she is from what she used to be so you wouldn't hardly know her,' asserted Lewis. 'It's just as if she had been – well, thawed out, if you know what I mean.'

'Same,' confirmed the cook, 'as if her young days had come back to her, like it was before her poor mother died.' .

'It's love 'as done it,' said the 'tweenie' in a whisper, her eyes shining, 'it's because they worship the ground they tread on – I mean,' she added, perceiving a slight confusion here, 'the ground each other treads on.'

'Well, don't you get worshipping the ground the baker's young man treads on,' the cook warned her tartly, 'not if it makes you spend half an hour taking in the bread when you ought to be washing up the breakfast things.'

'Ah, all that,' said Lewis benevolently, coming to the rescue of the blushing 'tweenie', 'is before marriage. But afterwards – well, look at them other two, Mr Carsley and Miss Jennie that was.'

'Why? Are they quarrelling already?' Bobby asked.

'I wouldn't say that,' Lewis answered cautiously, 'only there's – well, there's something if you know what I mean.'

'It's only the worry and the trouble,' the cook protested; 'the gentlemen from the papers always here, and the police that aren't all quite the gentleman like Mr Owen, and even when they try to be, it would get on anyone's nerves to be asked questions hour after hour and all put down in writing, too, which makes it all so much worse, because when you say a thing, you just say it, but when it's all put down in writing, it's different altogether to my mind, so what I say is it's no wonder if Mrs Carsley and Mr Carsley look like ghosts risen from the dead or worse still – especial,' she added with an indignant look at Lewis, 'when there's some as isn't above dropping hints and insinuations, without ever saying what's in their minds.'

'And there's some,' retorted Lewis, helping himself again to the whisky, 'as know very well what they mean, which, if others don't, that's their affair.'

'What we want,' Bobby pointed out, 'are facts. If we could identify the man who escaped over the wall next door, or even if we could trace the revolver used, it would be different. Facts are what we want.'

'If it's facts,' Lewis said, 'it's a certain fact none can deny that Mr Carsley – well, drink I should have put it down to, only for there not being time, because, though drink could do it, drink's not so quick as that. But if that man hasn't something on his mind that he never gets rid of by day or by night, then I' – he sought for a comparison tremendous enough, and, not finding it, concluded rather lamely – 'then I'm wrong, that's all. But you can always tell when there's something on anyone's mind – didn't we all know it from his guilty ways when the gardener that was here before Mr James was taking the grapes out of the conservatory home to his sick wife? And when I was with the old Duchess of Kew, didn't we all know there was something heavy on her mind and weren't we shown right when she up and married the piano tuner – though there was finer men on her own staff if she had had the eyes to see.'

Bobby was aware already that Peter looked strangely ill and worn, but he was not inclined to attach much importance to that, for he knew, what these good people did not, of the conflict raging in the offices of the firm between the two partners. It was enough to give anyone a worried and a troubled air.

He talked a little longer and then took his leave earlier than usual, alleging as an excuse that he was tired from a long day's fruitless tramping to and fro. His way led him round the house into the drive and when he reached it he found the two stepsisters there, Brenda and Jennie. He guessed at once that they knew of his nightly visits and were waiting for him, and he heard Jennie say:

'He's here again to-night, just as they said.'

Bobby thought it well to stop and offer an explanation.

'Your servants are still a little nervous,' he said; 'they asked me to look in sometimes, so that they could feel safer in a way, if they knew we were watching the house.'

'They told us,' Brenda said in her slow, deep voice. 'Of course, that is not why you come.'

Bobby made no answer. Jennie said with sudden passion that shook violently her slight and slender frame:

'You're trying to find out things against Mr Carsley, you think it was Mr Carsley and you want to get them to say things ... you think it was Peter did it and it never was. Do you think my husband would murder my father?'

'It's not what we think that matters,' Bobby answered slowly; 'we have to do our best, we have to do our duty. When murder's been done' – and then something made him add – 'if it was murder.'

'What do you mean?' Jennie asked in a quick, puzzled voice, but Brenda said nothing at all, and somehow Bobby thought that she saw a meaning in his words, a meaning that had entirely escaped her stepsister and that even to him himself was not entirely clear. 'What do you mean?' Jennie repeated in the same puzzled tone. 'You can't think ... he would never, never have killed himself. Why should he?'

'It's not possible he could have done it himself, the doctor's evidence shows that,' Bobby agreed, and Jennie said:

'Well, then.'

But upon Brenda it appeared that her old cloak of silence and of stillness had descended again, for she did not move or speak, and yet in some way made her presence more vital and more forceful than that of either of the other two.

Bobby waited, determined to be as silent as she was, and yet aware that his silence was nothing more than silence, but hers was that of a swift, deep-running current. He thought to himself:

'She knows something, there's something, but is what she

knows so tranquilly the same that Carsley knows that
makes him look the way he does? And that Mark Lester
knows that makes him get drunk at a night club? And that
the little man at "The Green Man" knows that made him
clear out so quickly?'

Jennie said:

'You only come to try to get the servants to talk – well,
there's nothing they can tell you.'

'Perhaps not,' Bobby agreed, 'but there are some who
could tell us everything if they would.'

Then Brenda spoke:

'There is always someone who knows, there must be.
Only you cannot always tell what you know, not even if you
want to, not even if you try.' She paused and then added:
'Why do you trouble yourself so much? Murderers are not
always hanged, why should they be? But they never escape,
never. Always in the end they pay for what they've done.'

Again she was silent; and when neither of the others
answered, she began to move slowly back towards the house.
Jennie followed, a little as if she were compelled to do so.
The last glimpse Bobby had of the two tragic stepsisters was
as they paused together for an instant on the threshold of
the lighted hall before they entered.

Puzzled and troubled, even more than before, he went on
to his lodgings where he found waiting for him a message
instructing him to report to Mitchell in the morning. When
he did so, he found the Superintendent a good deal worried
by the suggestion now put forward by Marsden that Peter
might not only be guilty of the first murder, but might also
be planning a second, in order to get his wife's fortune into
his own hands.

'It's a thing that'll bear looking into,' he said, rather dismally; 'but what's a poor department to do with one fellow
saying another chap means to do him in and that other chap
declaring on his side that the first fellow means to murder
his wife, and all the time the very strong probability existing

that the two of them are working together to confuse the issues, to put us off altogether? How's this for a theory? Carsley shot the old man, Marsden robbed the safe, and the two of them were working together then and now are working together to fool us? How does that strike you?'

'If it's that,' observed Bobby, 'I don't see, sir, where the little chap at "The Green Man" comes in, or what he can have told Lester that gave him the horrors, as the barmaid said. I've a feeling myself that if only we could lay hands on him . . .'

'I daresay,' agreed Mitchell, 'but we can't – at least, we haven't so far. Carry on with "The Green Man" though, he may turn up there, though it looks to me as if he were keeping out of the way on purpose. Perhaps it might be as well to try some of the other pubs in the neighbourhood, he may be using one of them now. Only why does he want to keep away from us? But that's the worst of this case. It's not only the facts we can't get at, we don't know what motives people have, why one gets drunk, and another comes "unfrozen" as your butler says, and another won't come forward. There's that elderly man you saw who left a footprint in the garden and spoke to Doran, we can't trace him either. You saw the appeals in the paper asking him to come forward?'

'Yes, sir. I suppose he hasn't responded?'

Mitchell shook his head.

'No one will tell us anything in this case,' he complained. 'How's a poor detective to find anything out, if no one will tell him anything?'

'It makes it very difficult,' agreed Bobby. 'I hope the tickets for the Regency were what you wanted, sir?' he added as Mitchell seemed to lapse into silence.

'Oh, yes, thanks,' answered Mitchell, 'quite good seats, very good show, rather a lot of corpses in the last act, if you ask me, bit of a surprise, too, because I always thought Shakespeare was all spouting blank verse, and that last act had any gangster film I ever saw beat to a frazzle. Yes, a good show – and gave us a lot to think about, quite a lot to think about.'

That was the end of the interview; and Bobby, finding himself dismissed, went back to his task of inquiring at the theatres for some trace of the man he was looking for. His lack of success was complete, however, and when he had come to the end of his list, he went back to the Regency merely to gratify a piece of private curiosity, for somehow he had got it into his head, from what Mitchell had said, that it was not only entertainment the Superintendent had been in search of in his visit to the theatre. Moreover, Mitchell came from Aberdeen and was not therefore, in Bobby's considered opinion, very likely to have spent twelve and six on a stall, when cheaper seats were available, unless for some special reason, or unless he hoped to put it down on his expenses list.

The six-foot-six commissionaire Bobby remembered noticing before was still magnificent outside the Regency, and Bobby introduced himself.

'You remember that sketch I showed you the other day?' he said. 'I suppose you haven't seen anyone like it round here since, have you?'

But the commissionaire shook his head and looked blank. He did not remember Bobby, he was sure neither Bobby nor anyone else had shown him any sketch, he had not in fact any idea what Bobby was talking about, and Bobby remembered then that in his hurry to get Mitchell the required tickets he had gone straight to the box office and after obtaining them and making his inquiries there about the sketch had hurried away, quite forgetting that he had not questioned the commissionaire. A stupid oversight, Bobby thought with some vexation, though one not likely to be of any importance, and as he began to hunt for his copy of the sketch he still had with him in his pocket-book, he asked a few casual questions from which it appeared that, by good luck, the commissionaire knew Mitchell by sight. He had a nephew in the police who had pointed the famous Superintendent out to him, and he had seen him again when he had had occasion to go to Scotland Yard on some unimportant errand or another. He remembered Mitchell's visit the other night quite well, having noticed him at once, and was certain he had been accompanied, not by a lady, but by a gentleman, in whom, from the description given, Bobby was sure he recognized the Assistant Commissioner himself.

And what on earth had made Mitchell and the Assistant Commissioner want to spend an evening together watching a Shakespearian play, was more than Bobby could imagine.

He gave it up finally as no business of his, and, producing his sketch, showed it. The commissionaire said: ·

'Why, that's Mr Harrison; he's brother-in-law of Mr Lamb at the box office. Not been doing anything, has he?'

'Why, no,' laughed Bobby, 'at least, not that we know of. But we think he could give us some information in a case we are interested in. Do you mean he works here?'

'Oh, no,' answered the other, 'but he's come a cropper in the City and now he's got nothing left – says he was done down by some of them there, skinned and nothing left, so he is glad enough of any little job Mr Lamb can find him, us being so busy with the rush there's been,' and the commissionaire puffed out his chest with pride, for proud though author and actor and manager may be of a West End success, their pride is but a poor thing to that of the average commissionaire, who almost visibly grows in stature on those rare occasions when he is able to watch a real rush for the box office window.

'Do you know his address?' asked Bobby.

The commissionaire didn't, but supposed they would know it at the box office, and thither therefore Bobby proceeded.

'When I showed you this sketch the other day,' Bobby demanded severely of Mr Lamb, 'why didn't you tell me it was your brother-in-law, Mr Harrison?'

'Harrison?' repeated Mr Lamb, quite surprised. 'You don't mean that's meant for Joe Harrison? Well, you do surprise me. I hadn't an idea. If you had showed me a photograph now, but how could anyone tell what that was meant for?'

He gave a glance of contempt and disdain at the sketch as he spoke and the offended artist picked it up.

'It's a very good drawing,' he said firmly, 'and it's my belief you knew who it was all the time.'

Mr Lamb shook his head.

'I am looking at it right way up, aren't I?' he asked innocently.

Bobby put the sketch away.

'I'll trouble you for Harrison's address,' he said coldly, and though Mr Lamb still hesitated a little, in the end he produced it.

CHAPTER 22

A Strange Warning

BOBBY's first act was to get on the phone and report to his superiors that he had discovered at last the name and address of the man they had been looking for so long, and to suggest that it would be wise to follow up the information immediately.

Neither Mitchell nor Gibbons was at the Yard as it happened, but the officer in charge agreed it was very important that no time should be lost, since nothing was more likely than that his brother-in-law might already be warning Harrison, by phone or wire, that his identity was known.

'Get over there as fast as you know how,' Bobby was instructed, 'and bring him along to the Yard. If he wants to make a statement, let him, but don't press him till Mr Mitchell's seen him.'

Taxis are not much in the line of men drawing a constable's pay, but on this occasion Bobby decided to hire one and risk getting the fare allowed. It seemed to him there was not a minute to lose; it was essential, he thought, to find Harrison and get him to talk before any warning could reach him; and during the long drive to the remote suburb to which he had been directed, Bobby's mind was all one tumult of conflicting thoughts, theories, fancies. For one thing he felt certain that Mitchell either knew or suspected something, something that had induced him to take the Assistant Commissioner to spend an evening at the theatre, yet how an evening at the theatre could help in the solution of the mystery was more than Bobby could even begin to imagine. He was convinced, too, that Mitchell took seriously, and was a good deal worried – 'rattled' was the word Bobby employed – by the twin suggestions that on the one hand Marsden planned to murder Peter Carsley, and that

on the other hand Peter himself proposed to complete plans
for obtaining full possession of Sir Christopher Clarke's
money by next disposing of his young wife. But then again
what could a visit to the theatre have to do with either of
these contingencies?

At last, while he was still racking his brains to find some
probable explanation, his taxi turned into the street for
which they were bound. The driver slowed down, looking
for the number he wanted, and there went by them very
swiftly a small, two-seater car in which as it sped by Bobby
saw at the wheel Mark Lester. For just that second their
eyes met, and there was that in Mark's expression Bobby
never forgot, so full was it of horror and despair, as of one
for whom no longer any hope existed. Yet there was something, too, of triumph in the gesture Mark made with one
quick, lifted hand, as if to tell Bobby he had come too late.
Then he was passed, and gone, and the taxi stopped, and at
the open door the driver said:

'Here you are, sir.'

'Did you see that small car go by?' Bobby said to him.

'Going at a fairish rate,' agreed the driver, 'some of these
young chaps; nothing under forty m.p.h. is any good to 'em,
and I don't know as that chap wasn't doing more – fair
stepping on it, so he was.'

Bobby had some vague idea of pursuit in his mind, but he
abandoned it, pursuit would evidently have been useless
even if he had known what to say or do had it succeeded.
But he had nothing to go on, save that one strange, fleeting
look which had seemed like that of one who despaired, and
the momentary gesture which had appeared like that of one
who triumphed.

One thing he noticed, though, was that the house he was
about to visit had no telephone, and certainly no telegram
could have beaten Bobby's taxi. Did that indicate that Mr
Lamb, of the Regency box office, had phoned to Mark, and
Mark had come on here at once to convey to Harrison the

warning that otherwise he could not have received in time?

But that meant collusion between Mark Lester and Harrison, collusion that must be of recent growth, for Bobby thought it certain that Mark and Harrison had met for the first time that evening in the 'The Green Man'.

'Can they have fixed something up together then, right under my nose, while I was looking?' Bobby asked himself bewilderedly. 'It doesn't seem possible, but then nothing seems possible in this case. Unless it is that Mark Lester is really the guilty man, and that Harrison knows it, and that Lester's afraid he'll tell. That might account for the way Lester looked just now.'

Bobby thought it best to tell his taxi-man to wait, and as it was evidently of little use to continue this riot of doubt and speculation in which he found his mind involved, he went to the house and knocked. He had to wait for a reply; and when at last a woman came Bobby felt more certain than ever from her manner that he was expected, and that Mark had been before him with a warning.

Mr Harrison lived there, the woman admitted. She was Mrs Harrison, she said, and her husband was ill in bed and could see no one.

'The gentleman who called just now saw him, I think,' Bobby retorted.

'That was a friend,' Mrs Harrison explained, but uneasily. 'He only came to see how my husband was getting on.'

'Then what made him look the way he did when he left?' Bobby demanded; and then realizing that it was only futile to stand there questioning the woman, he explained who he was, produced his warrant card, and told her it was necessary he should see her husband at once.

She still persisted that he must wait, at least till the doctor had been. They hadn't sent for the doctor before but they had now. It was a 'nervous breakdown', she explained, when Bobby asked what was the matter; and as that is an expression which may mean just anything or nothing, Bobby was not very much impressed. Apparently this breakdown of Mr Harrison's nerves had happened on the very night of the visit to 'The Green Man', and at last when Bobby still insisted and showed he meant to have his way, Mrs Harrison agreed to go and consult her husband.

Bobby warned his taxi-driver to see no one attempted to escape by the windows – for by now he was wrought up to be prepared for anything, and himself kept a careful watch from the foot of the stairs. He did not mean Harrison to slip away a second time, as he had done that night at 'The Green Man'. These precautions, however, proved unnecessary, for presently Mrs Harrison came out and took him back into the bedroom, where he found her husband sitting up in bed and looking very sulky and determined, so that Bobby knew at once it was going to be difficult to get a word out of him.

He was a small, pale, worried-looking man, with thin, grey hair and whiskers, two light-blue watery eyes, a long, thin nose, and a tight-lipped, obstinate mouth above a small pointed chin. The whole impression was that of a man who would not easily give up his aims, but who would seldom attain them, because, though certain of his aim, he would never be so of his means. He greeted Bobby ill-temperedly enough.

'What do you want?' he demanded. 'I'm not well, I don't want to be worried, what do you want to come worrying me for? Why can't you leave me alone?'

'I'm sorry to hear you're unwell,' Bobby answered. 'Have you been unwell ever since you met Mr Lester at "The Green Man"?'

'What do you mean? I don't know what you're talking about,' retorted Harrison with a mixture of discomfort and defiance in his voice.

'I think you do,' Bobby answered. 'What did Mr Lester come to see you for just now?'

'That's my business,' Harrison retorted sullenly.

'It's our business, too,' Bobby told him; 'and I'm afraid if you won't talk you will find yourself in a rather serious position. Are you able to come to Scotland Yard with me?'

'No, I'm not,' snapped Harrison very emphatically.

'I believe the doctor's coming to see you, isn't he?' Bobby asked. 'We'll have to wait and see what he says about that and if you really aren't fit to come to Scotland Yard, then I suppose Scotland Yard will have to come to you. There's good reason to believe you know something about the murder of Sir Christopher Clarke –'

The effect of these last words was startling and unexpected. The little man sat bolt upright, his scattered locks of grey hair tumbling over his forehead, the sudden light that flashed into his pale and watery eyes transfiguring him entirely with a certain wildness of appearance. Thrusting out a long, skinny arm straight at Bobby, he cried:

'Yes, I do know something, I know who did it, and, by God, I'll never tell.'

'Do you mean you wish to protect a murderer, Mr Harrison?' Bobby asked gravely.

'It wasn't murder,' Harrison answered sullenly, 'it was killing, but no murder. The swine got no more than he deserved, no more than I would have given him if I had had the chance.'

'Was it Mark Lester?' Bobby asked.

Exhausted, Harrison fell back on his pillow.

'Never you mind,' he said. 'What I know I'll never tell. Do your own job.'

'Do you know, too,' Bobby asked grimly, 'what is meant by being an accessory after the fact?'

'You don't frighten me,' Harrison retorted. 'The swine got no more than he deserved and I wish it had been me did it, but it wasn't, as I can prove all right. Only when I say I know, I only mean I know because I can put two and two together, because I've got eyes in my head and some sense as well. I don't know anything I could swear to. I mean I don't know facts I'm keeping back. Only what I know, I know, and I know I'm right, too.'

'You mean it was Mark Lester but you did not actually see him do it?' Bobby suggested, but Harrison only shook his head and looked more feebly obstinate than ever.

'You'll get nothing out of me,' he said, 'and it wouldn't do you any good if you did. There's nothing I could say you could tell a jury. Why do you come worrying me? Why don't you try old Belfort? He was hanging about there, for I saw him. Go and ask him.'

'Mr Belfort?' Bobby repeated, at a loss for a moment, and then remembering. 'Oh, yes, of course,' he said; and it seemed to him this piece of information might be as important as any of whatever it was Harrison was with-holding, for this was the first hint they had had that Mr Belfort had been on the scene of the murder before it occurred. 'Oh, we'll attend to him all right,' he said, 'but what we want to know now is what you told Mr Lester that made him leave here looking as he did.'

'I only told him I would do what he wanted,' Harrison replied slowly.

'What was that?'

'Hold my tongue and mind my own business,' Harrison retorted. He added slowly: 'But there's one thing I will tell you – you had better look after Mr Lester, you may be sorry if you don't.'

'What do you mean by that?' demanded Bobby crossly, for here was yet another vague and doubtful warning. 'Do you think he's going to murder Carsley? Or that Marsden's going to murder him? Or all of them murder each other? Or what?'

'I wasn't thinking of anything like that,' Harrison replied, in the same slow voice, 'but I daresay it might happen that way – I think in this affair anything might happen to anyone at any time. Did you know Mr Lester is to be married on Saturday?'

'What about it?'

'It's only an idea but if you ask me – well, I don't much think that marriage will come off, then or ever.'

'Why not?' Bobby asked, shrugging his shoulders at this fresh strange warning. 'They've got a licence, everything's arranged, nothing to stop them, is there? They seem fond of each other, too,' he added, remembering suddenly and vividly their parting he had been a witness to. 'They are fond of each other,' he repeated.

'Yes, they are, that's why,' Harrison replied. 'I think they're fond of each other more than most people ever are . . . very likely it wouldn't last but it's like that now . . . when you see them together you know that much without being told. He's fond of her, he's all there is to her, all she lives for . . . well, all the same, you mark my words, there'll be no marriage and that's the reason why.'

'I don't see why that should prevent it,' Bobby said. 'I don't see why anything should prevent it,' but all the same there was a certain uneasiness in his mind, as he remembered the look Mark had given him as he flashed by in his car.

CHAPTER 23

Mark's Way

THE doctor who had been sent for arrived. His verdict was that Harrison was emphatically not fit even to leave his bed, and he looked very serious and shook his head. He always did so when he saw a patient for the first time; one would not have a patient think one had been called in unnecessarily. To-morrow, he thought, Mr Harrison might be better or he might again be worse, but in any case he must stay where he was for the present; if the authorities wanted to interview him, then they must come to him.

'If Mr Harrison goes out to-night I will not be answerable for the consequences,' declared the doctor, and hearing that immemorial phrase, before whose vague terrors all must bow, Bobby knew there was no more to be said.

So he resorted to the nearest call box, whence he recounted his experiences to headquarters and asked for instructions. He was told to return at once to the Yard to report in more detail. As for the invalid Mr Harrison, the local people would be rung up and told to keep an eye on him, so that Bobby was freed from responsibility in that matter.

Back at the Yard, Bobby was questioned at length by Inspector Gibbons – Mitchell had not yet returned – and then was told he might go off duty.

'It's too late to do much to-night,' Gibbons decided, 'even if Mr Mitchell were here, and anyhow we must wait to know what he thinks. And it won't do any harm to give Harrison a night to think it over. I've told them out there to let themselves be seen, watching the house. That'll help to make Harrison understand it's pretty serious, though I don't suppose he'll go on holding his tongue once Mitchell gets after him. But he may be only talking through his hat, just a lot of vague notions and suspicions Treasury Counsel wouldn't look at for a minute. Still, it's one up to you we've been able to trace him at last, and I daresay Mitchell won't think you've done so badly.'

'Thank you, sir,' said Bobby, flushing a little at this praise. He ventured to add, though official superiors do not much encourage comment: 'I'm wondering a little what Harrison meant when he said Mr Lester's wedding wouldn't come off to-morrow. I thought myself Mr Lester looked very strange when he went by in his car.'

But Gibbons did not seem much impressed.

'I don't see what we can do,' he said, 'except make sure to-morrow whether there is a wedding or not. Most likely Lester only looked scared because he saw you and knew you would realize he had been to warn Harrison. Evidently there's some connexion. That's certain, and it'll have to be cleared up, but we must wait to know what Mr Mitchell thinks. I shouldn't wonder myself if you aren't right, and the truth is that Lester's guilty, and Harrison knows it, but won't tell if he can help it, because he's so bucked at Lester doing what he would have liked to do himself if he had had the guts for it.'

'Only there doesn't seem any motive,' said Bobby doubtfully, 'at least, I can't see any.'

'In my humble opinion,' declared Gibbons, 'it's a mistake to worry too much about motives. I've heard Mitchell say you can never tell a man's motive till you know it – and that's time enough. Lester may have thought the forty thou. Miss Laing was to have was only a put-off, and that if her stepfather died intestate she would take a half, or he may have had an idea that Miss Laing had been ill-treated in some way, or he may not have known about the proposed settlement, and thought because of the new will she was being left out altogether – or – or anything,' he concluded a little vaguely, 'and anyhow, we must wait for Mitchell.'

With that Bobby found himself dismissed, but his mind was restless and troubled as he walked away. He still remembered how wildly Mark Lester's eyes had seemed to stare as his car flashed by, how it had seemed as if he rushed in that speeding car to meet some unutterable doom. Nor had the impression then made been anything but heightened by Harrison's vague and uncertain warning. Bobby had had a long day, on his feet nearly all the time, much of it standing about in a way more wearying by far than straightforward walking would have been. But tired though he felt, and glad though he would have been of a rest, there had taken full possession of him by now that sombre passion of the chase the dreadful hunter knows when his quarry is man. Instead therefore of returning home to the bed and supper waiting for him, he made his way to the district where he knew Mark lived with his mother.

When he reached the house, it looked dark and deserted; in one room only, on the first floor, a light showed; and Bobby was leaning over the garden gate, watching it, when there came someone softly to his side.

'Hullo, Owen,' the newcomer said. 'I thought it was you. Anything fresh?'

Bobby started, for the soft voice had broken rudely on his troubled thoughts. But he recognized one of the C.I.D. men he had met during the course of the investigation. He had known, naturally, that Mark was under observation, though the fact was one that for the moment he had forgotten.

'That you, Jones?' he said. 'I didn't know you were on the job. Nothing new that I know of.'

'I thought something might have turned up to bring you along when I saw you,' Jones remarked.

'I didn't see you,' Bobby observed.

'Didn't mean to be seen,' returned Jones with a touch of professional complaisance. 'I had to report I had lost touch a little time ago,' he added. 'The chap got out his two-seater and went tearing off at such a pace I hadn't a chance to follow. But he turned up back again here all right.'

'I know,' Bobby said. 'There's a lot more going on than we've any idea of, I think. I feel somehow as if we weren't so much doing C.I.D. work as just scuttling about, trying to get good seats from which to watch what happens next.'

'Ah, you've had an education,' Jones said enviously, 'that's what makes you able to talk like that.'

'I don't know if it's education,' Bobby answered, 'but that's how I feel – just like when you're in the theatre, waiting for the curtain to go up on the last act. But in this play it's only the second act we've seen, we've no idea what the first act was, and only God knows how the third act is likely to turn out.'

'Nobody ever knows how anything's going to turn out,' declared Jones. 'Put a bob on a horse, and do you even know if it'll start? Not you. Put in a week's leave at the seaside, and do you know what the weather'll be? Not you. Same everywhere.'

'I suppose so,' agreed Bobby, 'and that great dark house – it looks to me just like a curtain that might be drawn back any moment when it's time for the third act to begin. Did you know Mr Lester was to be married to-morrow?'

Jones nodded.

'Looks to me as if he wanted to hurry it up before we pinched him,' he suggested. 'That is, if that's what we're after. I've got no orders to do more than keep him under observation as far as possible but not to obtrude myself – with chaps like you crowding into the Force the way they are, the language is getting so educated they'll have to serve us with dictionaries, soon.'

'We had a warning to-night,' Bobby remarked, 'that the wedding wouldn't come off.'

'It's all settled, isn't it?' Jones asked. 'They seem mighty far gone on each other, too. You can tell that much by seeing 'em when they're together, by the way they shake

178

hands as if no one else had ever done it except them. Why shouldn't it come off?'

As he spoke there sounded through the still night air a loud and sharp report, breaking upon the silence with a significance they both understood.

'Good God! What's that?' Jones exclaimed.

Bobby began to run towards the house. Jones followed close behind him. They knocked; there was no answer.

'Who else lives here? Do you know?' Bobby asked his companion.

'Only Mrs Lester and an old housekeeper, besides a woman who comes in daily,' Jones answered. 'Mrs Lester went to Brighton yesterday, and it looks as if the house-keeper wasn't in.'

'We must get in somehow,' Bobby said.

One of the windows on the ground floor was open a few inches. With the help of his companion Bobby climbed on the sill and pushed up the sash. He scrambled through into the room and Jones followed. They groped their way into the hall and though the house was very quiet they thought they could detect a faint groaning sound coming from somewhere upstairs.

'Anyone here?' Bobby shouted and got no reply.

They shouted again, and when there was still no answer they went up the stairs together, Jones lighting the way with the beam from his electric pocket torch. The house was provided only with gas that they did not stop to light. At the head of the stairs they saw a thread of light showing beneath one of the doors. They went to it quickly and opened it. Within, as they had more than half anticipated, lay Mark Lester, full length upon the floor, moaning faintly, a pistol in his hand, the blood flowing slowly from a wound where he had shot himself through the body.

'Done himself in,' Jones said. 'Knew it wouldn't be long before we pinched him and thought this way better than hanging.'

Bobby knelt by the prostrate man.

'He's not dead,' he said, and indeed Mark, opening his eyes and looking at him, seemed to be trying to speak. 'Do you know me?' Bobby asked. 'Can you speak? Do you want to say something?'

'My way ... Mark's way ... did it myself,' Mark muttered and then: 'Brenda, Brenda,' he whispered, 'fetch her, will you? Say ... good-bye.'

He closed his eyes and Bobby said to his companion:

'You stay here with him, will you? He may want to say something. I'll ring up a doctor, and the Yard, too, to let them know. Is there a phone?'

'In the hall,' Jones answered, 'near the door.'

Bobby went down and rang up the local police whom he asked to come along at once and to bring a doctor with them, and next his own superiors. To Scotland Yard he suggested that Miss Laing ought to be informed, as apparently the dying man wished for her presence, and he received permission to go to her at once.

It was some little distance to 'The Cedars', but he was lucky in finding a belated cab, and when he got to the house, lights there showed that all the inmates were not yet in bed. When he knocked it was Brenda herself who came to the door.

'Ah, you,' she said, recognizing him at once, 'what has happened?' And it seemed she had some idea, for she added immediately: 'Mark ... Mr Lester ... is it?'

'He is hurt, there has been an accident,' Bobby answered gravely. 'I think he wants to see you, he asked for you. Will you come at once? I have a taxi.'

She came down the steps immediately, without waiting to put on either hat or coat.

'Won't you get a wrap or something?' Bobby asked.

She shook her head and went on to the waiting taxi.

'We were to be married to-morrow,' she said, and then: 'Was it an accident?'

He did not answer. Somehow he felt it was unnecessary to reply; he had a very clear idea that what Mark had done was no surprise to her, that in some way she had anticipated his action. He signed to the driver to start and took his seat by her side. He said to her:

'Can you tell us why he did it?'

In her turn she made no answer and he asked again:

'Was it because he was afraid he would be arrested?'

'No,' she answered.

'Was it because there was something he knew?'

'It might be,' she answered then, 'I think it might be that.'

'Will you tell us what you think he might have known?' he asked again.

She turned her sombre, heavy eyes upon him, and did not speak. But she made a slight, negative gesture, and he knew that until she was ready, and that was not yet, she would say no word.

But he tried once more.

'If you keep anything from us, you help the murderer to escape,' he reminded her.

'No murderer escapes,' she answered moodily. 'What is done is done, and there's no escape.'

'I don't know about that,' Bobby said. 'Our duty is to see criminals are caught.'

With another faint gesture she seemed to put that aside as unimportant. She said presently:

'Shall we be in time? We shall be too late, I think.'

Bobby put his head out of the window and asked the driver to go faster if he could. Brenda said nothing more. Though Bobby spoke to her once or twice, she did not seem even to hear. But when at last the taxi drew up, she said, to herself as it seemed:

'Too late, it's too late now.'

She was right, for Mark Lester had died only a few minutes after Bobby left the house.

CHAPTER 24

Mr Belfort Speaks

THERE was so much to be done, so many of those details to be attended to that such tragedies involve: so far as Bobby himself was concerned he had to explain at such length how he happened to be on the spot after having been sent off duty – for in official eyes, zeal bears always a suspicious air – that it was far on in the small hours before he found himself free.

He had, indeed, not much leisure for anything more than a bath, a change of clothing, and a bare two hours' sleep, before it was time to appear again at headquarters, where he had to repeat to Mitchell the full story of his experiences.

'I've never noticed,' observed Mitchell reflectively, when Bobby had finished his story and he himself had finished asking questions about it, 'I've never noticed that your brains are any better than most, but you do seem somehow to have a way of being on the spot when things happen – I suppose it's luck.'

'I suppose so, sir,' agreed Bobby, considering the point.

'There's two kinds of luck if you've noticed,' Mitchell observed still more thoughtfully. 'One is the kind of luck you take advantage of. The other is the kind you don't. We've all our share of luck, but some get one kind and some the other, and now I suppose I shall have to spend most of to-day, with forty other things needing attention, interviewing Miss Laing and this Harrison fellow. Do you think I shall get anything out of them?'

'No, sir.'

'I'm rather inclined to agree with you,' admitted Mitchell. 'As for Miss Laing, her silence is a living thing. But this

Harrison seems quite a commonplace little man, doesn't
he?'

'Yes, sir,' agreed Bobby, 'but he hated Sir Christopher
so much, I think his hate will keep him from talking.'

'I've turned two or three of our best men on to finding
out all they can about him,' Mitchell commented. 'A
lot of our people – the Assistant Commissioner, too – think
what happened last night shows Mark Lester was guilty.
Some of the papers are hinting the same thing, I see.
The Assistant Commissioner thinks all we have to do now
is to wind up the investigation.'

'If I may say so, sir,' Bobby answered, 'it looks to me
as if it had hardly begun yet – as if so far we hadn't done
much more than look on, watching what's happening.'

'You mean you think there's more that's to happen
yet?'

'Well, sir, we've no idea yet what's behind it all, have
we? And I don't think Mark Lester's death means much
more than that one of the actors has left the stage – the
others have still to play out their parts.'

'Maybe,' agreed Mitchell, 'it may be that – and it's a
fact there's a lot about the theatre in all this business. The
whole affair is rather like watching a play – only you've
missed the beginning, so you can't quite tell what it's
all about or how it's likely to end. That is, if this affair
last night isn't the end already.'

'If I may say so, sir,' Bobby exclaimed earnestly, 'I'm
sure it isn't, I'm sure there's more to come. We've had
three warnings: that Miss Laing's wedding wouldn't
happen, that Mrs Carsley – Miss Jennie that was – is in
danger, and that trouble between Peter Carsley and
Marsden may come to a head any moment. The first
warning's proved true. So may the others.'

'Can you suggest any line of investigation?'

'Only the one you're following up yourself, sir,' answered
Bobby.

'What the dickens do you mean by that?' snapped Mitchell.

'The connexion with the Regency Theatre, sir,' answered Bobby. 'I take it, sir, you and the Assistant Commissioner didn't go there simply to see a Shakespearian production that happens to have caught on?'

'Does this mean,' demanded Mitchell formidably, 'that you've had the infernal cheek and impudence to trail your Superintendent?'

'Oh, no, sir,' protested Bobby, quite shocked at such an idea.

'Then how in thunder do you know where I spend my evenings and in whose company, heh?'

'They recognized you at the theatre, sir,' explained Bobby, 'and just happened to mention it.'

'Happened to mention it,' grumbled Mitchell, 'the way you happen to be on the spot when things happen, I suppose. Well, young man, I do think there's some connexion – the question is, what? Those tickets weren't sent to Sir Christopher merely for fun. It's not a pure coincidence that Harrison's brother-in-law is in charge of the box office where they were bought. There is a sort of vague idea running in my mind; but the Assistant Commissioner thinks it's rot, and I can't get an atom of confirmation in fact, so I'm mentioning it to no one else. For one thing I don't want to put ideas into other people's heads that may have nothing in them – the ideas I mean, of course. Though if the same notion occurred to anyone else –'

He paused as if half hoping, half-expecting, a reply. But Bobby could do no more than look blank, and once again Mitchell had a faint air of disappointment as he continued:

'I expect Harrison could tell us if he chose, but I expect you're right and he won't talk – hate's a silent thing, not like love; love's on the chattering side, every lover likes to tell you all about it but hate keeps quiet.'

'There's one thing I should like to suggest, if I may,' Bobby went on. 'You remember, sir, Harrison said he saw Mr Belfort near "The Cedars" on the night of the murder. I thought it might be as well if I saw if I could identify him with the oldish man I remember noticing – probably the same who spoke to Sergeant Doran and who seems to have left a footprint in the garden near the billiard-room window.'

'And I suppose,' observed Mitchell, 'if I assign you another job, you'll go trotting off on your own as soon as you're off duty, to see for yourself?'

'Yes, sir,' said Bobby.

'Sometimes,' complained Mitchell bitterly, 'I feel like going on my knees and asking God who's running this investigation – whether it's Superintendent Mitchell or Constable Owen with three years and two months' service behind him. Perhaps you know?'

'Well, sir,' answered Bobby, 'I think myself it's what I said before – we are not so much running the investigation as looking on while it runs itself.'

'Most investigations do,' retorted Mitchell. 'You'll know that when you've a bit more experience. Thank heaven, I shall be drawing my pension before then. You can get off now and see if you can find this Belfort man and if you can identify him. Don't press him at all but if he wants to talk, don't stop him. I don't know about sending Doran with you. I think on the whole I won't. If you find Belfort, Doran had better see him separately. The identification will be more certain that way. I suppose you remember him well enough to be sure of knowing him again?'

'Yes, sir,' answered Bobby confidently, and retired.

He had no great difficulty in obtaining Mr Belfort's address. He lived at Eastbourne, and Bobby took the next train there, wished duty led him to the sea front and a bathe instead of to the hinterland of the town where the villas pullulate, and presently arrived at the particular habitation in red brick that sheltered Mr Belfort.

The maid, once persuaded that he had no desire to sell her a vacuum cleaner, showed him into the breakfast-room where Mr Belfort, surrounded by abstruse works of reference, was busy trying to solve a crossword puzzle of the most complicated kind. Bobby knew him again at once, and was almost sure from Mr Belfort's manner that he had been recognized in his turn. So he went direct to the point.

'Mr Belfort, I think?' he said. 'I believe you are the gentleman I saw near Sir Christopher Clarke's house the evening he was murdered?'

'Were you the policeman on duty there?' Mr Belfort asked. 'I've been half expecting some of you would come along. But there's nothing I can tell you.'

'You can tell us why you didn't communicate with us,' Bobby pointed out. 'Didn't you see the notice in the papers asking you to come forward?'

'No,' answered Belfort stoutly, though Bobby did not for even one moment believe him. 'I supposed if you wanted me, you would let me know. I saw nothing in the papers and the whole thing had nothing to do with me.'

'You told one of our men, a sergeant you met, that it was a case of suicide?' Bobby reminded him.

'I thought it was, I took it for granted it was,' Belfort answered. 'I knew very well there was something wrong with the Trust fund. It's true it was put straight again, so there's been no need to take any action, as the fund is intact. But my lawyers agree with me that it is certain it's been tampered with. I had been given a hint of what was going on, and I thought it was certain Clarke had committed suicide rather than face me and confess.'

'Sir Christopher was a wealthy man,' Bobby said. 'He left nearly a quarter of a million, I believe. It's impossible to suppose he could have done anything like that.'

'Why?' snapped Belfort. 'Anyhow, if he didn't, someone did – possibly without his knowledge. But the fund has been put straight again, quite all right, so there's nothing more to be said. All the same something dishonest has been going on and I had the evidence in my pocket to show. When I knew he had been shot, I thought it was certain that was why – that he hadn't dared face exposure. I could hardly believe it when my lawyers told me they had examined the fund and found it intact.'

'A footmark was found in a flower bed near the billiard-room window,' Bobby said. 'It is believed to be yours. What were you doing there?'

'Sir Christopher had asked me to dine with him,' Mr Belfort answered. 'I came by tube and got there much too early. I walked round to have a look at the house first. I expect I was a little nervous and excited. The loss of the money would be serious enough and I anticipated a highly unpleasant interview with Sir Christopher when I made it plain I knew something of what had been going on. I saw a man walking up the drive to the house, and I saw him leave the drive, and walk across the lawn, and go into the house by an open french window. I thought perhaps it was Sir Christopher himself, and I thought, if so, I could have my talk with him at once. I followed up the drive, and then I saw, through the open window, the man inside the billiard-room stooping over something on the floor. I could see his face distinctly, and I saw it wasn't Sir Christopher, and I saw, too, something serious had happened. I ran across, and looked in the room, and I saw Sir Christopher on the ground with a pistol lying near-by. I felt sure at once he had committed suicide to avoid having to face confessing he had embezzled the Trust fund. That made it important certain steps should be taken at once, certain people informed. I went away to do that. The suicide itself was nothing to do with me, but what had to be seen to at once was important. On the way I met a policeman, so I told him, and sent him to the house. It seems now it was a murder but I had no idea of that; that never occurred to me at the time.'

'When you knew it was murder, why didn't you come forward?' Bobby asked.

'It wasn't anything to do with me,' Mr Belfort repeated, 'and I knew if I did the papers would rake up the old scandal again. The Belfort Trust was founded as a result of a very painful family scandal that all the papers were full of thirty years ago. I knew the penny press' – Mr Belfort, who paid twopence for his own daily paper, pronounced 'penny press' with that scorn with which once people used to say the 'ha'penny press' – 'would rake it all up again. I wished very much to avoid that happening. I knew the pain any raking up of the old scandal would cause to a lady, a very old lady now, who is a very dear friend of mine.'

Bobby guessed, too, that Mr Belfort had not been uninfluenced by a certain fear that his presence on the spot, if it were known, might lead to his coming under suspicion himself. Whether Mr Belfort could really be guilty was an idea that indeed suggested itself to Bobby, but for which he did not see much support, though he decided to mention it to his superiors for their consideration. He said:

'Your silence has helped to make things very difficult for us, Mr Belfort. It's a serious matter to hold back information from the police in a case of murder.'

'I've held back nothing of any value,' declared Mr Belfort stoutly; 'all I thought I knew turns out quite wrong – the Trust fund is intact, Sir Christopher didn't commit suicide. I should only have misled you if I had said anything, and I had no intention of letting the gutter press get hold of that old scandal, and rake it up again, if I could help it. We had that experience once, we don't want it again, it would probably have killed the lady I spoke of. It's true I did think sometimes I ought to tell you of the man I saw climbing the garden wall next door, but he had only been stealing fruit, so he couldn't have had anything to do with the murder.'

But Bobby was listening intently.

'You saw someone climb into the road over the wall of the next door garden?' he asked.

'A young fellow,' Mr Belfort answered. 'I heard someone shouting that a man was after the apples, and then I saw this man jumping over the wall in a great hurry. Apparently someone had thrown something at him, for I noticed his coat was stained and dirty. He ran off for dear . life.'

'Could you describe him?' Bobby asked, and Mr Belfort replied with a very good and clear description that made it certain the man he had seen was young Peter Carsley.

CHAPTER 25

Marsden Expresses Suspicions

THIS information given him by old Mr Belfort seemed to Bobby of such importance that when presently, after a few more questions had been asked and answered, he left the house, he went to the Eastbourne police station where he got permission to phone directly to Scotland Yard. He was put through to Mitchell, who listened with interest to what he had to say and told him to take the next train back to town to report in greater detail.

When he arrived at headquarters, however, Bobby found that Mitchell had unexpectedly been called away on other business, and so he had to spend the rest of the day dawdling about, yawning, reading the papers, playing a game of a hundred up with the C.I.D. billiards champion and losing half a crown for his temerity. Finally he was dismissed from duty for that day.

The next morning he had another long wait, but just as he was beginning to think that both he and his information had been entirely forgotten, he was sent for by Inspector Gibbons.

'It's been decided to put the papers before Treasury Counsel,' Gibbons told him. 'Seems to me the case is good enough, though the Treasury lot will pick a hole in it if they can – they don't want their cases cast iron, they want them cold steel, double lined, armour plated, jewelled in every hole, good enough for the kingdom of heaven, let alone a world like this. But when a murder puts a fortune in a man's pocket and that man is seen at the time escaping over a garden wall – well, even Treasury Counsel might be able to get a conviction if they chose to put in a bit of work for once in a way themselves, instead of expecting us to do it all.'

'Only,' Bobby pointed out, 'it didn't put a fortune into Carsley's pocket, but into his wife's.'

'The wife may go next,' Gibbons remarked, and when Bobby started slightly at the grim suggestion, he said: 'Thought that yourself, have you?'

'No, sir,' answered Bobby, 'but Marsden, Carsley's partner, hinted the same thing to me. I made a report.'

'Did you, though?' exclaimed Gibbons. 'I hadn't seen that, Mitchell kept it to himself, I suppose. Just like him, he's always doing that and then expects you to know it all. But if it's going to be like that, it's pretty tough – first the father-in-law and then the wife. Risky, too, one after the other, unless of course she suspects something and he has got to – to keep her quiet.'

Bobby perpended.

'I saw Carsley run straight the length of the whole field at Cardiff once,' he said slowly. 'If a fellow runs straight in one thing –'

'Doesn't follow he'll run straight in everything else,' interrupted Gibbons, 'human nature's not so simple as all that. Though Mitchell has rather the same idea as you, only he puts it that Rugby footballers haven't the brains for murder – unless of course it's a referee. But there are two weak points – we can't identify the revolver. If it's really the one Sir Christopher is supposed to have had, and that is missing now, if it ever existed, then, since Carsley was often at the house, he might have managed to get hold of it, or he might have got his wife to give it him. If it's that way, and if she has any suspicions, that might be why . . . what do you think?'

'Rather a lot of "ifs", if I may say so,' Bobby pointed out.

'Yes,' agreed Gibbons, 'I suppose we shall simply have to say a revolver was certainly used but that the point is, who used it? not, where did it come from? Then there are the theatre tickets as well. Mitchell is worrying quite a lot about them. He's got some idea about them he won't say because he can't get any confirmation, thinks we shan't understand the case till they're accounted for. What I say is we don't want to understand the case, all we want is the evidence on which to ask Treasury Counsel to act. Nothing need ever be said in court about those tickets, very likely they don't really come into the case at all.'

He went on to give Bobby his instructions for the day. They seemed of no great importance, being concerned chiefly with minor details, but they all clearly pointed to a general acceptance of the theory of Peter Carsley's guilt.

For indeed this identification of Peter with the man seen escaping over the garden wall seemed to suggest conclusions it was not easy to avoid.

One of the minor errands Bobby had been assigned took him to Lincoln's Inn, to the office of Marsden, Carsley, and Marsden. It was merely a date he had to verify, and one that seemed to Bobby of no importance or significance whatever. However, orders had to be obeyed.

He found the office in a state bordering on chaos. For some time now the two partners had ceased to be on speaking terms. The struggle between them, between Carsley's determination to examine in detail every recent transaction, and Marsden's resolve that he should do nothing of the kind, was, apparently, now approaching a climax.

'Mr Carsley says he'll circularize all the clients, telling them he believes something's wrong unless Mr Marsden lets him have all the information he wants,' one of the distracted clerks told Bobby. 'It'll be a pretty serious thing, if he does – criminal libel, if you ask me.'

'Surely Mr Carsley has a right to see and know everything if he's a partner, hasn't he?' Bobby asked.

'I suppose so,' agreed the clerk, 'but Mr Marsden says he knows there are things Mr Carsley could twist round to ruin the practice. Mr Marsden says he won't let that happen, not just to satisfy Mr Carsley's crazy spite. What Mr Marsden says is that the interests of every client have been and are fully protected, even if now and again one fund has been used to pay another. What's the sense of selling one client's securities at a loss when you can borrow from another whose money is lying idle in the bank?'

'Suppose the first man's securities happen to drop heavily and suddenly? That does occur sometimes.'

'That's easy,' retorted the clerk; 'it costs very little to insure at Lloyd's against that happening.'

'I suppose there's that,' agreed Bobby. 'What do you in the office think?'

'Well, we're all looking out for fresh posts,' the other answered rather dismally, 'but none of us believe there's anything seriously wrong, though there may have been irregularities.'

But what the clerk meant by 'irregularities', what he really believed, whether he did not think it wiser on the whole to exercise a prudent restraint upon his speech, Bobby was not sure. What he was sure of was that the whole office was thoroughly scared, and that a crisis was approaching.

For he remembered Peter's square, aggressive chin, and was still inclined to think him one not easily turned from his purpose – though what that purpose might be, Bobby could not even yet make up his mind, not even with the apparently damning testimony of Mr Belfort fresh in his mind.

His date verified, he went off, now a little inclined to suspect that this had only been a pretext, and that what Mitchell would be likely to ask him about would be the general state of feeling in the office, among the staff. Perhaps, Bobby thought, it had been another little test of his aptness for intelligence work and the gathering of information. Well, if so, he would be able to give some answer to any question that might be put him, and then he noticed Marsden himself coming towards him. He was rather inclined to suspect indeed that Marsden had been waiting for him; at any rate, it was with no air of surprise, but rather with a pleasant recognition, that Marsden was approaching.

'Hullo, you again,' Marsden said amiably. 'I almost thought you people had forgotten me. Aren't you shadowing us any longer?'

'I don't know,' Bobby answered. 'I've not heard, but I should think it's likely.'

'Well, you would know, I suppose, wouldn't you?' Marsden asked smilingly.

Bobby shook his head.

'I'm not directing the investigation,' he said. 'I just have orders and don't get told anything else.'

'Oh, just as you like,' Marsden answered with an incredulous smile. 'I suppose you chaps have got to be careful what you say, only I don't notice fellows dodging after me now the way they were before. Nor after Carsley, either.'

He uttered this last sentence quite carelessly, as if it were the merest afterthought. Yet Bobby thought that unless his imagination deceived him gravely, he could detect an odd note of anxiety, almost of fear, in the other's voice, a look that seemed of the same anxious fear flickering in the lawyer's sharp, dark eyes. Yet why Marsden should care, one way or the other, whether Peter was still being watched or not, Bobby was quite unable to imagine. There seemed no possible reason why that should or should not cause Marsden any concern, much less any fear. The notion that it should be so, indeed, Bobby labelled in his own mind as preposterous, and yet he kept it there, as something for which an explanation was required. Only this case consisted almost entirely of points for which more explanation was required. He said slowly:

'I don't know anything about it, but after what you told

us I should think it's certain Mr Carsley is being very closely watched indeed. Not that that means there's bound to be someone always on his heels. When we do it like that, it's generally because we rather want whoever is being trailed, to know it. It's the business of the police to stop crime just as much as to arrest criminals.'

'Well, you didn't manage to stop the murder of poor old Sir Christopher Clarke, did you?' Marsden retorted somewhat tartly, and yet again Bobby had the impression that his assurance that Peter was being closely watched had come to Marsden as an intense relief. Could it be that Marsden really feared his young partner, really thought he himself was in danger from him? That seemed to Bobby quite incredible and yet – who could tell? At any rate, it seemed clear that Marsden wanted to be assured that a close watch was being kept on Peter, and now he went on: 'You haven't got very far towards catching the murderer yet, have you? The sooner he's hanged the better, if you ask me. And you haven't found out much about the robbery of the safe, either, have you?'

'I don't know anything about that side of it,' Bobby answered. 'I've not been working on it at all, or heard anything from anyone who has.'

'Well, when you arrest the man who committed the murder and the man who robbed the safe, you'll only need one pair of handcuffs – at least, that's my opinion,' declared Marsden. 'I suppose you don't think much of the old saying "Who profited?"'

'What we want is evidence, not presumptions,' Bobby answered. 'Every lawyer knows that, I suppose. What we want is evidence we can put to a jury.'

'Well, I can't help you there,' Marsden admitted. 'But "who benefits?" is good enough for me, though of course, speaking professionally, I quite agree you can't put that to a jury. I only meant it as a pointer to work from. Of course, you'll say I'm prejudiced, and when a man's own partner is doing his best to ruin him and the practice together – well, it doesn't make you feel too charitable. Carsley has actually threatened to send round circulars to all our clients, appealing to them to investigate for themselves. In a way, I hope he does. I can have him then in an action for damages – it would be ruin all the same, but I might get enough for a fresh start somewhere else. Now Carsley's got a rich wife, he's worth powder and shot.'

'I don't see why it should ruin you, if you win your action and get damages,' Bobby remarked.

Marsden shrugged his shoulders.

'I don't deny there have been a few irregularities,' he answered. 'No one carries on thinking of strict professional etiquette all the time. Everyone strains it a bit now and then. All I do say is that all our clients' interests are safe and always have been safe – it's Caesar's wife over again. No woman's character is any good once it's been whispered about, and no solicitor's practice, either.'

'I don't understand why Mr Carsley –' began Bobby.

'Oh, personal reasons,' Marsden interrupted. 'I daresay I haven't always been as tactful as I might have been – showed him too plainly what an utter young fool I thought him. Of course, now, the practice is nothing to him. It means no more to him than a cab fare does to me. Why, do you know, only yesterday ... it's only a trifling matter but still ... of course, it's nothing to do with you but I would like to tell you just to show ... then you can see why I'm prejudiced ... help you to understand ... it's gospel truth Carsley went to any amount of trouble to get out of my hands into his own the disposal of the lease of a house belonging to a client of ours. Lord knows, he's welcome to the job, but it just shows you the spirit. It's a tumble-down old place in an out-of-the-way spot you can hardly get at, made out of an old mill turned into a dwelling-house, most inconvenient and with a suspected water supply. Not likely we shall ever find a tenant or a purchaser, unless we try

Bedlam, and yet Carsley went to immense trouble to get the whole business of dealing with it into his own hands. Now why? Do you know? Just to spite me. Silly, but it shows the sort of nagging I have to put up with.'

CHAPTER 26

A Doubtful Question

BOBBY's suspicion that he had been sent to the Marsden
and Carsley office less for the purpose of obtaining confirmation of an entirely unimportant date than to see what
impression the condition of affairs there made upon him,
turned into certainty the next time he saw Mitchell. For
the first thing the Superintendent asked him was what it
seemed to him the office staff thought of recent events,
and of the now open breach between the partners. So
Bobby recounted the conversation he had had with one of
the clerks and Mitchell appeared satisfied.

'I've got three men trying to make friends with the
different clerks working there,' he remarked, 'but I don't
think any of them really knows anything. You didn't tell
Marsden anything about Peter Carsley having been identified by Mr Belfort?'

'Oh, no, sir, of course not,' answered Bobby.

'The Assistant Commissioner has all the papers in the
case now,' Mitchell went on, 'and he is sending them on
at once to Treasury Counsel. Unless they can pick rather
more holes in it than I expect, they'll probably agree it's
good enough and we can proceed to arrest.'

'There's one point, if I may mention it, sir,' Bobby said,
and when Mitchell nodded consent, he went on: 'The
theory of Carsley's guilt doesn't throw any light on Mark
Lester's suicide.'

'Is there any reason why it should?' Mitchell returned,
though Bobby thought he looked worried. 'There may
be some connexion but it's just as likely there's none.
Anyhow, what we've to find out is not why Mark Lester
shot himself, but who shot Sir Christopher Clarke. For the
moment, there doesn't seem much else we can do, and in

any case I don't suppose we shall proceed to arrest Carsley till we hear from New York.'

'From New York?' repeated Bobby, surprised.

'Yes,' answered Mitchell. 'We had an anonymous letter the other day. Anonymous letters are generally lies written to mislead, but not always, and even if they are lies, they are still useful, for at any rate they prove what it is someone wants to be believed. This one says Sir Christopher bought a revolver from a friend in New York when he was over there just before his marriage to Mrs Laing, as she was then. The friend is named and the business he's connected with is mentioned, so it should be easy to trace him, and confirm, and we've sent a cable to the New York police to ask them to do that for us. If they succeed it will be important, for that would go to prove the murder was committed by someone who was a member of the household or a frequent visitor to the house – like Carsley.'

'But the pistol is supposed to have been kept in Sir Christopher's dressing-room, in a drawer that was always locked,' Bobby objected. 'Carsley surely wouldn't have found it easy to get hold of it there.'

'No great difficulty,' Mitchell answered. 'Besides, there's the Jennie girl, Mrs Carsley now. He might have got her to get the thing for him.'

'If that's so . . .' began Bobby and paused.

'If it is, she may suspect now,' Mitchell observed.

'I can't believe . . .' Bobby began and paused again. Mitchell smiled, a little sadly.

'Never believe anything, my boy,' he said, 'or disbelieve it, either. Nothing's too bad for human nature. Nothing's too good, either, thank God, or else a few years in the police service would drive you clean out of your mind. It's quite possible a man might use his wife to help him murder her father and then plot to get rid of her, too, if he thought that she suspected – especially if he stood to inherit a large fortune on her death. On the other hand, he might not;

and though at present it's a pattern that seems all to point one way, still it's a pattern that leaves out a good deal. There's too much altogether left out to my mind, though maybe what's left in is enough to hang Peter Carsley, even if he did run straight at Cardiff the day you saw him there. And it's a comfort anyhow that someone's started at last to tell us things. Perhaps they'll go on now, it's about the only way I know of you can really get to find things out – when the people who know already, come and tell you.'

'Yes, sir,' agreed Bobby, 'only in this case they don't seem to want to, and there's so much – I can't understand for instance why Marsden seemed worried at the idea that perhaps we hadn't kept Mr Carsley under observation.'

'Well, we have and are,' said Mitchell, 'we're watching him pretty closely, though that doesn't mean we're on his heels every second. But we're watching him all right – did you tell Marsden so?'

'I said I didn't know but I supposed we were,' Bobby answered. 'I can't understand why he should care, one way or the other.'

'Perhaps he's afraid Carsley may do him in next,' suggested Mitchell, 'and feels safer if he thinks Carsley's being trailed. So far as I can see the investigation will be rather at a standstill until we hear from New York about the revolver, and as you've had a busy time of it just lately, you can have twenty-four hours' leave, if you like. But don't go far away. I want you to stay in touch. You had better ring up two or three times during the day to ask if there are any orders. I suppose you'll have breakfast in bed and go to the pictures afterwards – that's my idea of a holiday.'

'I don't think I'll go to the pictures, sir,' answered Bobby. 'I think I'll go for a walk instead, and try to think things out, and see if I can't get them clearer in my mind.'

'I find the pictures rather good for that myself,' observed Mitchell. 'Nice, comfortable seat, temper unruffled because you haven't been rooked out of sixpence extra to pay for a programme that's two-thirds advertisements, and then it's so soothing to watch the screen go flickering on, just one long, long kiss after another, and all the time your mind busy with what you're trying to think out. Try it some day.'

'Yes, sir,' said Bobby, but doubtfully.

'Ah, you're young,' commented Mitchell. 'Perhaps all those long, long kisses don't soothe you the way they do me – well, stick to a walk in the open. It's a better way perhaps, and less risk of dropping off to sleep. Or there's the Regency – why not have an evening there? Jolly good show, I thought it.'

'Yes, sir,' agreed Bobby, 'but I don't think I feel up to Shakespeare just now.'

'No one does, no one does nowadays,' sighed Mitchell, looking quite disappointed. 'Well, get along, and spend your holiday the way you want to.'

'Thank you, sir,' said Bobby, and went back to his lodgings, just a little disappointed himself in that he had not been awarded any further task, and even a little worried in his mind because of a vague feeling he had that it was not merely pure Shakespearian enthusiasm which had made Mitchell suggest Bobby should spend an evening at the Regency, and look a trifle disappointed when that idea had not seemed very warmly welcomed.

Worrying, too, Bobby found it, the way in which the Regency and Shakespeare and all that crush seemed always turning up in the case, as if in some way the explanation of the mystery of Sir Christopher's murder was wrapped up with the excellence of this successful 'silver and grey' *Hamlet*, as the advertisements called it. A fantastic notion, of course, and Bobby tried to forget it, and then, for he was more tired and more worried than he quite realized, he began to fret over the possibility that this unasked-for twenty-four hours' leave was merely a way of breaking to him that it was intended to return him to uniform duty. So it was in a somewhat despondent mood that Bobby went to bed that night, and in the middle of it, somewhere in the small hours, he woke with a violent start and the question ringing in his mind, almost as if someone had shouted it at him: Why was Marsden so careful to give such exact particulars of the lonely house in which he declared Carsley to have shown so unusual an interest?

Bobby sat upright in bed and slept no more. He really almost had the illusion that this question had been asked him by some outside entity, for he had no knowledge of how well the sub-conscious can dramatize our hidden thoughts. In the dark night, in the silence, the question seemed to him to assume an immense importance, an importance, too, as obscure and threatening as the surrounding night itself.

'Why? why?' he asked himself, and there was terror in his mind, a terror of some unknown threat of which he seemed to sense the heavy menace.

Uselessly he told himself it was mere folly to let himself be troubled by such fancies. Marsden had simply mentioned the incident as an example of the bad terms on which he was with his partner and of how any trifle was good enough for quarrelling about. That he had mentioned that the dwelling concerned was in an out-of-the-way spot and likely to remain unoccupied for years, was purely accidental – absurd to suppose anything more, the height of absurdity to suppose any threat or danger lay behind. Yet in the darkness Bobby was aware that he was trembling slightly, that a great dread possessed him.

A lonely house in a lonely spot, he told himself again, and Carsley had the key and no one else – nothing in all that, why should there be? There's no lack of lonely houses in lonely inconvenient spots, likely to remain unoccupied for long periods, and someone has to have the key.

But all the same he could not sleep and in the morning

he was up even earlier than usual and poring over the list of house and estate agents in the directory – a dismaying list, for the profession is popular and easily entered.

In spite of his unsought leave, he thought of appealing to Scotland Yard. Scotland Yard, with its immense, ever-ready organization, could within a few hours put the inquiry before every house agent in London – in the country almost. But then he had so little to go on. In his written report he had already referred to the matter; and it was the responsibility of his superiors to decide whether any further steps should be taken regarding it. Bobby had, too, an uneasy feeling that some of those superiors were a little inclined to regard him as a pushing, interfering, officious youngster, badly in need of being taught his place. Better not to give them any further ground for criticism by what might look like a fresh attempt to teach his chiefs their business.

To his troubled and restless mind indeed the twenty-four hours' special leave that had been given him began to look uncommonly like twenty-four hours' suspension from duty, or at any rate a hint to try not to meddle quite so much.

He made up his mind firmly to forget all about the case, to spend the morning loafing, the afternoon at the pictures, the evening at the Regency, and so for that day at least avoid all risk of annoying his seniors by a display of too much energy. There was a friend of his who was always ready for a night out; and though he was a young man who in a general way preferred a song and dance show, yet Bobby felt it would do him all the good in the world, and probably improve his mind quite a lot, to introduce him to Shakespeare. So Bobby went out to find him, but on his way to the tube station, where he meant to take the train, he happened to pass an estate agent's. Before he well knew what had happened, Bobby found himself inside, explaining that he had an eccentric friend, an artist, who was looking for an appropriate residence, old-fashioned, quiet, out of the way – something like an old windmill turned into a dwelling-house would suit him admirably. Did the estate agent know of anything like that?

The estate agent did not, but since he did know that few people know what they want so clearly that they will not take something else if it is pressed upon them with sufficient energy, he recommended in turn a semi-detached villa in Golders Green, a wonderfully cheap luxury mansion flat practically in the heart of the West End, Bayswater district, and an attractive half-house in Chelsea. Bobby said he thought these were not quite what his friend was looking for, and managed to escape, but not till twenty minutes had elapsed. At twenty minutes to a visit, that meant three estate agents questioned an hour, without allowing for the time occupied going from one to another. It seemed at that rate as though progress would be slow, and Bobby wondered whether it would not be better to go straight to Lincoln's Inn and ask for the information direct from Marsden or one of the clerks. But something seemed to warn him against doing that. If the reference to the lonely windmill turned into a house meant anything, then it would be wiser not to risk putting those concerned on their guard. He felt he did not trust Marsden, better not give Marsden any hint of what was being done, and then he had a new idea as he noticed that just across the way stood a public library.

CHAPTER 27

Search for a Windmill

ENTERING the library, he asked for the librarian. He was, he explained to that official, interested in windmills; he was, so to say, collecting windmills, windmills were the passion of his life, the sole interest of his passing days. Could the librarian tell him where and how he could get information about the sites of all the old windmills in or near London?

The librarian received the request quite calmly. He was used to such demands. The earnest young lady wanting a book giving a brief, bright and complete account of the Kantian philosophy, the currency reformer requiring information on the monetary system of Ur, the biblical student wishing for a complete list of all contemporary references to the book of Daniel, the local antiquarian needing direction to the exact spot where stood the last old oaks that had flourished in the borough, the amateur of languages in a spasm of indignation because the library had no copy of the recently-published *Elements of Iroquois Grammar in its Primitive Period* – the sad librarian knew them all, and a little inquiry about the sites of windmills left him quite unruffled. He provided Bobby at once with an armful of books, and added that one that might be useful, *Picturesque Windmills and Watermills of the Southern Counties*, was in the reference department of the central branch but could be got down by the afternoon, if Bobby would like to see it.

Bobby said he would, expressed his gratitude, and retired with his armful of books, searched them diligently without coming across anything that seemed likely to be useful, and then retired to seek some lunch. In the afternoon he went back and found *Picturesque Windmills and Watermills* waiting for him. It was a formidable and ponderous tome, written three-quarters of a century ago, and when he had searched it half way through he came to a description that seemed to him as if it might be that of the house Marsden had spoken of.

At any rate the district was one that even yet London's all-pervading tide had not entirely flooded, and the author of the book had added to his account of this particular windmill an indignant protest against the impending vandalism which was threatening to turn it into a dwelling-house. Nothing else in the book seemed of interest, so Bobby returned it to the librarian, expressed his thanks once more, and then, after having a cup of tea and ringing up Scotland Yard to be assured there were no orders for him, started off to find the spot described.

Rather a wild goose chase, he supposed, but still it was something to occupy his mind and prevent his thoughts beating so restlessly against the bars of the problem in which it felt itself confined.

The task did not prove an easy one, for the directions given in the book had not been explicit. Even when he reached what he thought must be the right locality, an old gentleman, smoking his pipe outside his cottage door, from whom Bobby made inquiries, declared emphatically, and with some amusement at the suggestion, that there was no windmill there and never had been, and he had known the neighbourhood, man and boy, for seventy year.

Disappointed, Bobby made up his mind to abandon the hunt and return home, for by now it was growing dark, and then a young woman made her appearance from the cottage, curious probably to know what the good-looking young stranger wanted.

'Gentleman's looking for a windmill,' explained the patriarch, chuckling at an idea that seemed to him as extraordinary as humorous, for never before in all his long life had he known anyone come looking for a windmill – a public-house, now, that would be different, but a windmill! 'There's no windmill here and never has been,' he repeated. 'and I've known these parts man and boy for seventy year.'

'I've heard tell the house down the lane used to be a windmill at one time, and I'm sure it looks it,' the young woman remarked.

'But it's a house now and always has been long as I've known it,' retorted the patriarch triumphantly, 'and that's seventy year –'

Bobby interrupted with a word of thanks to the young woman, who then added the information that the house was uninhabited and had been so for some time, and could only be seen by an order to view. At one time a neighbour had had the key, but now that was in the hands of the lawyers.

'That's what I told the lady, as she couldn't get in no ways,' observed the patriarch, 'but she went on just the same.'

'The lady? What lady?' asked Bobby sharply.

'The lady what asked the way,' explained the patriarch, 'but it wasn't no windmill she was looking for – "Prospect House, that's to let", she named it, same as it always has been in my time, and I've known these parts man and boy –'

'Exactly,' interrupted Bobby. 'What was the lady like?'

'Well, she was very nice spoken,' replied the old gentleman after due consideration, 'and she might be youngish, or it might be not so youngish as she looked, but looked a lady as was a lady and hadn't ever done a stroke of work in her life.'

The young woman added the information that the stranger had worn a blue leather motoring coat, with a blue hat trimmed with red and adorned with a crystal ornament in the shape of a dog. The lady's face, unfortunately, she had not seen, but she described her as taller than most, and Bobby remembered clearly the tall, slim form of Jennie Carsley as he had last seen her in a blue leather motoring

coat and a blue hat to match, trimmed with red and showing
a crystal ornament in the shape of a dog.

Uneasily he told himself it must be a mere coincidence.
No doubt plenty of youngish women possessed blue leather
motoring coats and wore hats to match. Certainly crystal
dogs are common enough as hat ornaments. He told himself
again, yet with a vague, growing unease, that it was a pure
coincidence, for surely it was impossible Jennie Carsley could
have come to-day to this lonely, deserted spot. The patriarch
coughed, expectorated, and observed:

'She ain't come back yet.'

'Are you sure?' Bobby asked, and noticed that his voice
had suddenly taken on a higher note than usual.

'She might have gone by without your seeing her, grand-
dad,' the young woman remarked.

'I've been here ever since, ain't I?' retorted the old man
impatiently. 'How could she have gone by without me seeing
her? Except she's gone away by the fields at the back, and
she wouldn't do that, a lady like her, and if she hasn't then
she's there still, ain't she?'

The young woman said in an aside to Bobby:

'He drops off to sleep sometimes and then anyone might
go by and he wouldn't know.'

Her grandfather saw her whispering.

'I tell you the lady ain't come back,' he repeated irritably,
'so she's there still, and making a long stay of it, too, she is
that.'

'It's only three minutes' walk down the lane,' the young
woman said to Bobby, and he thanked her and walked
on.

A tall clump of trees had hitherto hidden the house from
him, but when he was past them and the turning just beyond,
it came clearly into view, crowning a low eminence, showing
dark and heavy against the dark and heavy northern
sky.

It may have been nothing more than the gathering shades

of evening that seemed to give it to Bobby's troubled imagination so frowning and sinister an appearance as it crouched there on its low eminence, as if preparing to hurl itself upon its prey in the meadows below. A tangle of trees and bushes in a neglected garden compassed it about, hiding its lower portion, but above one could see plainly where once, when its life had been busy and useful, its swift, revolving arms had hung.

For a moment or two Bobby stood still watching it and noting its lonely and deserted aspect, its shuttered windows and the broken steps to the front door, as though no living creature had been near it for long years. Yet a woman had asked the way to it only a short time before, and if she had come here and had not returned, what could be keeping her so long? It did not look a place where one would linger by choice.

The gate admitting to the garden hung broken on its hinges, and the gravel path leading up to the door was overgrown with moss and weed. There was no sign Bobby could distinguish to tell that anyone had really entered recently, and he wished he had the skill he had read that some possess, whereby a bent blade of grass, an overturned stone, can be made to tell who has passed that way.

If the old man he had been talking to could be trusted, a woman, wearing such clothes as Jennie Carsley often wore, had arrived here not long ago, and, again if the old man were correct, had not yet departed.

Yet the tumble-down old place, with its shuttered windows and neglected, overgrown garden, had so lonely and desolate an air it was hard to believe any visitor had recently troubled its brooding solitude.

For a moment or two Bobby stood hesitating, half reluctant to go on. Then he advanced slowly up the path, watching the transformed mill closely for any sign of life or movement. A low whistle close behind him made him start violently, so much did it take him by surprise, and when he turned he saw someone, half hidden by a tree, beckoning to him. He went across and recognized a man named Paul, one of the C.I.D. men.

'Paul?' he exclaimed, 'what on earth .. what are you doing here?' he asked uneasily.

'Have they sent you along?' Paul asked. 'How did they get hold of you so quick?'

'I'm only mooching around,' Bobby answered. 'Is anything up?'

'I don't know,' Paul answered, 'but it looks queer to me – more than queer. I thought I had better let 'em know I had trailed my bird here – as rummy a place as I ever saw. I tell you, Owen, I don't half like it. When I reported, they said they'd be along as soon as they could manage it. I thought when I saw you – it would have been quick work, though. What do you mean – mooching around?'

'I'm not on duty,' Bobby explained.

'Well, then, how did you ... I mean ... what's brought you along?'

'I just came along. I had heard of this place and I came along to have a look,' Bobby answered. 'Do you mean you've trailed Mrs Carsley here?'

'Mrs Carsley?' Paul repeated. 'What's she got to do with it? It's Carsley himself that's here, not his wife – she's not in the game, is she?'

'I don't know ... she may be,' Bobby answered. 'Do you mean ... do you say Mr Carsley – Peter Carsley's here?'

'Yes, and a rummy place to come to, if you ask me. Up to something he is, or I'll miss a month's pay. What do you mean – Mrs Carsley? What makes you look like that?'

'Some people down the road,' Bobby answered, 'told me they had seen a lady, answering Mrs Carsley's description, go past just now towards this place – and they said that she hadn't come back again.'

Paul was a little pale himself, now.

'Having tea, are they?' he said, trying to make a joke of

it. 'Or fixing up something together – I'm glad I rang up, anyhow. A rummy place,' he said, 'for a husband to ask his wife to meet him.'

'Yes,' agreed Bobby.

'I suppose she's got lots of money,' Paul said. 'Piles of money she's got, I suppose.'

'Yes,' said Bobby again.

'Come round this way,' Paul said. 'I'll show you something.'

He led the way round to the back of the building, where a small opening near the ground gave a measure of air and light to an inner cellar.

'Have a look,' Paul said.

Bobby lay upon the ground, the only way to see within.

Inside was Peter Carsley. On the cellar floor was a pile of freshly turned earth. In front of Peter was a large hole. Peter had a spade in his hands, and had evidently been digging, but for the moment was resting.

Paul said softly in Bobby's ear:

'I couldn't make it out at first, but now it looks to me as though it is a grave he is digging down there.'

CHAPTER 28

The Discovery

I т was perhaps the cold dampness of the earth, striking up as Bobby lay stretched full length, that set him shivering and shaking, like a man stricken with a fever. He scrambled to his feet. He knew now in literal truth what that old phrase means which speaks of the tongue cleaving to the roof of the mouth. For so now did his, and he could not speak. Paul said to him:

'Pull yourself together.'

'Yes. Yes,' Bobby muttered, getting the words out with difficulty. 'We must ... I mean we must ask him ... ask him what he's doing ... and stop him ...'

But Paul shook his head.

'No good,' he said, 'no good our doing anything ... too late to stop him.'

'We don't know,' Bobby muttered and paused and Paul said:

'If he hadn't done what he meant to do, he wouldn't be digging there.'

Bobby did not answer. He could not, for again the power of speech had left him. Paul said:

'He can't get away ... there's only the one door, the other door's boarded up. We had better wait, Mitchell'll be along soon, they said he would come himself.'

They had returned again to the front of the building and in fact almost at once heard the sound of an approaching car. It glided up to the garden entrance and stopped, and Mitchell and Gibbons and another man got out. They came up the garden path together; Mitchell, voluble as ever, holding forth to the other two. Paul and Owen showed themselves. Mitchell broke off his discourse to survey them with his most benevolent expression. Then he said to Gibbons:

'There's Owen all right enough and that's half a crown you owe me.'

Gibbons produced it reluctantly.

'And five bob more to come from the Assistant Commissioner,' Mitchell observed, pocketing the coin with satisfaction, 'picking up money I call it.'

'Twenty-four hours' leave you had,' Gibbons said reproachfully to the somewhat bewildered Owen.

'When you've had as much to do with Constable Robert Owen as the good Lord for my sins has inflicted on me,' said Mitchell, 'you'll find it takes more than twenty-four hours' leave to keep him quiet – cheap at half a crown to know that, too, if you ask me. Now then, Paul, was it you brought Owen here, or did Owen bring you?'

'I trailed Mr Carsley here, sir,' Paul answered, 'and according to instruction to report unusual happenings, and this place seeming so, I rang up.'

'Quite right,' said Mitchell. 'But where does Owen come in?'

'He said he was just mooching around, sir,' explained Paul.

'He would be,' agreed Mitchell, 'worth seven and six to me, too, that I bet we should find him on the spot or thereabouts – at least, if the Assistant Commissioner pays up. Inspectors have got to pay supers, but you can't be so sure of Assistant Commissioners – abuse of authority, I call it. Anything happened to make the two of you look the way you do and Owen do a sort of step dance because he wants to get a word in and discipline won't let him?'

Owen, who had been fidgeting uneasily at one side, subsided into stillness, reminding himself that Mitchell's flow of talk generally hid some purpose and that most likely he had been gaining a moment or two to take stock of the situation. Paul answered:

'We don't know, sir, we don't know if anything's happened at all. I thought we had better wait till you came before beginning investigations. Mr Carsley is in there – at least, I saw him go in and I haven't seen him come out again. Owen thinks there's reason to believe Mrs Carsley is there, too, but I don't know about that myself and I haven't seen her.'

'Mrs Carsley?' Mitchell repeated. He turned sharply on Owen. 'How do you know that?' he asked. 'Been trailing her?'

'No, sir,' Owen answered. 'I had no idea she was here, but an old man at a cottage down the road, when I asked the way, told me a tall young lady, answering Mrs Carsley's description, came up here a little while ago and he hadn't seen her go away again.'

'Ah, yes, yes,' Mitchell said slowly, evidently thinking deeply; 'and then Carsley arrived?'

'Now he's digging in the cellar, sir,' Paul said.

'Digging? Digging what? What for?'

'I couldn't say,' Paul answered. 'But it looked to me as though it might be a grave.'

There was a silence then, a silence in which could have been heard the slow breaths they took. Instinctively their eyes turned towards that shuttered, solitary building. It was as though they questioned it and it made no reply, guarding its secret well.

'Well, now, you know, that's funny,' Gibbons said at last, 'funny I call that, digging . . .'

'Very funny,' agreed Mitchell in a grim enough tone. He was still intently watching the old windmill as though his glance could penetrate its ancient walls. 'Have they been there long?' he asked.

'It's about an hour since Mr Carsley got here,' Paul answered. 'Mrs Carsley was apparently here already.'

'You've not heard anything?'

'No, sir. But I was away a few minutes when I went to ring up and report.'

'You're sure Carsley is still there?'

'It's not five minutes since we saw him, Owen and me,' Paul replied. 'In the cellar, digging.'

'Ah,' said Mitchell. 'Come on.'

He went on to the house, followed by the others. At the door he said:

'Gibbons, you and Paul search the house and see what you can find. If Mrs Carsley's there, detain her and report. You others, come with me.'

They found the steps leading down to the cellar. As they were descending they could hear distinctly the sound of someone working in the inner cellar. It ceased. Their own approach had evidently been heard, for as they reached the bottom of the steps Peter Carsley came out of an inner cellar. He was in his shirt sleeves. He had a spade in his hands, and his face and clothing were stained with earth. In the dim half-light that struggled in through one tiny opening high up in the cellar wall they could see him but imperfectly. But apparently he was able to recognize them for he said loudly and angrily.

'You lot again? What the mischief are you doing here?'

'I think, Mr Carsley,' Mitchell answered slowly, 'I think that is a question we have to ask of you.'

'Oh, you do, do you?' snapped Peter. 'It's like your cheek barging in here at all – what do you think you are doing, anyhow?'

'Our duty,' Mitchell answered in the same grave, level tones, 'our duty as officers of police. Where is Mrs Carsley?'

'Mrs Carsley? At home, I suppose. Why? What do you mean?'

'We have information that she was seen entering here shortly before your arrival,' Mitchell said.

'Nonsense,' retorted Peter briefly.

Mitchell had gone towards the inner cellar, and now, standing between the two, the outer one and the inner, he turned the light of his electric torch on the hole Peter had been digging.

'You've been busy here, I see,' he said.

'What's that to do with you?' Peter demanded.

'Only that it seems a strange thing to be digging in the cellar of an empty house,' Mitchell answered. 'Do you wish to say anything?'

'Well, if you want to know,' Peter answered, though somewhat sullenly, 'I was told the diamonds and bonds stolen from "The Cedars" the night Sir Christopher was murdered, were buried here. I didn't much believe it but anyhow I thought I had better come along and see. I was told there was no time to lose, they might be removed any minute. Also that they were buried rather deep, but I could tell the place because I could see where the ground had been disturbed. Well, that was right enough. A bit about six foot long has been dug up some time quite recently. Whoever did it has left his spade here, so I took it and started work. But I've not found anything. I expect it's a fake. But someone's been digging here quite recently.'

'Yes,' agreed Mitchell, 'someone's certainly been digging here,' and he swung the light of his torch on the fresh turned earth, on the darkness of the long deep trench Peter had been making.

'Only what for?' Peter said, 'and who and why?'

'We've got to find that out,' Mitchell said. 'Owen here, he says he saw you once run straight the whole length of the field at Cardiff.'

'What the devil are you talking about?' Peter demanded.

'Nothing,' Mitchell answered. 'I wasn't talking, I was thinking, a bad habit I know. Mr Carsley, who gave you this information about these diamonds buried in a trench six feet long and about two feet wide – an odd shape, isn't it? Who told you?'

'I don't know.'

'You don't know?'

'No, someone rang me up on the phone and told me to be at a certain address and I would be rung up there. It was one of those shops where they let anyone use their phone who wants to. Someone rung up right enough and sent me to another place and from there I was sent on here. If it's just a fake or a joke of some sort, it was a jolly elaborate one.'

'Do you think Mrs Carsley came here to look for the stolen diamonds, too?'

'Why do you keep talking about my wife?' Peter demanded, his voice troubled and uneasy now. 'She's not here.'

They heard footsteps descending the cellar steps. It was Paul. He said:

'We found a locked room at the top of the house. We opened it. Inside is the body of a young woman, wearing a blue leather motoring coat and hat to match. She has been shot through the back of the head. Death must have been instantaneous. The body is still warm. Inspector Gibbons is staying with the body and ordered me to report.'

CHAPTER 29

Murder Again

INSTINCTIVELY they had all turned to watch Peter. He did not speak or move, but for a certain tenseness in his attitude one might have thought he had not heard. The light, grow· ing fainter every moment, had now almost vanished. They saw him only as a tall, still figure in the gloom. They heard him say twice over in a harsh, strained voice:

'A dead woman . . . a dead woman . . .'

They were still silent nor did they move. He said again, his voice bewildered now:

'But it can't . . . I mean . . . there can't . . .'

His voice trailed into silence.

Paul said:

'Well, it is . . . she's there and the room was locked . . . outside . . . through the back of the head . . . it must have killed her on the spot . . . instantaneous.' He added, very slowly, his voice dropping to little more than a whisper, though one that in this silence was clear and distinct enough: 'I only saw her once, but she looks to me like a lady I saw talking to Mr Carsley where he lives. I can't be sure, for I only saw her once, but that's what she looks like to me.'

Peter did not speak. Very carefully he placed the spade he held against the wall. It seemed what he was chiefly thinking of at the moment was to make sure that the thing was well placed and would not fall. He went back into the inner cellar and put on his coat, slowly, with jerky motions, like a man in a dream. He said:

'I must go and see.' Then he paused and stood staring at the long narrow trench where he had been digging. 'It does look rather like a grave,' he said.

'Yes,' agreed Mitchell.

'I'll go and see,' Peter said again. He walked towards the

steps that led up from the cellar. Opposite Paul, he stopped and looked at him.

'There's a locked room and a dead woman . . .?' he asked. 'She was wearing a blue leather coat. .. she's like someone you saw me with?'

'That's what I thought,' Paul answered, 'I don't know but it's what I thought.'

'Jennie has a blue motor coat,' Peter remarked abstractedly, as though dropping an observation without any possible interest either for himself or anyone else.

He began to ascend the steps. The others followed him. He was muttering something to himself, but what it was Bobby, who was next behind him, could not clearly hear, though the name 'Jennie' seemed audible once or twice. They came into the entrance passage, and then began to ascend the stairs that led to the upper part of the building. Peter was hurrying now, so that the others, too, had to hasten. But when they came out on to the wide upper landing, Peter paused. There were two doors opening from it. One was wide open, and showed, so far as they could see in the darkness, only an expanse of bare, uncarpeted flooring. The other door was closed. Peter, suddenly still again, stood looking at it, and Bobby understood that he was in the grip of an appalling, an unutterable terror. Mitchell and the others, crowding together at the head of the stairs, were all waiting, as though to see what Peter would do and he remained motionless, his eyes burning on that closed door, burning, too, with awful terror of what that closed door might hide. Slowly the door swung open while he watched, almost as if it were his intent gaze that had forced it, and Inspector Gibbons appeared. He did not speak either. It was very dark here on the landing, and now they all showed to each other as little more than sombre, silent shadows. Inside the room it was no lighter, for the windows were closely shuttered. But an electric torch in Gibbons's hand made a splash of light that he directed slowly towards a still form that lay quiet and huddled just behind him. Peter moved forward and took the torch from Gibbons. He knelt down by that quiet figure. The others watched him. The silence remained unbroken, to Bobby the strain seemed intolerable. He could feel his heart thumping wildly. He thought to himself:

'Is it her? Is it his wife? God in heaven, why doesn't he speak?'

As if he, too, could bear the strain no longer, Mitchell moved across to where Bobby stood. He said:

'You can't see a thing ... it's so dark. Gibbons, smash those blasted shutters ... no, don't ... it'll be dark outside by now as well. Paul, cut along and get one of the car lamps and bring it.'

Paul hurried away to obey, and Peter, apparently roused by the sound of Mitchell's voice, looked round and said very quietly:

'It is not my wife; it is Brenda, Miss Laing, her half-sister, you know. It is Jennie's coat, I think, and her hat as well, but it's Brenda who is wearing them.' He got to his feet and came out on the landing. He leaned against the wall as if for support and they could see that now he was trembling violently. He said: 'Thank God for that ... God forgive me for saying so ... it is Brenda and not Jennie.'

Mitchell glanced at Bobby.

'You've seen them both,' he said. 'Go and look.'

Peter said:

'It's Brenda, it's Miss Laing right enough. Why was she here and why was she wearing Jennie's coat and hat? Why was she here at all?' He paused and then went on: 'It was like a grave I was digging down there. I never thought of that before but I see it now. Do you think I murdered her? Why should I, poor girl? We always got on well enough, though she was so quiet; the way she never said a word, it got on people's nerves sometimes ... not on mine, I didn't mind ... I suppose you think I did it ... digging like that down there in the cellar ... well, I didn't ... I suppose it might just as well have been Jennie but it's not ... thank God, it's Brenda ... God forgive me for saying so ... I don't know what I am saying ... In God's name, what was she doing here and why was she wearing Jennie's coat and hat?'

Bobby came out of the room.

'It's Miss Brenda Laing,' he said. 'There's no doubt of that. I think it's Mrs Carsley's coat and hat she's wearing but I can't be sure.'

'Why should she be wearing Jennie's things?' Peter asked again. 'I can't make it out ... why was I sent to go digging in the cellar ... there's no sense to that. .. I think there's something damnable about all this.'

Paul came back with the car lamp. It gave them light, but showed them little more than they had seen already. There was Brenda lying, silent and enigmatic in death as she had been in life, surrounded by a strange silence still as she had ever been. At a little distance lay a revolver, a clean white handkerchief placed carefully by Gibbons underneath it. The room was otherwise bare and empty, and the doors of two large cupboards at one end hung loosely open, showing they held nothing. The windows were closely shuttered. There was no fireplace. The only other object visible in the room was a walking stick that Mitchell picked up.

'What's this?' he asked.

'It was lying there when we got in,' Gibbons said. 'If the murderer left it, it may be useful.'

Mitchell saw that Bobby was looking at it. He said to him: Recognize it?'

'It's rather like one I've seen Mr Carsley carrying,' Bobby answered.

'Go and ask him,' Mitchell said.

Bobby took it outside to Peter, still standing against the wall on the landing, still evidently terribly shaken, but fighting hard for his self-control.

'Do you know whose this is?' Bobby said to him.

'It's mine, where did you get it?' Peter returned immediately.

'It was in there, lying near Miss Laing's body,' Bobby answered.

'How did it get there?' Peter asked. 'She had Jennie's hat and coat, why should she have my stick, too? I had it at the office ... or at home ... I forget ...'

'We found it in there,' Bobby repeated, 'near Miss Laing's body.'

'You think I killed her?' Peter said. 'I didn't. Why should I? Good God, man, why should I murder her, poor girl? Jennie liked her, so did I, why should I? ... Ah, God, I think I'm going mad ... who was it got me digging down there in the cellar? ... like a grave ... a grave for Brenda. What a fool I was, I knew I was, but still I thought there was a chance the diamonds were really there; and then why should anyone want to murder Brenda? What for? There's no sense ...' He flung out his hand and gripped Bobby fiercely by the arm. 'Why was she wearing Jennie's coat and hat?' he almost shouted. 'Tell me that!'

'Now, Mr Carsley,' Mitchell said soothingly, coming out to join them, 'you mustn't lose your head ... there's a lot about this that wants clearing up and we'll do our best. But it won't do any good getting excited. I'm going to ask you to go to Scotland Yard with two of our men, Inspector Gibbons and Paul. When you get there, if you like to make a statement, you can do so. You're a lawyer yourself, but it's for you to decide whether you want further assistance. I'm staying here with Constable Owen. There's always a lot to be done in these cases. I'm sending for assistance, and for a doctor, too, not that a doctor can do much for that poor soul. Silent she always was when she was alive, and she's silent still, but we'll do our best to find out what happened.'

'I must let Jennie know first,' Peter said.

'There's no hurry about that; never any hurry telling bad news,' replied Mitchell. He did not add that already he was planning to send one of his best men to interview Jennie, to try to obtain from her information as to Peter's movements and Brenda's. There were many thoughts in his mind and some of them were strange. He said again: 'Mrs Carsley will know soon enough and there's a lot to be thought of, if we're to make sure that whoever it was did this shall hang.'

'Yes, but I must see Jennie, tell her, I must see my wife first,' Peter persisted.

'I am afraid I can't permit that,' Mitchell said, more sternly, for the idea was in his mind that this looked as if Peter might be anxious for a chance to tell his wife both what to say and what not to say.

But Bobby had a surer intuition, and he said aside to Mitchell:

'I think he's afraid, sir ... afraid about her, I mean, I think he wants to make sure she's safe.'

'But I must, I tell you I must,' Peter was saying angrily, and then with a sudden change of tone: 'Do you mean you want to arrest me?'

'I wouldn't like to say that, Mr Carsley,' Mitchell protested. 'I wouldn't put it like that ... shall we say we're detaining you for necessary inquiries? You see you were on the spot, and now there's your walking stick, and then that digging business in the cellar – it all wants clearing up, doesn't it? And you needn't worry about Mrs Carsley. I'll ring up and make sure she's at home and safe and then I'll ring our people and they'll tell you at once, they'll know before you get to the Yard most likely.'

'If you'll do that,' Peter said, looking relieved. 'I suppose it's silly ... I feel as if I were going off my head ... it's all like some awful nightmare.'

'If you're ready, Mr Carsley, sir,' Gibbons said, 'we had best be moving ... lots to do, you know ... not much bed for any of us to-night, I expect.'

The three of them went down the stairs together and Mitchell turned to Bobby.

'If that had been Mrs Carsley lying there,' he said, 'the rope would be as good as round his neck already, if that were Mrs Carsley.'

'Yes, sir,' agreed Bobby, 'but it isn't – it's Brenda Laing.'

'And rum, too, that is,' Mitchell remarked. 'If you serve as long as I've done, Owen, I doubt if you'll ever have a rummier case than this to deal with.'

'No, sir,' agreed Bobby again.

'Got any ideas?' Mitchell asked.

'I can't get them clear in my mind, sir,' Bobby answered. 'They go whirling round and round and I can't get them to settle.' After a long pause he said: 'There's such a thing as being too clever by half.'

'So there is,' agreed Mitchell, 'and it's fatal. You can be not clever enough, and get away with it all right, but when you're too clever, then, sooner or later, you crash. And all this business looks to me just a little tiny bit too clever. But there's one thing I'll say again, if that were Mrs Carsley there, instead of only her coat and hat – why, then Carsley would swing sure as God's in heaven.'

'Yes, sir,' agreed Bobby, 'so he would, only – ' and he and Mitchell talked long and earnestly together, were still so talking indeed when at last there arrived the assistance Mitchell had sent for.

CHAPTER 30

Baiting a Trap

I T was late enough before Bobby got to bed, but he was able to allow himself an extra hour there or so, and then to enjoy a leisurely breakfast, during which he read his own paper, and borrowed the landlady's to look at hers, and was able to note with satisfaction that not a word appeared of the previous night's tragic happenings.

'Good old Mitchell,' he said to himself, 'he's managed to keep it dark so far, though I suppose the newspaper men will always play up if you put it to them nicely – hard on them, too, when they smell things out so quickly.'

He finished his meal and started out in time to arrive at Lincoln's Inn about eleven, at which hour he strolled into the office of Messrs Marsden, Carsley, and Marsden.

'Mr Carsley in?' he asked. 'Could I see him?'

It appeared Mr Carsley was not in, a fact which did not much surprise Bobby. Mr Carsley, the clerks explained, had not yet arrived. It was unusual for him to be so late and no message explaining his absence had been received, but no doubt he would not be long now. So Bobby looked worried, and said it was important, and would Mr Carsley's partner, Mr Marsden, know where he was?

The clerks all giggled at this, and said he might ask Mr Marsden himself if he liked. For their part, they would rather be excused. It was hardly safe, these days, to mention one partner's name to the other, and then Marsden appeared from his private room. To Bobby's inquiry he answered that he knew nothing about Carsley and didn't much want to, either. Why? Did Bobby want to see him?

'Oh, just one or two questions I've been instructed to ask him about last night,' Bobby answered carelessly. 'But I can't find him. I've been to the house and he's not there.

Mrs Carsley isn't there, either. It seems she didn't come home last night. The servants say they suppose Mr Carsley knows where she is, but he didn't say.'

'Funny,' said Marsden, 'very funny. But what happened last night? Nothing serious, I hope? Come in here.' He led the way back into his private room, and, producing a box of cigars, offered Bobby one. 'What about last night?' he repeated.

'Oh, nothing of any importance,' Bobby answered. 'Only, as you know, we've felt we had to keep Mr Carsley under observation, and last night our men trailed him to a rummy, out-of-the-way place, way out at the back of beyond, an old empty house.'

'Yes,' said Marsden. 'Yes.'

'Well, when he got there, he started digging in the cellar. Now, what can you make of that?'

'Digging in the cellar?' Marsden repeated. 'Why? Digging ... what for?'

'That's just it,' said Bobby, savouring his cigar. ' I am enjoying this, Mr Marsden, if I may say so – not often a cigar like this comes my way.'

'But ... but ... you did something ...? Surely you did something ...?'

'Oh, yes, our people asked him what he was up to,' Bobby answered. 'He told some sort of wild story about having been rung up about the diamonds stolen when Sir Christopher was murdered – you remember?'

'Yes, I remember,' said Marsden. 'Go on.'

'Well, his story was someone had rung him up and told him they were hidden there – buried in the cellar apparently. Sort of yarn you can't make head or tail of – might be true and mightn't.'

'But ... but ...' Marsden said, 'didn't you ... I mean ... you surely didn't accept that? Surely you ... you took further action?'

'What could we do?' asked Bobby. 'No law against

digging holes in cellar floors. Funny, of course, as suspicious as you like, most likely something behind it, but we can't act on suspicions and "most likely", can we?'

'Didn't you look round ... search the house?' Marsden asked.

'Why, of course,' Bobby answered. 'From top to bottom – rather.'

'You ... found ... found ...?'

'The whole place was as bare as the palm of your hand,' Bobby said. 'Looked as if no one had lived there for years – I expect no one has, either.'

'You looked everywhere?'

'Went over it with a fine tooth comb,' declared Bobby. 'The garden, too. We thought there must be something somewhere to explain why Mr Carsley went digging in the cellar. But as I said just now, no one might have been near the place since the beginning of the century. Funnily enough one room was locked – a room at the very top of the house.'

'You didn't open it – look there?'

'Oh, come, Mr Marsden, what do you take us for?' Bobby asked in mild protest. 'We have got some sense, you know, we have really.'

'Then ... inside ... you looked ...?'

'Oh, we had that door open in two shakes of a donkey's tail,' Bobby answered, puffing out a cloud of smoke and watching it curl upwards to the ceiling ... 'I can tell you, Mr Marsden, if ever the C.I.D. take to burglary ... there isn't a door or a safe in existence our people couldn't open.'

'And,' asked Marsden, 'when you opened it ... this locked door ... you found ...?'

'Why, that's almost the queerest part of it,' said Bobby, slowly knocking off the long ash from his cigar. 'Yes, I really think that's the queerest thing of all.'

'Yes ... what?' asked Marsden. 'What?'

'You would never guess,' said Bobby. 'I would lay anyone

a five-pound note to a bad threepenny bit, they'd never guess.'

'Wouldn't they?' said Marsden. 'What . . . what did you find?'

'Why, inside that locked room,' said Bobby, 'behind the door, lying there –'

'Yes,' said Marsden, 'yes.'

'– was Mr Carsley's walking stick,' Bobby concluded his sentence. 'What do you make of that? You know the one with the crooked handle in some kind of horn.'

'Nothing . . . else?'

'Well, they did have a good look round for his hat and gloves as well,' chuckled Bobby, 'because they felt those ought to be there, too. But they weren't. Not a sign of them. A locked room in an empty house, all bare as the top of the bald man's head in the advertisements before he starts using So-and-So's hair restorer, and inside that locked room – Mr Carsley's walking stick. What do you make of that, Mr Marsden?'

'I don't know,' said Marsden. 'Not at all.'

'Funny, too,' Bobby went on; 'when we showed it Mr Carsley he agreed at once it was his, but he swore up and down he hadn't brought it with him, hadn't been upstairs, didn't know there was a locked room in the place, or, if there was, how his walking stick came to be inside it. Told us we were drunk or dreaming, but we weren't, for that's where we found it. Now, Mr Marsden, what are poor, worried C.I.D. men to make of all that?'

'It seems funny, certainly,' agreed Marsden, 'there must be something . . . I don't know.'

'Well, I must be going,' declared Bobby, 'mustn't waste any more of your time – suppose we shall run up against Mr Carsley sooner or later.'

'Isn't he still under observation?' Marsden asked.

'Oh, yes. That's how it is he was followed last night to the place I've been telling you about. But we lost him afterwards.

Of course, anyone can always dodge us if he wants to –
tubes, lifts, shops with a dozen doors, and all the rest of it.
Big towns are just made for dodgers. We can't help that. But
I want to see him again as soon as possible. Mrs Carsley, too.
It's worrying us more than a bit to know what's really
behind his being in that old empty house last night.'

'I suppose you are keeping the house under observation,
too?' Marsden asked.

'What for?' Bobby demanded. 'Nothing there, it was
examined and searched from top to bottom, and I'll swear
there's nothing there.'

He went off then and round a corner at a little distance
found a car waiting. As he approached the door opened.
He entered. Mitchell was sitting there. The car started and
Mitchell said:

'Get on all right?'

'I think so, sir,' Bobby answered. 'I followed instructions
closely.'

'Good. You look a bit pale.'

'I remember reading,' Bobby said slowly, 'that St
Thomas Aquinas, I think it was, said one of the pleasures of
the saved in heaven would be leaning over to watch the
damned burning in the flames of hell. That's what I've been
doing.'

'How do you mean?'

'Watching the tortures of the damned – and I think
Thomas Aquinas overrated the fun to be had from doing
that.'

'I think in your place,' observed Mitchell meditatively,
'I should have enjoyed it all right enough – this time for once
in a way I'm on the side of the saints. Got any sandwiches?'

'No, sir.'

Mitchell shook his head gravely.

'A good detective never forgets his sandwiches,' he said.
'That's the first law of all sound detective work – don't forget
the sandwiches. We may have to wait there all day.'

'Yes, sir,' said Bobby, rather dispiritedly.

'Just as well,' observed Mitchell, 'that they always put me up enough for two.'

'Do they, sir?' said Bobby hopefully.

'That's because,' explained Mitchell, 'they know I've an appetite for two.'

'I see, sir,' said Bobby, less hopefully this time.

The car stopped and Mitchell got out. Bobby followed and Mitchell said:

'We'll do the rest of the way on foot, across the fields at the back. We have a wary bird to deal with and we don't want to give anyone any more chance than we can help of telling him two men, both outsize, have been seen entering the old mill.'

Evidently Mitchell had taken pains to find out the best way to take to accomplish his purpose of reaching their destination unseen. He led the way first by a field path, and then across some fields in the shadow of a tall hedge, till they reached the crumbling wall that bounded the old mill's garden. A gap let them through, and by the back door, purposely opened the previous night, they entered the building and made their way upstairs to the room where had been found the dead body, now removed, of Brenda Laing.

'Suppose he doesn't come, sir?' Bobby asked.

'Then we shall have wasted our time and had our trouble for nothing,' answered Mitchell. 'Most C.I.D. work is time wasted and trouble for nothing. You can make up your mind to that, young man. Which of those two cupboards looks the most uncomfortable?'

'I couldn't say, sir,' answered Bobby cautiously.

'It's the one I wanted you to choose,' explained Mitchell. He got inside one and closed the door, then opened it again. 'Get inside the other and see if you fit,' he ordered and when Bobby obeyed: 'That's all right,' he said, 'the door shuts all right and none of you is sticking out. Leave a crack or make one with your knife so you can see to take notes. How's your shorthand?'

'Fair to middling, sir,' answered Bobby.

'Can you do two hundred a minute?'

'Yes, sir,' answered Bobby confidently, 'but I can't read it again. A hundred a minute is as much as I can manage and be sure of being able to make it out afterwards.'

'Ought to be good enough,' observed Mitchell. 'Remember, we mustn't move, we mustn't speak, we mustn't smoke, we must only stand and suffer, and curse the day we told our mothers we were entering the police force.'

CHAPTER 31

In the Attic

AFTER several years – at least, so it seemed to Bobby, suffo-
cating, cramped, bored stiff in a very literal sense, but
really after a couple of hours or so by a more normal meas-
urement of time – they both heard an approaching sound.
Rather, they both heard amid the other sounds of which
the still, old house seemed full, one that was like that of a
footstep on the stairs.

They lost it. They heard it again. It was doubtful, hesi-
tant, uncertain. They both knew, with an intuition surer
than any formal knowledge could ever be, that on the
landing outside there was someone driven very horribly by
a fear that urged him on to enter, held back as terribly by
another that told him he must not. And to both of them,
hidden and waiting, there came the same thought:

'Suppose the second fear proves the greater and he goes
away again and we do not even see him.'

The door of the room was dashed violently open. With a
kind of rush Marsden appeared on the threshold. A stray
ray of sunshine through a crack in the shuttered window il-
lumined his features and showed them, no longer smooth,
controlled, set in an unchanging mask as formerly, but
twisted, contorted, agonized beyond all imagining. For a
moment he stood there glaring – there is no other word –
glaring all around in a panic of wonder, doubt, and terror.

He came a step or two forward, peering anxiously, doubtfully, at the spot upon the bare boards where a little before
a dead body had lain. He made a kind of gesture with one
hand towards it, and then quite suddenly, as it seemed, his
self-control broke down, and he burst into a screaming
torrent of words from which it was hard to pick out any
two that made coherent sense. He swore, gesticulated,

shouted, he made appeal to unseen powers, his arms waved
frantically, hysteria had him in its grip, he blasphemed
aloud, defying his Creator; alone, as he thought, he raved
there in that quiet, silent, and unheeding room, and the two
hidden watchers waited in grim patience the outcome of
this extraordinary scene.

As for trying to take down that torrent of incoherent rav-
ing, Bobby, though he had note-book and pencil ready,
gave up the attempt. All he could do was to try to catch
now and again distinguishable words and to remember
them.

At last, breathless, panting, exhausted, Marsden ceased,
and leaned against the wall, wiping with his handkerchief
his face down which the sweat ran like a young girl's tears.

'Who moved her?' he said aloud, muttering to himself,
'she couldn't have moved herself ... that's certain, not
when she was dead ... who's done it then? ... what for?
... where is she? ... she couldn't herself ... I didn't miss ...
well, then, someone must have moved her ... who? ...
what? ... why? ... what for? what for? what for?' He went
unsteadily across the room and stood staring down at the
spot where the body had lain, where the fresh bloodstains
were clearly visible. 'They couldn't see that,' he muttered,
'those cursed police ... the fools, the fools,' he screamed,
'not to see that, the fools.' Then he fell to his muttering
again. 'Everything arranged so perfectly and then for it to
go wrong like this because those fools ... those utter fools
... well, she didn't move herself, that's certain, but who did?
What for? What for? I shall go mad, I think ... there's
madness somewhere ... where can her body be?'

He wiped his streaming face again and seemed on the
brink of a fresh attack of hysteria. With an effort he appeared to conquer it and for the first time to notice the cupboards.

For a moment or two he stood staring. Then slowly he
went across the room to them.

'Oh, impossible,' he said, 'only it's all impossible ...
impossible.'

He tore open the door of the cupboard in which Mitchell
was hidden.

'Oh, oh,' he said.

'Good day, Mr Marsden,' Mitchell said, coming forward, 'not impossible at all, you see, but deucedly uncomfortable,' and then as Marsden slowly, terribly recoiled,
slowly staggering backwards till he was half-way across the
room again, Mitchell added: 'I'm afraid you didn't expect
to see me.'

'You were there all the time?' Marsden asked, recovering
himself a little, 'you heard ... you saw ... you know ... it
was you who moved her body ... you've hidden it ... you
found her body and you've hidden it?'

'The dead body of a woman was found in this room last
night,' Mitchell agreed. 'It was subsequently removed. I
think it will be necessary for you to explain how it is you
were acquainted with that fact. You are a lawyer, Mr Marsden, so I needn't go into explanations with you as to your
rights or your position. If you wish to make a statement we
are ready to hear it, but probably you prefer to wait.'

'Oh, I'll make a statement all right,' Marsden snarled.
'You think you've trapped me, I suppose? That spy of yours
who came to see me this morning ... all a put up job, eh?
Oh, very clever, but not so clever as you think, perhaps, for
I've still a card or two to play. I'll tell you, though, I'll tell
you all right' – his voice rose almost to a scream – 'I knew,
I knew because I did it. I did it, I did it, listen to that as
much as you like, I shot her, I shot Mrs Carsley, I waited
behind that door till I saw her coming up the stairs in the
dark, till I saw her head show against the crack in the
shutters in here ... then I fired ... just one shot ... blew the
back of her head all to bits. Are you listening? Hear that?
... just one shot ... then I locked the door and got out and I
waited to see Carsley come and your fellow following him ...

Why, it was perfect, man, not a flaw in it, superb ... his dead wife in a locked room upstairs and Carsley digging a grave in the cellar ... perfect, I tell you,' he raved, and now flecks of foam were on his lips. He wiped them away and went on more quietly: 'What went wrong? Why didn't you arrest him? Wasn't the evidence good enough? It was good enough to hang a bishop on if you had arrested him then. Oh, you fools, you utter fools, I had it all arranged so well you couldn't help but think ... why didn't you?'

'It was quite good,' Mitchell agreed. 'Her dead upstairs and him digging in the cellar ... I suppose you had been there before?'

'Yes,' agreed Marsden, 'I dug a hole there like a grave and then filled it up again and told him the diamonds were hidden there so he would dig in the same place and shape and way ... his own gardener's spade, too, I had taken from their toolshed at "The Cedars".'

'No detail forgotten,' Mitchell mused. 'Even the walking stick by her side up here. I'm sure, very well arranged, indeed, but wasn't it just a little hard on him?'

'He deserved it,' Marsden retorted. 'He had murdered his father-in-law, so it was all right getting him hung for murdering his wife, even if he didn't do that.'

'You think he murdered Sir Christopher?' Mitchell asked.

'Of course I do, so do you, don't you? Of course he did, who else?'

'Well, after this performance,' observed Mitchell, 'some may think it was you.'

'Me? Oh, nonsense,' Marsden answered. 'I had nothing to do with that. Why should I? It was nothing to do with me. It was Carsley shot him, of course. I've always been sure of that Then he started trying to ruin me, trying to get a reputation for honesty, trying to act the honest man who can't let fraud go by – and he a murderer! I had to stop that, I had to, it was ruin if I didn't ... why shouldn't he hang when he was a murderer? He had earned it. I was only getting him what he deserved.'

'Rather rough on Mrs Carsley, wasn't it?' Mitchell remarked mildly, 'to bring her in.'

'I couldn't help that,' Marsden answered sullenly. 'I didn't want to. I had to, that was all. I had to think of myself first, hadn't I? Everyone does. Don't you?'

'Well, some of us may think there are limits,' observed Mitchell, 'but indeed I think you had it all very well worked out, and Mr Carsley would certainly have hung, with evidence and motive all complete, since his wife's death meant a fortune for him. Yes, I don't think any man ever had a narrower escape from the gallows, for we should have sent him there and he would certainly have hung – but for one little, little flaw. Oh, a trifle, and yet it counted.'

'What was it? I would like to know.'

'Only that it wasn't Mrs Carsley you shot, it was her half-sister, Brenda Laing.'

Marsden stood quite still, staring stupidly.

'Oh, that's impossible,' he said, 'that's quite impossible ... another lie.'

'What did you do to get Mrs Carsley here?' Mitchell asked.

'Two birds with one stone,' Marsden answered. 'I told her the stolen diamonds were here in this top room. I told her the door would be open – I had all the keys, of course. I told her she must come at once and alone. Or else the diamonds would be gone. The same tale I told Carsley over the phone, making my voice different so that he wouldn't know it. That's a lie, isn't it? Another lie, another trap, that it was Brenda Laing who came?'

'It's the truth,' Mitchell answered. 'It was Brenda Laing who was murdered here last night.'

'Then that's why ... I might have guessed ... how could I, though? I never did ... that's why she asked ... she knew something from the start, somehow she knew something ... '

He burst into wild laughter. 'Well, it doesn't matter now what she knew, if you're telling the truth, for now she'll never tell it ... never be able to tell it. Silent she always was and now silent she'll stay for ever.'

'Yes,' Mitchell agreed, 'she'll tell us nothing now, but I hardly think it's necessary ... not when you've told so much.'

'Yes, I've told you a lot,' Marsden answered. 'Do you think you're going to have a chance to tell it to anyone else? Not you, you fool, you double fool.' All at once a small automatic pistol showed deadly in his hand. 'You fool,' he said again, 'do you think I've told you all this, for you to tell everyone else?'

He swung the pistol up as he spoke. His eyes were deadly, his bare teeth snarled. Behind the features of the conventional, civilized, twentieth-century citizen glared the primeval killer. It all happened in a moment. Twice the pistol spat across the room its tongue of fire, its trail of smoke. From the cupboard behind, Bobby leaped out, flinging note-book and pencil at Marsden's head, grabbing at his levelled arm. One bullet splashed against the wall, another brought down a shower of plaster from the ceiling. Mitchell had tripped and fallen on his hands and knees. Another shot shrilled by, missing his head by an inch or two. In the middle of the room Bobby and Marsden threshed to and fro, Bobby trying to wrench the pistol away, Marsden trying to level the muzzle at him or at Mitchell. Marsden got another shot loose, but Bobby twisted his arm, and the bullet went harmlessly through the open doorway. Mitchell was on his feet again now. Bobby wrenched his own arm free and dashed his clenched fist with all his force full into Marsden's face, that seemed as it were to fall away beneath the force and impact of that one great blow. He went down heavily before it, with a crash that seemed to shake the whole of the rickety old building. His pistol flew from his grasp into one corner of the room. He lay unconscious.

They noticed that blood, streaming from his face, from his mouth and nose, crawled in a little stream across the bare boards of the floor towards and to join that other dark stain left there from the night before.

CHAPTER 32

Brenda Breaks Her Silence

SUPERINTENDENT MITCHELL, seated next morning at his desk at which he had been working long and hard, looked up when Bobby, following instructions, appeared to report.

'Sit down there,' he said, and went on with his writing.

It was a transcript of Bobby's shorthand note of what had passed between Mitchell, himself, and Marsden in the top room of the old transformed mill that the Superintendent was working on, and there were one or two points he wanted cleared up. When that had presently been accomplished to his satisfaction, Mitchell observed thoughtfully:

'So far as Marsden is concerned, it's good enough. Not even Treasury Counsel can pick a hole in that evidence. It's too strong even for them to muck up, and if they can't get a conviction on it, they can't on anything. I don't believe even old Marshall Hall would have been able to get Marsden off, and he could have got Old Nick himself acquitted nine times out of ten. But the Commissioner has been in here this morning, grumbling like blazes.'

'Has he, sir?' said Bobby, alarmed, for when the Commissioner grumbles, the sun itself stands still at noon – or ought to.

'Because,' explained Mitchell, 'we haven't got whoever it was did in Sir Christopher Clarke. He asked me what we were doing about it, and I said we were taking all possible steps to follow up the clues in our possession, and he said, didn't I know any better than to hand out that sort of official tripe to him, and what were we Doing? And I said we were up against a blank wall, and he said he supposed when thick heads came up against blank walls, nothing much did happen. So I said, no, nothing much except headaches, and then he said it looked to him like Marsden, and anyhow if Marsden was going to be hanged for one thing he might as well be hanged for the other as well. And of course there is that, but Marsden declared he had nothing to do with Sir Christopher's death, and I am inclined to believe him, because I think in the state he was in just then, he was too excited and upset to lie. Hysterical he was, and couldn't think of anything but the truth. Besides, if he stole the diamonds and bonds from the safe in the study, how could he have shot at the same time poor old Clarke at the other end of the house?'

'Seems difficult,' agreed Bobby.

'Only someone did it,' Mitchell went on, 'and the funniest thing about it all is that before last night's happenings, I was fairly sure it really was Carsley. If only Marsden had known enough to keep quiet, Carsley would have been under arrest by now most likely – it's really Marsden who saved him in trying to destroy him. Funny that, you know, Owen. For things were working out just exactly as Marsden wanted and we were well on the way to rid him of Carsley all right – a bit ironic all that, makes one almost believe there is some power after all that does look after things in this dull old muddle of a world. Of course, logically speaking, what happened last night has nothing whatever to do with the strength of the evidence against Carsley, and doesn't in the least affect the fact that he has been identified as doing a bolt from the scene of the murder immediately after it was committed. But you can imagine how defending counsel would let himself go, and how he would put it to the jury that the police themselves admitted that evidence had been faked to make them believe Carsley guilty of the second murder, and who was to say the same thing hadn't happened before? No sense or reason to the argument, but any K.C. would get a verdict from any jury every time by taking that line. Do you think it was Carsley?'

'No, sir.'

'Because you saw him once run straight the whole length of the field at Cardiff?'

'No, sir,' answered Bobby, flushing a little and wishing to goodness he had never made that unlucky reference, of which it seemed Mitchell never tired of reminding him. 'But when you have got the truth, everything fits. I think that's the main test of truth. It fits, it makes a harmony, one pattern all through. But there's only a good case against Carsley if you leave a whole lot out – unexplained.'

'If it was explained, if we knew the explanation, it might point the same way, too,' Mitchell observed. 'There's a cable from New York confirming that Sir Christopher was in possession there of a pistol of the same make as that found by his body. That suggests who ever shot him was an inmate of the house, or had access to it, and somehow got possession of his own pistol, as Carsley might have done through the Jennie girl.'

'Do you think it was Marsden sent the anonymous letter telling us about that?' Bobby asked.

'I'm sure of it,' Mitchell asserted. 'But there's other things I would like to know more about. Those theatre tickets – the stalls for the Regency. Where do they come in? Let me see, the play was – *Hamlet*, wasn't it?'

'Yes, sir,' answered Bobby, surprised at the question, for he was quite sure Mitchell knew that well enough.

'The Assistant Commissioner and I went to see it,' Mitchell went on musingly. 'Rather a jolly evening, too, even if I did get told I had too much imagination for a policeman, whose business is facts. By the way, there's a note from the administrator of the Clarke estate – you knew Carsley declined to have anything to do with that and another firm is acting? Apparently he's found trace of another sum of about five hundred lent to Dr Gregory and nothing to show it was ever repaid. But Gregory sticks to it he repaid it all right and he has the torn I.O.U. to show. But he can't show any cancelled cheque or any other trace of the transaction. He accounts for that by saying he paid in cash, mostly in notes he won racing. Everyone who has money he can't account for always says he won it racing – that's classic. We can't disprove that, anyhow, but it is possible that when he found Sir Christopher dead, he thought of his debt, and saw a chance to get hold of the I.O.U. from the dead man's pocket-book. If it happened like that, it would account for his delay you noticed and reported. But it wouldn't prove or even suggest that the doctor did the shooting.'

'No, sir,' agreed Bobby.

'It might be – oh, lots of theories and "might be's",' Mitchell went on, drumming on his desk with his fingertips. 'Looks to me we shall never know – not now, not now Brenda Laing will never tell us what she knew.'

'You think she knew something?' Bobby asked.

'You heard Marsden say so. Marsden's a good steady liar, but last night I think it was the truth came out. Yes, I think she knew something but what she knew she'll never tell. Silent she was all the days of her life, and silent she'll stay now she's in her grave – silent in life and death, too.'

There was a knock at the door and Inspector Gibbons entered. He was carrying a large sealed envelope he handed to Mitchell.

'I thought I had better let you have this at once, sir,' he said. 'A young lady brought it. She is here still, if you would like to see her. I asked her to wait. She says she knew Miss Brenda Laing, but hadn't seen or heard from her for some time. The day before yesterday she got that envelope from Miss Laing, with a note asking her to keep it by her unless anything happened to make her think she ought to bring it to us. So when she read the paper this morning and what had happened to Miss Laing, she supposed that was what was meant, and she took the first train up and brought it here.'

When he had finished Mitchell was silent for a moment, looking thoughtfully at the packet in his hand. Bobby rose to his feet, his intense excitement making it impossible for him to keep still. Mitchell said slowly, half to himself:

'Has she spoken at last, has she broken her silence at last now she is dead?'

He broke the seal of the packet and settling himself in his chair began to read.

CHAPTER 33

Information Received

'"I AM writing this because I want to tell you how it is I came to shoot dead my stepfather, Sir Christopher Clarke.

'"When I did it I thought it was my duty and my right.

'"But now I am not sure.

'"I was five, exactly five, it was my fifth birthday, when I first understood that there was something wrong between my own father and my mother.

'"I can remember it as clearly and as vividly as anything that happened half an hour ago, that day when I was five.

'"I was standing at the top of the stairs that led to the nursery. They were very narrow stairs and they were covered with a kind of oilcloth, not carpeting. There was a stain on the wall near the top, shaped like a bear, that used to terrify me, because the nurse told me that if I were not good it would come alive and eat me all up. So I used to try very hard to be good, only it is difficult to tell what is being good when one is only five – and when one is older, then it is more difficult still.

'"Father was standing just a little way down the stairs. He was holding out a marvellous new doll. It had blue eyes and fair hair, I remember, and the fair hair was tied up with pink ribbon, and if you pressed it, it said 'pa-pa', and 'ma-ma'. I have that bit of pink ribbon still somewhere, I believe.

'"Mother was standing behind father, and I knew she was angry, and did not want me to have the doll.

'"But father passed it to me over her head, and I took it, and ran as fast as I could into the nursery, into a corner there, for fear mother would come and take it from me. I heard her say:

'"'You said it was too expensive when I asked you, you said it cost too much. Then you go and buy it yourself.'

'"I did not hear what father answered, but I understood very well. I could not have put it into words but I knew as clearly as any grown-up could have done that father was bidding against my mother for my love.

'"And I knew why.

'"It was because he knew he was losing hers.

'"He was losing his wife and so he was trying to bribe his child that he should not lose her, too.

'"I think there were two little five-year-olds in the nursery that day. There was the happy babe, absorbed in an ecstasy of rare joy because of this great wonder miraculously issued from the shop window to become a part and portion of every day existence. There was another child who knew that the joint life which should have been her protection and her stay had been torn asunder.

'"I suppose this attempt to bribe a little child's love is a proof of some essential weakness in my father's character. I imagine it was this weakness in him that cost him his wife's love. It was a weakness that would, I think, have made some women love him more. I think it would have me. I think if I had found a man leaning on me, depending on me, that would have called out all the best I had to give. But my mother did not feel like that, because she was weak, too, weaker than he was, very weak and yielding and gentle, and ready to take the impress of any near her. If she had found strength in him, then perhaps she would have been strong, too. And if he had found strength in her, then in his turn he would have been stronger. But their two weaknesses clashed, reacted, each on the other, and I think there was unconscious anger and distrust between them, because each knew what the other might have given, but could not.

'"Yet there was so much in them both that was sweet and gentle and very tender. I think it would have been all right in the end, only that one day my father brought home a business friend, Mr Clarke, he was not Sir Christopher then.

' "That happened before the doll episode, but it was not till some time after it that I began to associate Mr Clarke with the trouble in the house, with mother's occasional tears and father's fits of gloomy silence. I remember once he had me in his arms in the hall, and was laughing and kissing me, and I tried to pull mother towards him, and he put me down suddenly and went into the drawing-room, and mother went back upstairs, and I was left alone in that cold passage.

' "Mr Clarke was altogether different from father. He was loud-voiced, vigorous, competent. He knew what he wanted and what he wanted he took; and if it was something that happened to belong to you, why, so much the worse for you. Oh, he was strong, strong as brute, elemental things are strong. It was like a struggle between the fine flower of sheltered city life and some raw force of nature, it was like a sudden storm of wind and rain breaking into a carefully guarded conservatory, it was like the matching of a vase of beaten gold against one of wrought iron. With all that, there was a certain rough good nature about the man; he was not malicious, no more malicious than the wind and rain bringing ruin on the delicate, hot-house plants. If you were in a difficulty, and he had time, he would often help you, even if very often chiefly in order to show his greater strength and skill. If you bent before him, he did you no harm; if you ran for shelter, he passed you by.

' "So much justice it is right and fitting I should do him, now that I have killed him.

' "But it was my father's great misfortune that he possessed something Mr Clarke wanted with all the force of his strong, narrow, seeking self.

' "I suppose he fascinated mother from the first. She felt the contrast with my father, who was always so hesitating and uncertain, and who would have turned aside from picking up a fortune rather than hurt the feelings of a blind beggar standing near. Mr Clarke – Sir Christopher – my stepfather – he wouldn't even have seen the blind beggar, no, not even if everyone near had combined to point him out. He would have seen nothing but the fortune and he would have taken it and kept it.

'"Why is it that the fine things of the world must break when they come against the coarser?

'"Or must they?

'"My father broke at any rate, as is shown, I suppose, by his pathetic attempt to bribe my love. But it was not for the doll I loved him but because I knew he had great need that I should. But I loved my mother, too. She was very gentle and very, very lovely, and so fragile you thought a breath would be enough to blow her right away.

'"Two things happened. Mr Clarke went away on business that took him to New York. That didn't make things any easier. He was gone in the body, but his memory was with us, like a living thing, always there.

'"The other thing that happened was that father fell ill. His health was always weak, and it had grown worse. Mr Clarke came back from America and came to see us and then had to go back there again. My father grew worse. Mother nursed him. The doctor wanted a professional nurse but mother would not hear of it. She would hardly let anyone else into the room, she wanted to do everything, though she was so very far from strong. She tried to keep me away, but I used to slip in every opportunity that I got, and sit by him. We never spoke, father and I. But I knew he wanted me there. Perhaps it was then I first learnt to be silent as people say I am. The maids used to talk about how devoted mother was. So did the doctor. And he told us there was no real danger; with care and good nursing there was every reason to think father would get well again.

'"One day I was in the room, sitting by the side of the bed. We had been silent as usual. He had his eyes closed. He opened them. Mother had just gone out of the room. He looked at me for a little and then he said:

'"'Brenda, had your mother a letter to-day?'

' " I knew there had been letters that morning but I did not know anything about them.

' " He said:

' " ' I should not ask you that.'

' " Mother came back into the room and I said to her:

' " ' Mummy, daddy wants to know if you had a letter this morning.'

' " I saw them look at each other. They looked at each other for a long time. They did not say anything. I was very frightened. I did not understand, but I was horribly afraid. I do not think anyone can understand how afraid I was.

' " I began to cry and mother took me out of the room and called one of the maids. The maid thought it was because of father I was crying. So it was, but not as she thought.

' " That night the same maid came and woke me up.

' " ' Your father wants you,' she said.

' " She carried me down into his room. The doctor was there and my mother. Father put out his hand and held mine. The doctor was standing quite close. My mother was standing at the foot of the bed. Her face was in shadow and I could not see it. I heard the doctor say:

' " ' I can't make it out. I can't understand what's happened.'

' " Then he said again:

' " ' He's no right to be like this, not when he was going on so well.'

' " Suddenly father pulled me close to him.

' " ' Brenda, remember,' he said very loudly, 'remember, Brenda.'

' " He never spoke or moved again though he lived some hours.

' " But I think I knew very well, even then, what it was he had told me I was to remember." '

CHAPTER 34

Information Received (continued)

'"WITHIN six months mother had married again. I do not think anyone was very much surprised. Mr Clarke cabled as soon as he heard of father's death and returned at once, though he still had business in New York that needed his attention. But he left all that to his associates and took the next steamer home. Father's affairs were in great confusion. There were debts and nothing to pay them with.

'"Mr Clarke took all that in hand. I remember very well the difference there was after his return, how tradespeople became civil and attentive again, and a horrible man who had been about the house a lot suddenly disappeared. Mr Clarke cleared up everything, settled with the creditors, arranged everything, did everything. I suppose but for him we should have had to go to the workhouse. When mother told me we were going to live with him always, it hardly seemed a change. He had been so constantly with us ever since he came back.

'"He was always quite kind to me. He didn't take much notice of me, but mother had everything she wanted for me quite naturally. He took it for granted that mother would see I had all it was right and necessary a child should have, whether in the way of necessity or pleasure. He would pat me on the head or cheek when we met and give me sixpences and shillings, and at Christmas and on my birthday there were always generous treats and presents.

'"But I do not think all that ever gave me any pleasure, ever gave me any of that joy which there should be in a little child's existence.

'"It was from him I first learnt I was silent. I heard him say one day:

'"'She's a silent little thing.'

249

' " Afterwards I asked mother:

' " ' Mummy, why am I a silent little thing?'

' " She did not answer me but I remember still how pale she became and later on I heard him ask her why she had been crying.

' " He was always very good to her. He was really fond of her; somehow his hard, aggressive, thrusting self seemed to find delight in her gentle, yielding personality, so strangely receptive as it was to stronger characters. He was really fond of her in his possessive kind of way, he took possession of her as he did of everything; she was a part of him and everything that belonged to him became at once important and valuable – and valued. I believe he would have grown fond of me if I had let him, if I had surrendered, too. But I never did, and he hardly noticed it or minded. My conquest did not seem to him of any importance, he no more bothered about me or conquering my personality, or knowing if I had one to conquer, than he did about his office clerks.

' " Presently Jennie was born. He was very pleased, very proud, here was another witness to his power, to his success, another possession, and he measured all things by possession. Anything that was his had, so to say, from that mere fact, a kind of halo about it.

' " He wanted a boy, too. So mother did her best, but she died instead because she was never very strong.

' " She knew she was dying. So did I. I knew it from the first. It was when she knew it herself and knew I knew it, too, that she said to me:

' " ' Brenda, what did your father mean when he told you to remember?'

' " It angered me that she should ask that, ask me what we both knew so well. I said:

' " ' I don't know.'

' " Of course that was not true and she was not deceived. She said:

' " ' I daren't pray ... I daren't pray.'

'"I didn't speak. I knew she wanted me to, but I kept silent. After a long time she said:

'"'It's all true about hell because I've been there ever since.'

'"I did not ask her ever since what. Presently the nurse who had been out of the room on some errand or another came back, and then Sir Christopher – he was that by now – came tip-toeing in. I don't know why exactly, but that he should come in on tip-toe like that made me mad, I think. I remember the feeling that came over me. I spoke to the nurse. I think perhaps what I did then was the most dreadful thing any woman has ever done since the world began. I don't think I would have done it had he not come in like that on tip-toe. I said:

'"'You won't mistake the medicine, nurse, will you?'

'"I don't think Sir Christopher understood then. Perhaps he did later. But mother heard. Mother understood. I saw how she shrank and trembled and was still again, and, ah – how she looked at me, how terribly she looked at me. The nurse began to laugh. I daresay she would have been vexed if she had not laughed. But she stopped laughing. She felt laughter was not right and I expect she explained that by reminding herself that it was a sick-room. But it was not that that made laughter wrong. She stopped laughing and said:

'"'Good gracious, no, indeed I won't.'

'"I remember that scene so well. By now the nurse was staring at the three of us, her eyes, her mouth wide open. She looked so bewildered I could have burst out laughing in my turn. Sir Christopher was staring at me. He was puzzled, just puzzled. That was all, vaguely puzzled, vaguely annoyed that he was puzzled. I knew he thought I was not behaving nicely and I suppose I wasn't. He was a man with a great gift for not understanding – especially when he did not want to understand. Mother lay quite still, one does lie still when one has suddenly been stabbed right through the heart. I think she hardly moved or spoke again, though it was nearly two days before – before her second death.

'"I think Sir Christopher soon put the scene out of his mind. He decided not to think of it any more. He was so strong he had the power to do that – to put the things he did not wish to remember clean out of his mind. I had not.

'"I know her death was a great sorrow to him and he missed her, but I think he was almost as much puzzled and annoyed as he was grieved. It was astonishing to him that events he had always been so well able to control should thus escape his grasp; he had a sense of having been unfairly treated, he was angry as though a rightful possession of his had been suddenly snatched away behind his back.

'"It was, I am quite sure, for my mother's sake that he showed he wished to do all he could for me. He told somebody who had spoken about me:

'"'I look upon Brenda's future as my responsibility.'

'"Even a responsibility he thought of as 'his', and my future, too, he thought should belong to him as well.

'"Not that he took much notice of me. He was a busy man and work helped him to forget, both his real grief for my mother's loss and the insult that had been offered to his sense of property. He made up for that by accumulating still more, very successfully, but he never forgot mother, and for her sake he still continued to do what he thought his duty by me. Also I think he knew I was fond of Jennie and that Jennie was fond of me; and then quite naturally the house management fell into my hands and I know I did it well. I have a kind of gift for organizing and managing, at any rate it was never any trouble to me, and everything in the house ran smoothly, as he liked it to.

'"He was not a subtle man. A thing had to be very obvious before it impressed itself on him. I remember once when something was said about my silence, he laughed, and pulled my ear, and said:

'"'Anyhow, I am glad my little girl is not a chatterbox.'

'"Always that 'my', you see.

'"But I wasn't a little girl any more and it was some time after this that I began to see him watching me. I never said anything. I never referred to either my father or my mother. I was, I am sure, no more silent than I had always been, than I had been when he laughed about it.

'"But now I could see he was watching me, and, when I was there, he began to change a little from his usual boisterous, confident self. I wonder if it was the intensity of my thoughts that he became aware of? Perhaps it is because thought can be felt that after a time I began to be aware that he was afraid. I knew that before he did, I think at first he was only conscious of a vague unease, but it was not very long before he knew that it was fear he felt. When I came into a room when he was there, I could see it from the way he looked up. When he went out of a room where I was sitting, I could see it in the way he walked. When we remained together in a room, then I knew it still more certainly. But yet it often seemed to me that he did not know what it was he feared or what he was afraid of. Only every day that passed he knew just a little tiny bit more clearly. Once or twice he even tried to make me talk.

'"The next thing was that he began to encourage young men to come to the house. But what had I to do with young men when there was no room in my mind save for the one thought that never left it?

'"All the time his fear was growing and all the time he never knew whether there was any reason for it. Perhaps if he had been more certain he could have faced it better, known better what to do. But there was nothing that he could do, because, if he sent me away, then that would have been to acknowledge his fear, and he would not.

'" I wonder if there are other houses like ours, houses that look so calmly prosperous, so placidly content, proud houses where nothing seems to be but wealth and ease, and yet where doubt and fear and guilt brood day and night?

'"Then Mark Lester appeared. I think really he had been there a long time only I had never noticed him much. I hardly realized that he was constant in the changing crowd of young men who came and went. It never occurred to me that his great ill-fortune had been to fall in love with me. How should I have known? Love and hate do not go well together.

'"Sir Christopher noticed Mark, became aware of his assiduity, saw he was in earnest. In his direct, determined way he spoke to Mark himself. Then he spoke to me. He made himself quite clear. I think the chance of escape offered him made him desperate it should be taken. Mark wanted to marry me. I was to accept him. Of course, any other young man would have done as well, but Mark was there, he wanted me, he was eligible. If I refused – but a refusal was not contemplated. In his relief at the thought of getting rid of me, Sir Christopher was his old masterful, certain self once more.

'"He told me he would settle forty thousand pounds on me, absolutely.

'"An enormous sum! An incredibly generous sum for a man to settle on a stepdaughter who had so little real claim on him.

'"But I understood, very well I understood.

'"I knew that forty thousand pounds, that huge fortune, was just a bribe. Just as my father had tried to bribe my love, so now my stepfather tried to bribe my hate!

'"It is strange how sometimes things seem to return upon themselves and happen all over again and yet so differently.

'"Mark loved me. I knew that now. I saw the choice quite clearly. I could have a fortune, love, happiness, content – all that was offered me.

'"A bribe!

'"I do not think it ever occurred to me to accept.

'"I do not think it ever occurred to my stepfather that I would refuse."'

CHAPTER 35

Information Received (continued)

'"But this offer of a bribe did one thing. It made me certain. It took all my doubts away.

'"Now I knew.

'"Already I had all my preparations complete. For long and long I had had every detail worked out in my mind – and variations of every detail to meet every conceivable chance and change.

'"No wonder that when I had so much to think of, I got the name for being silent. How could I talk and chatter when in my mind I was rehearsing step by step the task that lay before me, that I had been called upon so dreadfully to accomplish, when always there was present to me my father's ghost: 'Remember'?

'"Long and long ago I had had a key made of the private drawer where I knew my stepfather kept his revolver. No one else had ever seen it, no one except me. I had not only seen it, but handled it as well, and made sure it was loaded and in working order.

'"I went to a gunsmith, too, and got him to show me how to use a pistol and practised with one to get accustomed to it.

'"Oh, there was nothing that I overlooked.

'"He was very fond of billiards and often spent the hour before dinner in the billiard-room. He used to say that it was while he was 'knocking the balls about' that all his best ideas came to him, and that he found the solution to all his business worries.

'"I made a point of using the same hour for my music. He liked me to play. He used to say he was fond of music. Really he meant that he was fond of noise and silence worried him. He would not have cared, he would hardly

255

have known, whether I was playing Beethoven or jazz. It was all one to him so long as it was not silence.

'"There was one piece I played very often so that everyone in the house knew it well. I secured a record of it. I obliterated the first half of the record so that when it was put on, for that first half no sound came. Then I practised playing that first half on the piano, and stopping at the exact point where the record began. I got to do that on the dot, so that no one could have told when my piano stopped and the record began.

'"All this time I had a sort of odd certainty that when the moment came, I should know. I was certain somehow that it could not pass without summoning me to my task.

'"I knew it would be revealed to me, and it was.

'"There was a production of *Hamlet* at the Regency Theatre that Jennie was very keen on seeing. She and I went together.

'"She enjoyed it very much, she said. To me, the play was not an enjoyment, but a message.

'"Indeed, it was as if it had been put on for me alone.

'"How well I understood him – Hamlet himself, I mean. I knew so well that shrinking, trembling terror that he showed, because he had been called to such a task. How well I understood his hesitation and his doubts, for he, too, was not certain; how well I recognized the agony with which he tried to persuade himself the monstrous truth was not. In the interview with his mother, it was myself I saw with my mother, and her great cry of anguish was my own mother's. All that scene had been my experience, too. Even when he threw away Ophelia's love with his cry: 'Get thee to a nunnery, go!' I knew it was because he could not help it, since love and hate are opposites, and to choose the one is to reject the other. So I saw myself rejecting the claim that Jennie's love made on me. That was wrong, all wrong, but at the time I did not know that I loved Mark. That came later. I thought there was no one but Jennie I cared anything about, and I knew I must put her aside – as Hamlet put aside Ophelia – because, if I did not, I could not do what had to be done.

'"But all that part of my thought was wrong, how wrong I found out afterwards. Jennie and I were in no way like Hamlet and Ophelia; how could we be. And I had forgotten that Ophelia killed herself. I was to be reminded of that, too. She killed herself because she knew what Hamlet had to do – it was easier like that than if she had waited till she knew what he had done!

'"I imagine no one has ever understood the play as well as I did that night. It was my own soul I watched. Sometimes I have heard people talk about Hamlet as if there were some puzzle about him, or as if his character and motives were hard to understand.

'"That's so silly.

'"He could do no other, things being what they were.

'"And he, too, felt he had to make quite, quite sure. That is why he got the strolling players to give their performance before the two he suspected, and then he watched, and then was sure.

'"Because even his father's ghost might have deceived him just as in the same way my father's 'Remember' might have deceived me.

'"So he invented a test, and I did, too. I bought two stalls and sent them to Sir Christopher. I did it again, and another time as well, three nights in succession, and then I was sure.

'"For all his fears came back to him that he had put aside when he hit on the splendid idea of bribing me with a husband and a fortune!

'"How wonderful it is how foolish, strong, clever men can be. It was his very attempt to bribe me made me certain and now I was more certain still, certain enough to act.

'"On the night itself, I was in the drawing-room as usual for the hour before dinner. I knew the time was near, for twice over I had wakened in the night to hear a thin and ghostly 'Remember' whispering in the corners of my room. I knew, too, Sir Christopher was hurrying on the wedding, and that papers settling all that money on me were nearly ready. So it had to be done quickly, since afterwards, as soon as the money was mine, as soon as I should have seemed to accept his bribe, then I should have had no right to act. Once his money belonged to me, my vengeance would do so no longer.

'"Therefore I knew the hour had come and I knew it still more certainly when I saw a strange man go creeping past the drawing-room window. I did not turn my head, and he did not know I saw, but there was a mirror that showed him plainly, and that he had his face covered with an old scarf. I realized at once it was a burglar after the contents of the safe in the study, where Sir Christopher often kept valuable papers and diamonds worth much money.

'"I saw immediately that by doing what had to be done while there was also a burglar in the house, I should make myself much more secure. And I had always felt that my own safety was an essential part of my task. I did not wish that in taking my revenge for his crime, I should give him his for my just deed. It seemed to me essential what I did should go undetected and unpunished. I did not expect then that before long I should be myself writing out exactly how and why it all came about.

'"But I realized immediately my chance to confuse from the very start the investigation that I had to expect – and baffle. I saw I could put the police on a false track at once. They would spend their time trying to trace a connexion between burglary and murder that did not exist. I thought I was very clever to see all that, but circumstances are more clever still, for how was I to know he was not an ordinary burglar but Mr Marsden, Peter's partner?

'"I put on the half-obliterated record I had specially prepared and I plunged into my rendering of the same piece. At the exact moment I stopped and the record went on. I don't think anyone could have suspected I was not still at the piano, still playing.

"'I kicked off my shoes. That was another detail I had long thought out. I always wore heavy shoes and I had trained myself to walk heavily, so that people should get to think I had a heavy step and to suppose subconsciously that they would always hear me when I moved about. In my stockings I ran upstairs and opened the drawer in Sir Christopher's room. I took out his pistol and saw that it was loaded and ready. Of course, I held it in my handkerchief so as to leave no finger marks. I ran downstairs again and went into the billiard-room. Sir Christopher was there. He was knocking the balls about. I said to him:

"'"I have come to kill you.'

"'He went all horrible with terror, all soft and saggy. He did not make a sound. He would have screamed, I think, only he did not dare, for he knew the moment he made a sound, I would fire. But I wanted him to understand. I said:

"'"Because you murdered my father.'

"'I saw he wanted lamentably to deny it, so I said:

"'"Because you made my mother murder my father.'

"'He managed to stammer out:

"'"I never knew ... I wasn't there ... I gave her something once to give him ... but we threw it away again ... I was in New York when it happened ... I knew nothing, I swear I didn't...'

"'I did not wait for any more excuses. I knew very well what had happened. He had talked about it to her. The opportunity came. Easy enough to pour the medicine away. Yes, he was in America, but his spirit, his will, was there, at her side, urging her, pressing her on, compelling her though absent. I knew all that so well and I did not want to hear it said again. Besides, he looked so disgusting in his terror that I was afraid, if I was not quick, I would never do it at all. I fired twice. He fell down, right down, and lay there, and I looked at him and saw that he was dead, and the thought came strangely into my mind that I had avenged, not my father, but my mother.

'"I took one of the cues standing in the rack and threw it on the table and I moved the pointers on the scoring-board. I wanted it to look as if a game had been in progress.

'"Then I put the pistol down by his side and went back to the piano in the drawing-room."'

CHAPTER 36

Information Received (concluded)

'"My first sensation was that of an enormous, an overpowering relief.

'"I was as one who has at last found peace after long days of grief and trouble, I felt as Christian in the *Pilgrim's Progress* felt when at last the burden fell from his shoulders, like the traveller who after weary journeying reaches his destination at last. I experienced a content that was too calm and tranquil to be called joy and yet was greater than joy, it was so perfect and so all pervading.

'"I suppose a result of this was the complete change that seemed to come over me. I do not know if others noticed it but I felt almost like an entirely new person. Everything around appeared in an absolutely new light, like a new world.

'"I saw things, so to say, as they really were. Now the world around me existed in its own right, not merely to subserve my mission. Things had become ends in themselves, not merely means to one narrow purpose. I stepped into a new life and I found it wonderful, like an enchanted kingdom.

'"To the past I never gave a thought, I had done my job and it was over and finished, so I thought. As for remorse or regret, such ideas never entered my mind. Why should they? A task had been laid upon me and I had been its slave. Now it was accomplished and I was free, gloriously free.

'"I remember that night I said to a young policeman, a good-looking boy, who was at the house:

'"'If it was murder, it will be punished, for murder is always punished.'

'"What I meant was that now at last due punishment had been exacted for the murder of my father so long ago – and of my mother, too, for she had been murdered, just like my father, body and soul together, by what she had been made to do. Now at last a righteous punishment had been inflicted. That was what I meant, but I meant also what I said as a challenge to the Unknown Powers. I felt as if I said to them:

"'"Well, there it is. If it's murder, punish me. You know why I did it.'

"'That was my challenge. I made it with supreme confidence. It was heard, accepted. Now it has been answered. That is why I am writing this.

"'But at the time I was quite easy in my mind, content and satisfied. Besides, I knew I had laid all my plans so well I was in no danger of discovery. In case anyone else had seen the burglar pass the drawing-room window and wondered why I had not, I explained I had seen someone but had taken him for Mark. I thought that would confuse them still more, and I knew Mark was at home, because he had said he would have to stay in to prepare a lecture he was giving.

"'But now almost the first thing I was conscious of in the rush and glow of my released feelings was a new understanding of what Mark meant when he said he loved me.

"'It was very bewildering.

"'Before, when he said he loved me, I thought that only meant he wanted to marry me, and that people only wanted to marry because it was the sort of thing one did, and one had to, and the world couldn't go on very well without it. Of course, obviously people wouldn't marry each other if they disliked each other. Naturally they wouldn't. But I didn't imagine that there was any real difference between saying you loved a man and saying you loved music or dancing or your pekingese dog. I thought it was all a question of degree; and if you loved a man more than your pekingese, that was only because the man was more important and counted for more, just as it was more important and counted for more to love music than to love cream buns.

What I mean is that I thought it was all the same thing, only graded in value and degree.

'"But now I knew the difference; and then the second thing I became conscious of was that I loved Mark.

'"The emotion that had controlled me before in carrying out my mission had been like the dull smouldering of half-extinguished embers, but this was a great rushing fire that altogether burnt me up.

'"It was ecstasy. It ran through me in every nerve and fibre of my being. I touched, I think, real life then, not mere everyday existence, but life itself glowing and real. My love was my self, as fierce as it was steady, a great, fierce, leaping, roaring flame that never changed. My every thought was quickened, every emotion heightened, I lived altogether on a higher plane. Whether in the body or out of the body I hardly knew, but I was caught up into another sphere.

'"For the Unknown Powers had heard my challenge and accepted it; and so that they might utterly cast me down, first they had to lift me up to a great height.

'"How else could my fall have been so great?

'"But at least I have known great and wonderful things, I have lived hours more great and wonderful than any others can have known. Or is that wrong and have others also known such ecstasy as mine? Have the ordinary, every-day people around me also known such heights? The man who drives your taxi, who brings the milk to the door, who goes to the City all the week and plays golf all the week-end, the girl who sells you your stockings, or the one who spends her time rushing about from cocktail to cocktail; have all of them, or some of them at least, issued for a while from the narrow confines of their everyday existence to know what I knew then?

'"But the challenge I had offered the Unknown Powers they heard and accepted, and I knew that first when Mark declared he would find out who was guilty. He swore an oath that he would, he said it came to him as a thing that he had to do, and I knew well it was the Unknown Powers that had laid it on him – and I knew he would succeed.

'"Also there was a little man who was their instrument. I do not even know his name, I only saw him once, I hardly remember him at all. He had some grudge or grievance against my stepfather and he hung about the house trying to see him, so he came to know me by sight. Also he had something to do with the box office at the Regency and he knew I bought tickets for the stalls three nights running and to whom I sent them. He thought it strange. I think he suspected something. I think he hated also and his hate gave him insight and imagination. At any rate he watched, and he was watching the house the night I did what I did. He was convinced it was someone in the house had fired the shots. He knew something of my story and guessed more. But he did not say anything for what I had done he had talked of doing himself. So he remained silent, but one day, I don't know how, Mark found him and talked to him and he told Mark all he knew, all he suspected.

'"Mark knew at once it was the truth. I am not sure if he had suspected before. I don't think so, but anyhow he knew at once quite certainly that he had been told the truth.

'"I suppose it was a great shock to him. Somehow he got rid of his informant, making him promise to keep silent, and then he came straight to me. I did not know why. I had no idea. I only knew that now his love, that mine in its sudden growth had outstripped, had flowered suddenly to be its equal. He told me we were to be married as soon as possible. It was not very long we were together. I mean not long in time, but all the same for us it was like a thousand years – like the tiniest fraction of a second, too. For we measured that moment by what we knew and felt and were, not by the ticking of a clock, and then in the twinkling of an eye it was past and gone.

'"But he knew, he knew, and when the knowledge grew too much for him, he shot himself.

'"I knew why. I knew the Unknown Powers had heard my challenge and accepted it. I knew they had decreed it was murder I had done, and that Mark should pay.

'"For the life that I had taken he had offered his own that was mine as well.

'"He had understood, and now I knew it also, that our love had no right to life, because it was born of death, and death lay between us, and death must separate us.

'"So he paid my penalty and died, for he could not live knowing what he knew.

'"I was left.

'"But now that penalty was paid, the Unknown Powers, placated, showed me great mercy.

'"In this way.

'"Jennie told me everything that Peter told her. What she said made me realize for the first time that the burglar I had seen, of whom the sight had told me that the moment had come, was really Peter's partner, Mr Marsden. From Jennie, too, I learnt of the struggle going on between Mr Marsden and Peter, and that Peter was determined to find out the truth about the practice and how the money of their firm's clients had been used. Mr Marsden made an opportunity to see me and talk – at least, he thought he made it, really I made it for him. There were things I wanted to know. He tried to pump me as it is called. He really fully believed that Peter was guilty, and he thought if he could get some evidence to that effect from me, then he could have Peter arrested, and tried; and, whatever the outcome, that would put an end to Peter's endeavour to find out the real state of affairs at the office.

'"But Peter was pressing him hard. I gave Mr Marsden no help, and he saw he had no chance of securing the evidence he wanted in time to stop Peter's activities. In sheer desperation, for it seems he saw exposure, ruin, gaol, very near, he determined to try another plan.

'"If he couldn't get Peter hung for the murder he truly

believed Peter had committed, then he thought he would get him hung for another one. And that other murder, and the evidence to prove Peter guilty of it, Mr Marsden decided to provide himself. I believe it was while he was talk-to me, and finding I was no help, that the idea first came to him. I suppose perhaps it was my own past experience, my own knowledge of how I had planned and thought, that made me recognize in his eyes what he meant to do.

'"It was a desperate plan but Mr Marsden was desperate, and he was not going to let a life stand between him and his own safety, even apart from his hate of Peter, and his fear that made his hate greater still. For he knew well that unless he stopped Peter somehow, his own fate was certain.

'"But I knew so well everything that was in his mind. I knew it all, his hate, his fear, his dread, his determination to do what he, too, felt he had to do. I think it was the will of the Unknown Powers that I should watch in another all I had experienced in myself, watch it in all its horror and abomination.

'"Why, I felt I knew every shade of every thought he had.

'"His plan was simple enough. He meant to entice Jennie to some lonely spot, and murder her, and arrange for Peter to be on the spot, and for the police to be there, too, and for them to arrest Peter, as it would seem, almost in the act. Who could doubt his guilt when he was already under suspicion for the murder of the father, and when Jennie's death would mean that her father's fortune would pass entirely to him?

'"But I was watching and I made Jennie tell me every-thing. And now she has had a message telling her to go secretly and alone to some old house where she is to be given evidence to show who really is guilty and therefore proof of Peter's innocence.

'"It is a trap and I know whose trap. But Peter's inno-cence will be known well enough when this is read, and meanwhile I am going in her place to keep this appoint-ment. I am going wearing her hat and coat, our figures are much the same, and it is my dear hope, my belief and expectation that I shall not come back alive. Peter will be safe then, and Jennie, too, and I don't think anything else will make them safe, for Mr Marsden knows the time is short, and he is very desperate.

'"I do not think he will recognize me but I must risk that. He has only seen me once or twice, and I don't think he took any special notice, and he will be expecting Jennie, and I shall be wearing her things. We often did, we have the same figure nearly, and I shall take a scarf to hide my face.

'"I think all will go well; I feel it somehow.

'"Mark took his way – Mark's way. This is my way – Brenda's way.

'"To-night I think the weaving of the pattern will be completed, the tangled web made straight, and that come to its appointed end which began the night my father brought home Mr Clarke to dinner, so that they might talk business together."'

CHAPTER 37

The End

SUPERINTENDENT MITCHELL laid down the paper when he had finished reading it.

'Now we know,' he said slowly, 'now we've been told. I always say it's the only way to find things out – to get someone who knows to tell you all about it. Information received.'

Bobby was looking at his superior and suddenly he blurted out:

'Then that's why you went to the Regency Theatre, sir, that's what you meant about the show there. I couldn't make it out but now I see. It's been *Hamlet* all over again from start to end, except that this time Hamlet's been a woman. And you knew that all the time.'

'In police work,' explained Mitchell, 'you never know anything till you can put it in a report, with all the "i's" dotted and all the "t's" crossed – lots of red lines as well. I had a kind of idea but ideas are no good. Treasury Counsel want facts, not ideas. Why, the Assistant Commissioner said I was fanciful – almost as good as asking me to resign. I dropped a hint or two to you, Owen, just to see if you would take them up. You didn't. So I took it your fancy didn't run as quick as mine and a good thing, too. I told Treasury Counsel in a non-professional way what I thought and they said it was very interesting in a non-professional way, but what they wanted was facts to put before a jury and where were they? Well, now we've got 'em because someone's come along and told us.'

'What about Peter Carsley?' Gibbons asked. 'Where does he come in? After all, he's been identified leaving the scene of the murder immediately after it happened.'

'That's right,' agreed Mitchell. 'I wonder if he's got here

yet. He rang up to ask if I could see him, wants to know about these new developments, I expect – Marsden's arrest and Miss Laing's death.'

He picked up his desk telephone and inquired and on being told that Mr Carsley was waiting directed that he should be brought up. In the interval before Peter appeared he picked up Brenda's statement and glanced at it again.

'"Good-looking young policeman,"' he mused abstractedly. 'I wonder who she means?'

Gibbons looked sourly at Bobby, who wriggled uncomfortably in his chair.

'It's the curl in his hair does it,' Gibbons pronounced. 'When he's in a Lyons shop he gets served practically before anyone else.'

'It won't lie flat,' Bobby protested. 'I've tried but it never will.'

'Making excuses isn't any help,' observed Mitchell, 'some day some girl will catch you by it – then you'll know.'

But this discussion on the aesthetics of the person was interrupted by the appearance of Peter, showing stronger evidence even than of late of the strain recent events had put upon him.

He, too, had apparently been the recipient of a note from Brenda explaining, though in only a few words, without the wealth of psychological details she had given in her longer statement, what she meant to do.

'But then I always knew it was Brenda who shot her step-father,' he explained, 'for I saw her do it.'

'You mean you were an eye-witness?' Mitchell asked, and when Peter nodded, he continued: 'Was it because of your having seen it happen that you went off the way you did through the next door garden? I may as well tell you now that we've suspected that was you for some time and finally we got you identified. In fact, but for this statement made by Miss Laing, you would probably have been arrested to-day.'

'I've been expecting that long enough,' Peter answered quietly. 'I didn't know anyone had seen me though. I thought I had managed very well, especially the way I changed after that fellow hit me with his ripe tomato.'

'I don't say you didn't,' sighed Mitchell, 'but it's meant the devil of a lot of worry and work for us. How was it you happened to be there at the time?'

'You knew my wife and I had been secretly married just before all this happened?' Peter asked. 'Well, there had been a bit of a dust up at the office and I saw a crisis had come. Sir Christopher very plainly suspected something. I could see there was bound to be a flare-up, and I went to "The Cedars" to try to see Jennie on the quiet. I didn't want her father to know or any of the servants. We had a way fixed up by which I could let her know, when she was in her room, that I was waiting. I knew Sir Christopher, when he was at home, nearly always spent the hour before dinner in the billiard-room – billiards was his great hobby. But just to make sure he was safely occupied and wouldn't be likely to interrupt us, before I let Jennie know I was waiting, I slipped round by the shrubbery, so as to have a look into the billiard-room and be certain he was there. And while I was looking, Brenda opened the door and came in, and I saw and heard it all. It was a bit of a shock. I thought my only plan was to clear out before I was seen. I didn't want to be called as a witness. It didn't strike me at the moment that I ran any risk of incurring suspicion myself. Anyhow, I think I should have run that risk. What I really felt was that it had better be kept quiet as far as possible. It was dreadful and horrible enough for Jennie that her father should be murdered, it would only make things worse if her sister were hanged for doing it. That's what I thought and then I suppose it's always a lawyer's instinct to try to hush things up, that's always the legal instinct. So I cleared off, but I didn't dare go by the drive for I had seen a policeman in uniform hanging about there as if he were waiting for someone. He hadn't seen me come, for he had had his back to me, and I thought it very much better not to give him any chance of seeing me going either. So I cut off across the next door garden, as I had done once or twice before, after seeing Jennie on the quiet, only of course this time I was bound to be spotted and some ass got after me with tomatoes and things.'

'I rather thought it must be like that,' observed Mitchell. 'Well, Mr Carsley, so far as that goes I suppose Miss Laing's statement clears you, but I think you've had a pretty narrow escape twice over – you might easily have been hanged for Sir Christopher Clarke's murder, and this last time Marsden had everything arranged so neatly, it was a hundred to one your guilt would have been taken as proved. The only weak point in the Marsden scene was that it was so ingenious as to be just a little too ingenious. Life's not so clever as all that, and so I think it's Marsden will hang and not you.'

In this Mitchell was a true prophet, for the jury before whom he presently appeared found the evidence overwhelming. Indeed Marsden hardly troubled himself to give much help to the lawyers charged with his defence or take any great interest in their efforts. Nor did he attempt to deny that it was he who had been responsible for the burglary on the night of the murder.

'I had had it in my mind for some time,' he said. 'I knew things couldn't go on much longer and I managed to find out the safe combination and to get a key. The job itself was easy enough. The mistake I made was coming back from Paris when once I was there. But I knew the hardest part is always to escape afterwards, with police looking for you everywhere, and I thought I could bluff my way to safety now the old man was dead. I calculated there wouldn't be anyone very energetic about following it up, now he was gone, and I didn't expect any trouble with Carsley. I was quite sure he had committed the murder, and you don't expect murderers to make trouble for others, you expect them to be too busy keeping out of it themselves. So I took what seemed the smallest risk, and that offered the biggest prize, for the only thing I had to hope for, if I stayed abroad, was escape; whereas if my bluff came off I was back in my old place, safe and respectable once more, able to pick up my career again. What did for me was the way Carsley turned stupid, and I never expected that, how could I? And if I hadn't been unlucky right to the end - for who could have expected that girl to interfere the way she did? - I could have settled him all right. If Brenda Laing hadn't played the fool the way she did, Carsley would have hung and I should have been safe for ever - and so would she herself. She threw it all away, her safety and mine, too, she spoilt it all. Never trust a woman.'

After that he said very little more and the inevitable sentence, duly pronounced, was carried out in due course.

By that time Peter and Jennie - Peter had wound up the practice after having seen that all his clients' accounts were straight and in good order - had gone abroad for a long holiday and rest, and the change of scene and company of which they both felt the need.

Peter's intention is to abandon the law and to put what money he has left into some small country estate, so that in quiet rural pursuits he and his wife may forget their tragic and unfortunate experiences.

As for Constable Robert Owen, he has received his transfer from the uniform ranks to the C.I.D., where, as he is known to stand rather well with Superintendent Mitchell, he will probably be called upon to play his part in any other difficult or complicated case that may arise.

THE END

Made in the USA
Middletown, DE
06 September 2016